HIDDEN HEARTS

HAVEN CROSSROADS
BOOK 2

EVEY LYON

HAVEN CROSSROADS SERIES

Clashing Hearts

Hidden Hearts

Bound Hearts

Copyright © 2026 by Evey Lyon

Written and published by: Evey Lyon, Lost Compass Press

Edited by: Contagious Edits

Proofreading: Rachel Rumble

E-book non-illustration Cover: Lost Compass Press

Illustration Cover: Concepts by Canea

Hardback Cover: Lost Compass Press

All rights reserved.

No part of this book may be reproduced in any form or by any electronic or mechanical means, including information storage and retrieval systems, without written permission from the author, except for the use of brief quotations in a book review.

This book is a work of fiction. The names, characters, places, and incidents are products of the writer's imagination and used fictitiously and are not to be perceived as real. Any resemblance to persons, venues, events, or businesses is entirely coincidental.

The author acknowledges the trademark status and trademark owners of various products referenced in this work of fiction, which have been used without permission. The publication/use of these trademarks is not authorized, associated with, or sponsored by the trademark owner.

The author expressly prohibits using this work in any manner for purposes of training artificial intelligence technologies to generate text, including, without limitation, technologies that are capable of generating works in the same style or genre as this work. The author reserves all rights to license uses of this work for generative AI training.

This book is U.S. copy registered and further protected under international copyright laws.

ABOUT

Hayes came to a friend's barbecue expecting burnt burgers and awkward small talk.

He left knowing my two-year-old daughter is his.

His anger hits fast and sharp, aimed straight at me for not knowing the truth, even if I could never find him after our one night. Worse? Fate isn't done with us. We're forced to work together, as he is our new high-powered executive in the office. To him, the only solution to our situation is to do things his way.

His constant demands and control should make me worry about his motives and the potential upheaval to our lives. What I don't expect is the way he softens around our daughter—complete devotion. Or the way his lingering eyes steal my breath. Then it's a kiss. A night. More.

One thing is clearly apparent.

I kept his secret—now he's decided I'm his.

Listening to the real estate agent jabber over my car speaker, I'm growing a little frustrated. I've looked at five different places in Chicago, and I've set my sights on the last property shown. A penthouse with three bedrooms, a small office, approaching the north side of the city, and high enough for a great view over the lake, too. So why is she going over the homeowners' association and fees? I don't know. This is the agent that HR sent to me while I prepare to relocate?

"Just get it done. I don't care if fees don't cover the parking spot. Let's wrap this conversation up. They're announcing my new role at the office later in the week, and I have enough to deal with right now." I'm moving to Chicago from Austin to become the Chief of Operations at Haven Crossroads. The owner, Julian Haven, who happens to be my best friend, wore me down until I said yes. It just hasn't been announced yet.

"Of course. It's the weekend. You won't hear from me until I have news." Steffy, on the other end, sounds apologetic.

"Thanks," I sigh and end the call. I've worked hard, striking gold investing in a few startups, to get the number of zeroes in my net worth, and I'm sure as hell going to enjoy it.

I squint as I begin to see fall-colored trees on the horizon on this blue-sky Saturday afternoon, and the landscape of dry cornfields turns slightly hilly when I exit the highway onto Lake Spark County Road. I've been out of the city and suburbs for a good hour, and all I've seen is flat farmland. A few times, I tried to guess the crop when it didn't look like corn. I just needed to pass the time.

Entering Everhope, the quaint town greets me with a classic Main Street and well-maintained storefronts and sidewalks. Definitely postcard-worthy. I find my way to Julian's weekend home and sputter a laugh. There's a field of wheat behind the large house with a sprawling front porch. Parking, I find my way around the house to the backyard and instantly spot my best friend by the grill with hanging streamers in the background.

Wasting no time to make myself at home, I grab two bottles of beer from the chilled bucket on the long table with a plaid tablecloth in passing. I continue my way to him.

"Look what the cows dragged in." He grins, and I hand him a bottle.

"Only for you did my navigation send me through corn fields to get to your weekend chalet."

We both use the side of the workstation edge to pop the caps before we clink our beers together.

The guy looks ridiculously relaxed, and I've never seen him this way. "It'll grow on you, just wait. Thanks for coming. Nothing's better than having a friend and new COO at my backyard BBQ for Savannah's birthday."

I give him the once-over. "All you need is an apron with some ridiculous phrase on it, and we're all set."

"Har-har."

"Where is the birthday girl? Contemplating her birthday wish and if it should involve you or not?" I tease him.

He holds out his bottle, wanting me to accept a toast. "It does, as we are getting married."

A wide grin finds me. "Ah, congrats." Another clink of our drinks. "You're settling down. Next thing you know, there will be a little one and a Labrador running around."

"We'll wait. Unless I get a little demanding on the honeymoon."

Kids.

That's already on his mind. Makes sense, we are at the age. I guess if I were with someone, then the topic would come up, too. A long discussion, actually. I have my career in full swing, but so does he.

I have to highlight caution to him because he has a tendency to go overboard. "Marriage and having a kid are two different things. Anyhow, where is the bride-to-be?" My eyes scan the yard.

I spot Savannah walking out of the kitchen carrying a tray of veggies. And then I freeze.

A chest-dropping, stomach-sinking, blood-rushing-in-my-ears type of freeze.

The woman following Savannah is holding a bowl of dip. Her hair is still long and slightly darker, and she seems happy, smiling with a warm, familiar smile. The forest-green sweater paired with those dark jeans screams natural beauty.

But what the hell?

I do a double take, it can't be. I feel perplexed. "Why is she here?"

Julian swings his gaze to his fiancée and must notice that

my eyes are on the woman next to her. "Elodie? She's Savannah's best friend and also works at the office."

My eyes go wide. That can't be right. "You mean Ellie?"

"I mean, Elodie," he repeats.

The corner of my mouth ticks before my thoughts swarm me, and it only causes me to laugh to myself, almost hysterically, because of a realization. "Of course, we used different names."

Even though I can't look away from the woman whose true name has now been revealed, I zone out into memory.

I spot her right away, sitting at the tropical bar. It's Vieques, Puerto Rico, with the clock almost noon and the sun bright, not a cloud in the sky, and the water a perfect blue. The woman, maybe ten years younger than me, seems content yet bored. A blue wrap covers her bikini-clad body as she stares aimlessly at a drink in a pineapple with a straw and an umbrella. Suddenly, I'm relieved that I didn't join my cousins for a group scuba diving trip to check out turtles. My win, because now I can casually slide onto the stool next to her, and I do just that.

"Please tell me there isn't rum in that. It would be too cliché," I say.

"Please tell me you're not about to order a fancy bottle of beer with a slice of lime," she counters and slowly angles my way, only for her to still and her lips to part open. She seems surprised.

I smirk proudly because I have a feeling it has to do with my looks. Today, I've skipped a suit and opted for a white, unbuttoned linen shirt with my shorts. I'm a man who keeps himself fit before conquering the office. I don't consider myself arrogant, but right now I'm playing that card.

"Gosh, you're gorgeous," she says.

Bingo.

"And you're beautiful and alone. I feel like that is a travesty."

She laughs and shakes her head slightly, amused. "Is that your usual line?"

"Not the travesty part," I promise.

She turns her attention to the barman who arrives. "Can we create a code word or something in case I need to escape this guy? You can save me." We all look around to see an empty pool area. "Okay, fine, you'll notice if I need to be saved."

"Why aren't you out on a beach somewhere enjoying the island?" I wonder. In the corner of my eye, I spot the bartender lifting his brows.

She sucks on her straw for a long drink, and I most definitely notice the way her lips move. "I'm here for a bachelorette trip for my cousin... not that I care, but it's a little awkward since she's marrying my high school boyfriend."

I feel my face contort. "Eek."

She waves me off. "Yeah. But it's okay, water under the bridge. I just didn't want to tag along on the cousin's boat excursion; they won't be back until late. You?"

"What a coincidence, I'm avoiding scuba diving with turtles on a bachelor party with my cousins. A getaway from Texas."

"You don't have an accent. What a shame. Those are kind of hot."

Chuckling, I like her candidness. "I'm only working there. My family is on the east coast. Do you have a name?"

She tilts her head slightly to the side, and her gorgeous blues squint. "Name territory means we might actually have a long conversation."

Shrugging, I feel my mouth begin to stretch. "I guess so."

She pauses for a second. "Ellie. You?"

"Hale."

"That's not really your name, is it?" she shoots back simply with a wide grin.

"Nope. And Ellie isn't yours."

"Nope."

"We'll stick to our island names then."

I'm completely puzzled as I watch her set items on the buffet table.

"You know her?" Julian is trying to catch up.

Confusion hits me hard, and I hiss a whistle to myself. "You can say that again. Kind of a one-night thing about three years ago."

His brows rise. "That's her?" Oh yeah, I've mentioned the mystery woman to him a few times. Borderline unhealthy how much she has occupied my mind.

Taking a deep breath, I'm utterly lost. "I didn't think I would see her again. I'm kind of caught off guard in this moment."

In the corner of my eye, I notice that Julian tips his head to the side. "Wait… did you say about three years ago?"

I take a long swig from my beer as my feet are cemented to the ground. "Yeah, why? Wait, you mentioned Savannah and the office? Tell me she doesn't work for you." I already know the answer, but it doesn't hurt to check.

The sound of a little girl giggling snaps my gaze to her as she wobbles during her run. She's smiling, part of her darker blonde, almost-brown hair up on top of her head, very cute, and races straight to the woman I now know is Elodie. She lifts her and tickles the girl's belly.

Huh.

I turn to my friend, and a feeling itches me, my forehead scrunching.

"She has a kid?"

Julian takes a very long drink from his bottle as though he is delaying the seconds. "Uh, yeah. Lola's a little over two years old, so plus nine months is… math, right?" His voice lacks his usual confident tone.

Math.

That's all it takes for me to drive my vision straight back to Elodie and Lola.

And the moment that Elodie's eyes tip up to meet mine, her smile wilts.

My chest gets tight like I've been stabbed in the heart.

2

ELODIE

It's like a knife cutting through me and pure elation. One moment I see him and our past flickers in my mind. I never thought I'd see him again. But then I remember Lola, this tiny human, binds Hale and me forever. I could have searched harder.

Fear fills me as he appears unexpectedly, one fact flooding his eyes—those same eyes that haunt my dreams.

He never knew he had a child.

And his fierce gaze, with his brown eyes turning stormy, tells me that I won't need to confirm what he just discovered.

Even with his hard face, chiseled jawline, and sandy-brown hair, he's undeniably handsome. His black sweater and dark blue jeans show he takes life seriously but can let loose. It's a crazy impression, but it's what I feel.

His breathing changes, chest rising rapidly. My heart pounds.

Did I ever imagine this day? Maybe in my dreams, but never at a BBQ with ranch dip in hand.

My daughter grabs my hair, snapping me into action.

Quickly, I hand her to Savannah, my best friend and Lola's godmother, who's oblivious but senses my urgency.

I dart back inside to the kitchen. Salads line the counter. Running my hands through my hair, I claw my head and exhale, flooded by memories.

The moment I saw Hale, I was entranced. The conversation led to the discovery that we approach life differently but both value a strong work ethic. I can easily sink into vacation time and relax. Him? He's adjusting, but there is a natural piece inside him that enjoys downtime. He even turned off his phone that was pinging with email notifications. He's well into his career, with ten years on me. It isn't exactly clear what he does, but he is definitely business-savvy.

Our groups wouldn't return until well after dinner. Our conversation continued on the beach and then for a bite to eat.

"You really should be out there, merman," I say as we continue to eat a late lunch at a bistro along the seafront.

"Hey, I said I was on the swim team in high school, but that doesn't mean I want to stay in the sea all day." He cuts into a piece of chicken.

"Disappointed you weren't captain of the hockey team? You'd have scored points on and off the ice." I've learned things about him, and I've shared things too.

His suave grin is infectious. I can't stop smiling. "My parents are good people. They never pushed me, even if hockey parents had better fundraisers. Enough about non-island life. Look at us—eating chicken on an island with fresh seafood," he says.

"We established I hate seafood, and so do you."

"Two peas in a pod."

He slips on sunglasses, hiding his eyes. The sun is bright, so I adjust my sunhat.

"You're headed back tomorrow? You don't want to spend it doing something, I don't know… islandy?" I ask.

"I'm sure this constitutes as islandy enough, considering I met you holding a pineapple."

"I was just checking that you aren't regretting something. I've already gathered you are not used to downtime."

"My dad always told me to be reckless once. This might be the start of that. Spontaneously ending up spending an afternoon with a stranger." A different look finds him. It's devilish, and I like that. "I'm not regretting anything right now. That's a very good thing." It sounds flirty, dangerous, and only keeps me wanting to stay in his presence. "Except…"

I wait for him to finish. I'm intrigued.

"You're burning. How have you not had a sunstroke yet?"

I check my arms—they're pink. "Oh. I didn't notice. I've been too absorbed in our conversation."

"I guess you don't have sunscreen with you, do you?" I shake my head. "Totally not me hitting on you," he holds his hands up in defense, "but my room has a perfect view of the sea, and I have sunscreen there."

At first, I want to reject his directness. But after talking with him all afternoon, I've noticed his polite manner. My intuition trusts him; I'm good at reading people.

"I'll send a text to my other cousin who isn't marrying my prom date, in case I disappear and can't be found. It would be a good story, though. The daughter of a preacher was last seen with a man corrupting her innocence."

Instantly, he grows still. "What?" He seems petrified.

All I can do is chuckle. "Relax. I was joking. My dad works in agriculture." The relief that hits him is honest. "Come on." I grin. "I might take a page from your father's book about being reckless, because I can assure you that this is new to me." I don't run off with a man I just met, but he's different. I feel it in my bones.

"Fair enough."

And ten minutes later, we're in his room in a boutique hotel with a balcony overlooking the sea. He keeps his word and hands me a bottle of sunscreen. Our fingers brush, and we both freeze, eyes locked. For a moment, we hover in stillness before we both lean in, and our lips meet suddenly.

I pace the kitchen, knowing I have seconds before Hale storms in. But that's not his real name, is it?

It connects to me that Savannah told me who was on the guest list, and I assume the guy close to Julian narrows down the options.

The sliding door opens. I look up and see that I was right. He quickly steps in, shuts the door, and we face each other at last.

"Elodie." With his gaze piercing my eyes and voice firm, I'm not sure what direction this conversation will go.

"You are not Hale. So what is your name?"

"Hayes."

I laugh once under my breath—this world just got smaller. We both used fake names that day, each not far from our own. "Right. Our real names suit us better, I think. I'm Elodie Miller, and you're Hayes Callahan." His brows knit, confused. I tug my sweater sleeve, nervous. "Savannah mentioned you a few times, a friend of Julian's. I just didn't realize it was *you*."

"Obviously. Otherwise, I would know about her. Wouldn't I?" His tone is measured, direct, not at all compassionate.

We both glance out the window. Lola is giggling in Savannah's arms on the lawn below, safe and unaware.

Swallowing emotion, I say, "You would." I step forward, but he steps back. "She's yours. In case—"

His jaw ticks, with his face remaining stone. "I know, Elodie. It's fucking obvious. We may have been together one day, but I never got the sense that you're a liar."

"I searched for—"

Hayes steps back. "And gave up," he accuses me.

This isn't the man I remember. Everything about him right now ignites a fear that he isn't the man I had hoped. His tone causes my mood to shift to angry. "I'm not the only one who kept details off the island," I say defensively.

He pinches the bridge of his nose. "Elodie, I don't fucking care. I have a kid out there that I didn't know about." He points outside.

My hands find my hips. I won't tolerate his mood, even if he has every right to be shocked. "She's not *a kid*. She's Lola," I bite out.

Remorse shades his face. "You're right."

A deathly silence surrounds us for a good long beat or two.

"Who does she think her dad is?"

My eyes drop to the floor. Unsure if my words will help his mind that is probably chaos right now, I meet his fiery gaze. "She's two—she doesn't get it yet. Her world is playing, snacks, and loud cartoons. All she knows is me as her parent. The only man in her life now is Julian. My brother Sam is deployed overseas; she's seen him just once. Her grandfather is in her life. So, to answer your question, there isn't a story yet."

His eyes grow. "A story *yet*. Well, that's going to fucking change."

There's a pit in my stomach because I'm unsure what he means, but it only makes me more determined to stay poised in this fragile situation. Hayes walks a few steps to the floor-to-ceiling sliding doors to watch the party, and I cautiously follow him. When Savannah and Julian see us, they quickly look away and, along with Lola, cross to the other side of the party.

"I thought we were careful. Wait…" His fingers find his temples to massage. "That one time."

We didn't just have sex once; it happened two more times.

"I got food poisoning the next day, and obviously that affected the efficiency of the pill too."

Another long inhale finds him, and he rubs his face. "Of course it would," he whispers. "Of course, we would be the 1%," he says cynically.

"Don't be mad, please."

He looks over his shoulder. "I'm not mad at that. I'm pissed I missed my daughter's first years. I won't shake that anger soon."

I close my eyes, feeling unfairly targeted. "Can we talk? Just not now. She's out there."

He nods gently once while he shoves his hands into his jeans pockets. "Okay."

I ease a little, still stuck in our standoff, emotions spinning in all directions.

Our silence doesn't last long, though.

"Wait. Julian mentioned something about the office."

I laugh nervously. It's not funny—I feel disaster looming. "I work at Haven Crossroads."

Hayes rubs his jaw, growling. "You've got to be kidding." I wince. "First Lola, now I'm your boss? My entire world changed in ten minutes."

"What do you mean?"

"I'm the new COO that they're announcing this week. They've been tight-lipped about it."

Yep, there is that other set of nerves that fears a looming disaster.

This can't be happening.

I couldn't care less that the man has more figures in his bank account than I can imagine. But my daughter's father, Julian's good friend in our social circle, working in the same building? This is effed up to epic proportions. Too many coincidences to make it even possible, yet here we are.

I take a tiny step forward, but our closer proximity feels like a bolt of lightning strikes between us. And the crazy thing is that even in our current states, it feels anything but edged. For a brief second, it comes back to me.

He helps tie the top of the bikini back into place as I sit on the edge of the bed, which is a mess of wrinkled white sheets. The feeling of his fingers feathering down my back awakens my body's sensitivity.

"To buy time, we can lie to our families and say we decided to go on some educational trip into the hills and check out a fluorescent pond."

I smile and make the mistake of looking at him with a sheet barely covering his waist. "Tempting. But we've now both crossed vacation fling off the reckless list." We got lucky, my cousins were too tired to meet up after their boat trip, and Hale's cousins were late back, so he blew them off. Fate let us have all night, talking while naked.

"I have to leave this room eventually, and we'll head back to our lives away from here. I don't do one-night stands." I think about it for a sec. "Or flings." Never. "So I'm just going to assume this is protocol when you have sex with a stranger." He is a man married to his career, it's obvious he would want nothing more. Nor am I someone capable of long-distance.

"For us, it seems to be," he jokes. His tongue is skilled,

and his cock hit the right spots. I assume he has experience. I'm not a virgin, but this guy's quality is unmatched in my life.

I want to stay, but that would make it worse. This is all it is.

I lean down to kiss him quickly on his lips that are firm yet have the ability to kiss softly. "I'm happy you missed the turtle dive."

"I'm happy you didn't throw the pineapple at me."

Gosh, that smirk. I'll miss it.

"Uh... I wouldn't know anyhow, but everything we've said to one another about our life minus the name part... it's true, isn't it?" I have to wonder.

He nods gingerly. "It is. Sure you don't want to burst the vacation fling bubble and tell me your real name?"

Thinking about it, I debate whether being wild and mysterious is really me. Once in a lifetime try, right? Besides... "Probably better if we don't. Even though we all might have that what-if person, I'll be more occupied with you in my head if I know who you really are."

He tilts his head, accepting my logic. "I agree." His knuckles slide down my cheek, a caress. It's a minute, maybe more, that our eyes lock, and we say nothing until he rasps, "If we ever meet again, then that'll be a sign to share our real names."

I grin at him. "Perhaps."

Our bodies remain in a standoff of recognition. Both of our lives just changed today.

"This all must sound messy, but I swear it wasn't my intention to keep this from you. I don't expect anything from yo—"

He steps back, and I feel a loss of connection, which is wild, as it was only magnetism in the air between us. "My mind is already made up. We'll be talking about this. I'm not waiting, either. Are you heading back to the city later today? I assume you live there if you work for me."

"I don't exactly work for you. More like the company." He isn't impressed. "Semantics," I rasp to myself and divert my gaze, my hands finding my back pockets. "We live there. I'm just staying here for the weekend to see my parents."

He chuckles to himself, bitterly amused, it seems. "Of course, you are from the same small town as my best friend's fiancée. Any other coincidences that we need to lay on the table?"

"No. I mean, if you really want to get into the details—"

He cuts me off. "Oh, I do," he says, adamant.

I met Hayes drinking from a damn pineapple. "Lola is allergic to pineapple, actually."

"Fitting," he responds flippantly.

This is one fucked-up circle of a conversation, and I'm getting exhausted. The sound of the door sliding open, though only partway, draws my attention to Savannah, who must have given Lola to Julian or one of the neighbors at the party. She is hesitantly perplexed and looking delicately at us. Searching for a clue about what the mood is in the room.

"Sorry to interrupt, but…" She swings her gaze between Hayes and me. "Uh, Lola seems to be a bit tired."

I check my watch. "Yeah, it's nap time. I'll… No, I'm going to go. I'll bring her to my parents'."

"No. I want to see her," Hayes grits out.

Savannah appears awkward and wants to escape but doesn't move an inch.

Momma bear instincts are in full force, and I step in front of him, my fingers pressing against his chest. This time, there is no spark, just pure protectiveness. "Not a chance. She has no clue who you are, and she's tired, and we need to talk. You know I'm right, too."

His nostrils flare slightly, but the way he darts his gaze deep into me feels tide-changing. "Fine. But I'm not leaving this damn town until we talk."

I nod in agreement. "Main Street, across from the coffeehouse, Foxy Rox, in an hour. Get my number from Julian."

Hurrying off, I trail behind Savannah to Julian, who is giving Lola a piece of watermelon.

"It's *him*!" Savannah whispers behind me.

I scoop up Lola from Julian. "Yes," I confirm in a hiss.

"Okay, so this is my sign to go check on Hayes while you two ladies… Yeah." He leaves us be.

Savannah seems as panicked as I am. "What happens now?"

"I don't know. I just need to get Lola to my parents', then I'll talk with him. He isn't exactly thrilled."

She watches the house. "What an a—"

Shaking my head, I still and blink to find myself digesting everything he has said. "But he seems to have already made up his mind on his role in Lola's life." I'm both weary and bewildered by his adamancy coming on so fast. "Now about…" I indicate with my head to my daughter without saying her name, because who knows what she hears or understands. "I'm trying to get a read on him, but all I'm getting is that he might be more pissed about missing so much, and I have a strange feeling that he will be taking that out on me."

Affectionately, she touches my arm. "No. Everything Julian has said to me about him means it will be okay. I have no idea how this happened, though. I realize that, well, names, Hayes not coming to the office while dealing with the business, and the lack of photos. All of it seems like it could happen. Small chance, but still."

"Trust me. If it's a one percent chance, then that's us.

Hence, why I have the cutest little girl in my arms," I coo at my daughter.

Savannah smiles at me with comfort, and I appreciate it because I need it.

———

Two hours later, I find Hayes sitting on a bench on Main Street, and I would rather have this conversation in complete privacy, but it's perhaps better that we're in public. It'll keep our tempers down, and if it really fails, there's a wine store on the corner to stock up for the night.

The way the autumn sun shines down causes his eyes to glint as I approach him. His look could slice right through me. Yet a glimmer of our time together whispers in my head.

I notice the expensive sports car parked across the street, and I assume it's his.

Sliding onto the bench, I ensure there is distance between us. Nothing about us right now is pulling us closer. Not like that day a few years ago.

"It's simple, Elodie." I gulp because he's stern and cold. "I'm not going to make this in any way easy on you."

And dread fills me to the brim.

"In fact, you are probably going to hate me, but I don't give a damn," he warns me.

3

HAYES

I spotted Elodie at the party and felt an instant rush of elation that I unexpectedly found her, but it was quickly replaced by confusion and anger. Now, I'm on a bench with a woman as beautiful as ever—except she's had two years with my daughter that I never got.

She seems nervous, and rightfully so. I'm not being the man who holds himself up to a high caliber. Because all I feel is determination not to make this easy for her—I want her to feel my anger for losing two years with my daughter, missing her milestones, and knowing I can't turn back time.

The last hour, I've been questioning my approach to the situation. I could be a man who hesitates, demands a paternity test, and puts his life on hold until evidence provides clarity. Or I can be a man who takes control of the situation, calls the shots, and approaches the news as I would with everything else in my life. Be determined and avoid failure. There is no middle ground for me. It's not in my nature. I'm doing my damn best to talk myself out of this approach, but my emotions keep winning the battle.

Fatherhood? It has everything to do with honor and

responsibility. Fatherhood and protectiveness are also simply a natural instinct that apparently I had and didn't even know it. I want this.

There is another reason deep down, but I'm not ready to fully confront it.

Sometimes in life, surprises awaken inner aspirations, right?

But holy mother of… I didn't know I had a daughter.

And I want to get straight to the point because my mind is running a thousand miles a minute.

"When did you find out?" I begin, my voice steady.

"When I was six weeks pregnant. I had a lot of nausea."

I'm beginning to take in the details. Elodie is younger, early in her career, and I wasn't in the picture. That begs me to wonder. "And you wanted to keep her?"

Her eyes move to cut right through me. "Yes." She's frustrated that I would even ask.

"You should have tried harder to find me."

Elodie sighs as we both look forward, probably at the stack of hay with a scarecrow sitting on top outside the coffeehouse called Foxy Rox. "Except privacy laws really make hotels unwilling to comply, *Hale.* Do you really want to go around in circles? What's most important is that you know this wasn't intentional."

It's a fair point. I look at her, and she meets me halfway. A quick memory of her in my arms, laughing and smelling of coconut, flashes by. We never ran out of things to say that night. But facts remain. "We barely know each other," I admit.

I can't read her facial expression, but she seems to accept it.

"I don't know what to do now," she admits. "I don't need your money or expect—"

I chuckle under my breath, bitterness tightening my voice because the facts of the matter return. "It's simple how this is going to go. I want you to know I'm determined to set things right with regard to Lola. Everything has come to mind while I waited for you. There are logistics. You will receive child support for all the years of missed payments. Lola can have her last name changed. A trust will be set up for her. My name is sure as hell going on that birth certificate, and I expect 50/50 on custody." Each word lands sharply.

She stands with her fists clenched and her face beginning to turn red. "No! You can't just waltz right in and uproot our lives. *Her* life."

I stretch my arm along the bench, jaw set. "'Waltz' is generous, sweetheart. I never even knew she existed. I lost two irreplaceable years, and that's not something I can just accept."

Elodie grasps that I'm not backing down with my requests and quickly sits down with panic glinting in her eyes. She angles her body to me, intent on making me listen. "Will you stop! I get it. You missed it all and I didn't, but you need to take a step back. This is a lot to process. I clearly move at a different pace than you. And you have yet to meet Lola." Her eyes pinch shut, then open, at the reality. "I mean properly, not spontaneously across a yard."

"Then we make that happen," I say, direct, even if every word she said is chipping away at this exterior I've chosen to wear today.

She grumbles in frustration, and in another fucked-up world where this wouldn't be our topic, I would consider it sexy as fuck.

Her hand movements signal for me to calm down. I pause, breathe, and reflect on where this conversation is heading. I perhaps need to take my foot off the gas pedal a bit. And I do, but I'm left in a cloud of curiosity.

"Allergic to pineapple," I say faintly, remembering our earlier conversation. I lean forward and rest my elbows on my knees.

A subtle ease finds her. "Yeah. Not serious but enough to keep being cautious."

Is this our starting point to step away from the legal talk of custody and those things? For me to calm down?

"When did she start to walk?"

"Thirteen months, though walk is an understatement—she ran. She's learning to talk: animals, people, cookies. She has a stuffed bunny named Bagel."

My mouth cracks into a half-smile from that. "Bagel?"

Elodie shrugs, smiling. "She named her at brunch a few weeks ago, and it stuck. Lola loves blueberry bagels with strawberry cream cheese."

It slips into my mind. The fact that this woman in front of me carried my child for nine months and brought her into the world. "Labor went okay?"

She nods. "Yeah, I mean, I guess average. Savannah was there. She's Lola's godmother." Our circles are even more entwined.

"Why the name Lola?"

Shrugging, she still maintains a soft smile. "I wanted something similar to me. Kind of had this view that it would be her and me, best friends hopefully. Plus, it's a cute and playful name."

"It's not going to be just you and her anymore." My voice is soft because the idea of her doing this all alone pings inside me. It's what she has been doing, but I'm in the picture now.

I like hearing things about Lola. I'm melting a bit. I can't help but wonder what it would've been like to witness her milestone moments. What would I have felt? Now, I can only imagine, as anger refuels inside me.

But then I recall seeing Lola for the first time and the lightning strike without doubt that she's mine. The shape of her mouth and nose was the giveaway; her eyes are far too familiar to my own. I tamp down my emotions and shock because I crave to learn every little detail about her.

"You'll send me photos?" I'm eager.

"Of course."

"What else does she like?"

"Playing. I think avoiding naps might be her hobby. She loves the small slide at daycare." Elodie's affection shows in her tone. I remember her as angelic and bright.

"Daycare?"

She glances sidelong at me, but with reassurance. "Yeah, Haven Crossroads has one. I'm sure you know all of those things, Mr. New COO."

Shit, I am.

The mother of my child works there, and no one knows I'm Lola's father—but that's about to change.

"We are going to have to address that dynamic. The office one. But Lola at daycare is perfect. I can check on her anytime."

Elodie inhales a sharp breath. "Right." Her voice is unsteady. "We have to go slow. You can't just show up when you want. She needs structure… I need to, well, figure you out and your intentions."

My lips quirk out as I consider. "Makes sense, but I'm not backing down from my original thought. I'm entering her life—because I have to, for Lola and for me—and I won't let this be simple. There's too much at stake to just let it go."

"Can we slow down? I'm also overwhelmed. I didn't think

I would see you again. This is big. Not just for me but for Lola, and she has no idea."

An instinct has my hand moving to comfort her, but I pull back before I touch her. We should keep a respectable wall between us while we figure out the basics. I'm probably being stubborn—any friend would say unreasonable—but right now, I ignore it. This situation stings.

"I'm not going to wait long. I want to meet her properly soon. It's a big week with the announcement of my joining Haven Crossroads, but now, Lola is an even bigger event."

She scoots away like I'm suddenly a hot plate. We both glance quickly at a car going by. This town is almost eerily calm. People say "good day" in passing, even if they notice that two people are in the most important conversation of their lives.

"By chance, in the city I got a place with three bedrooms, and there's a pool in the building. There's space for Lola." *And you.* That comes to my mind for a second, but that's a mistake. Or is it? We have to get to know one another a lot better.

Elodie tightens her sweater around her slim curves, disgruntled. "I'm at a loss for words. You'll meet her in a few days. After that, I hope we can find a way forward. It doesn't have to be messy, but it's always been her and me. I can't just let her go half the time."

I feel like an insufferable jerk, but the ache is still there— I want to scream, to demand why it had to be this way. Alas, this is the hand I'm forced to play, and I'll fight for every bit of lost time.

I stand, making my resolve unmistakable. "I warned you you'd hate me, but I keep my promises. This is happening— my lawyer will be in touch."

Her face turns pale, and her jaw drops. She stands, infuriated. "You have every right as her biological father to know Lola and play a role in her life if you're serious. But you know what? I'm getting the gist that so far today you are not being the best version of yourself. So figure it the fuck out so we can move forward."

And she storms away.

————

"You're being an asshole," Julian berates me as he sits behind his desk overlooking the city.

There's coffee and croissants on the table, but this breakfast meeting tanked in seconds.

"Am I? Tell me, oh wise one, what would you do in my shoes?" I challenge as I unbutton my blazer on my three-piece suit and saunter to the desk.

He folds his arms and gives me an unimpressed look but then slips into a sympathetic one. "Fine. I'm not sure. But Elodie, she's... sweet, kind... my fiancée's best friend, employee... did I mention a great mom?"

Sitting down in front of his desk, I don't argue his description. "I'm trying to navigate the next few days. I need to talk to her and balance the announcement."

"Agreed. I've already had my assistant ask marketing to reschedule interviews and such to give you a few days of breathing space."

"I appreciate that."

"But I'm also advising you as a friend that you need to find another approach when it comes to Elodie. You know I'm right."

I am listening.

But I'm a man capable of being two people. One is a man who seeks success and approaches it with structure. Out of the office, I'm the guy who is normally lower-key. Except, the whole weekend I treated life like a business deal, throwing around demands and seeing red.

Maybe the struggle is that I'm trying to figure out the alternate routes. I'm capable of operating a billion-dollar company, but my newly discovered daughter and her mom, who was a one-night stand? I'm clueless. Out of my realm. I'm resorting to what I know best, and that's a business approach fueled by innate instinct for my child. And an awareness that I can't even consider Elodie a one-night stand. It was a stronger connection, which is another slew of problems in itself.

But as I reflect, I'm aware I'm going to have re-evaluate my demeanor.

The knock on the door causes my attention to refocus, and I see our CFO, Foster, arrive. I've known him since before my career move, purely from social functions with Julian. He's our age, sharp, and we will be working closely together now.

"Hey." I don't sound too enthusiastic, and it isn't directed at him.

He grimaces humorously as he takes a seat next to me. "Yikes. Someone woke up on the wrong side of the bed. Or did Julian give you food poisoning at his BBQ? For once, I might be happy I missed it."

Julian scoffs a laugh. "Most definitely not food poisoning," he mutters.

Foster becomes puzzled, swinging his gaze between us, yet a grin remains. "What's going on? I have a feeling we're not running through the press announcement for tomorrow."

Julian indicates with his hand that the floor is all mine.

Taking a deep breath, I debate the best way to share my news. "Elodie is in your department, right?"

"Yeah. Just made her a manager. Great at accounts receivable. She's been working her way up since she joined us a few years ago. Why?"

Scratching my neck, I decide to just jump off the cliff. "Her daughter..." I drawl out.

"Her daughter, Lola. Yes?" He is still oblivious but trying to drag this sentence along faster.

"She's mine."

Foster's face slips to neutral, probably debating if I'm joking or not. "What?"

He needs me to repeat.

"Lola, I'm her dad. I just found out, too."

He gives a sideways glance to Julian to double-check, and he nods in agreement that this isn't a joke, but then he grasps the situation. "Wow… okay. This wasn't on my bingo card, but…" Tilting his head to the side, he appears to be contemplating. "I'm not going to ask for details, but fuck, this is…"

I stand with the intent to get a strong black coffee now that everyone is on the same page. "Look, I need to talk to Elodie. I'm sure we can all agree to keep this news between these walls, but that's not going to last forever," I say without looking over my shoulder. I pick up a cup and attempt to understand the machine, all the while considering if the news has sunk in for me now that it's been two days.

"We'll wait for your cue to do what we need to," Julian assures me.

Finding success with the machine, I give it a mere glance. "Thanks."

"What am I supposed to do when I see Elodie in the office this morning? I can't just pretend not to know. I'm not that good an actor." Foster sounds compassionate and frustrated rolled into one.

"Give me a few hours. I need to talk to her." I take a

quick sip of the coffee that is pretty damn good, definitely the kick of energy I need. I didn't sleep much last night.

"So the plan is the announcement of your new role tomorrow. Then the fact that you are now a father and the mother works for Haven Crossroads and just got promoted and might end up in meetings with you, will be out in the open when?" Foster asks facetiously.

The way he strung together the office obstacles into one shouldn't be funny, it's a mess, but it causes the corner of my mouth to tug, barely.

"We have some boundaries to set," I agree. "But I'm not going to keep this a secret forever. I have no reason to hide the reality."

Julian breaks out in an approving smile. "Didn't think you would." His face quickly turns stern. "Just take it down a notch on the legal BS that you wish to throw at Elodie."

Foster winces. "Geez."

"I'm a dad now, I need to think seriously about these things."

"Exactly, you're a dad now. Don't be like mine, though. Otherwise, you will end up with a kid who never wants to talk to you."

Foster throws his thumb over his shoulder in Julian's direction. "I second that. Be the dad who actually enjoys Saturday at the zoo with a thousand kids screaming."

That reminds me of my father. He was all those things growing up. Not a single event missed. If he's looking down on me right now, then I'm sure he would tell me that I can be a better man.

Setting my coffee down, I take a loud breath and rub my forehead with my hand. Coffee and my two friends are going against me this morning.

My approach obviously needs to be retailored, and I'm

beginning to feel it, too, if I'm honest. Is this what cooling off from this life-changing news feels like?

"I'm calm. I'll talk to her. Do you have a recommendation for where we can go for early lunch away from the office?"

Foster and Julian look at one another and chuckle before Foster zips his gaze back to me. "Do we? The city is ours. We have options. So what ambiance are you wanting?"

My phone begins to vibrate, and I fish it out of my pocket. "Hold on, the assistant has the time the movers are arriving at my new place."

But one glance at my home screen and dread fills me.

ELODIE

What the hell! We need to talk and fast!

"I need a spot with a table in the corner, private, and where nobody can hear. Food should be top-notch to ease the mood. And I need a reservation ASAP because I did something this morning that she already wants to kill me for…"

4

ELODIE

As soon as I enter the highly reviewed Italian restaurant with a dark interior, I'm ushered by the hostess to the back, to a circular corner booth with a white linen tablecloth tucked away from everyone, where Hayes is already waiting. The hostess seems to notice that my scowl isn't changing into a polite smile for her, which isn't like me, but I'm boiling. She skitters away.

Hayes looks up as I hover, standing stiffly beside the table, not taking my seat yet.

"If you want to play dirty, then I sure as hell will," I begin, with venom in my voice and my hand on my hip.

I hate two things right now. One is the way the corner of his mouth curls up into a sly smirk while he's in a three-piece suit, which causes me to forget to breathe for a beat. Two, he is doing everything to make me livid.

He begins to stand because the man has manners and waits for the woman to sit down. "I didn't order seafood since we both hate it." He remembers.

But I let go of that little fact when I recall our last conversation. "I'm not going to stay long. I want you to know that if you come at me with your fancy lawyers or legal documents, I won't hesitate to fight back with a lawyer of my own."

His lips roll in, and for a second, he appears remorseful.

"Elodie," he says, his tone firm.

I point my finger at him because I'm not going to let him take charge of this conversation. "You need to back it up. Imagine my surprise when I dropped Lola off at daycare this morning, and they let me know that *you* requested to be updated on her day and are now also an emergency contact."

"Well, they informed me they need your permission, but still. Why not?" My eyes drill into him with my face blank, waiting for the smart man to figure it out. He swings his eyes to the side before zooming back to meet my own. "I admit that was a step too far and should have checked in with you first. I apologize. I'm just eager to learn about Lola."

I pause, weighing what's best for my daughter against my memories of this man.

He senses it and spreads his hand out to the table. "Please, join me. We need to talk." I remain in place. "For Lola." His voice softens, not at all suited to the image of a man who has his own driver and meets with billionaires every day. Nor the man from the weekend whose wrath I faced.

With a deep breath, I slide into the booth opposite him. "I'm listening, but we have to figure something out."

He nods once in understanding. "Agreed."

I lift my chin slightly as I investigate him. He's different today, I sense it. "Have you decided to ditch the asshole approach for this conversation? Because our last one wasn't so great," I remind him.

He actually has a shade of a smirk on his face. "You might have had a point and I wasn't my best self when we spoke back in Everhope."

"Really? Who could have guessed?" I say, deadpan.

The corner of his mouth ticks due to my comment. Does he find me amusing? He clears his throat. "I would like to make up for that. I'm a better man, and you'll quickly learn that."

"I don't deserve the way you've approached this all," I quietly point out.

"No, you don't," he solemnly agrees. "Shock and adrenaline clearly don't bring out my finest qualities."

He sighs and nods a thanks to the college-aged waiter who delivers his whiskey on the rocks; Hayes gestures if I want one, and I shake my head. Water is safer, I need to focus.

"I'm trying to be a little more understanding because if I were in your shoes, then I would be losing my mind, too."

He smiles softly. "Understanding sounds like you. You saw a wounded crab on the sand and worried about it for a solid five minutes. You don't have an ounce of venom inside you."

Creases form on my forehead because the tiny detail grabs me. "Can't believe you remember that."

Hayes moves his glass in a circle, appraising the ice cubes as they swirl. "Hard to forget."

The sincerity dripping in his tone is overwhelming because deep down, my instincts tell me it's true.

"How do I know you won't disappear? I can't let Lola get attached just to be hurt."

Hayes's eyes nearly bug out, and he seems flabbergasted. "Do you really think I would do that? Like *really*?" He isn't at all impressed. "The man who literally, within two hours of finding out, was offering *legal* options to ensure that I see her and she is financially secure. The man you will be around a lot because of mutual friends and work. And you have the audacity to ask me that?"

My lips tighten, and I inhale. "Okay. You've had days to digest this. From the start, you were all in. I'm…" I glance down, nervously playing with a fork. "It's not what I expected. Most men in your situation would demand a paternity test or something."

"Why the hell would I? Let me highlight *again* that we will be around each other a lot and that there is no advantage to you in lying, nor do I sense that you would. Shall I point out how blatantly obvious it is that Lola is mine? One look is all it takes. A calendar makes it obvious, too." He's heating up a bit.

"You're right. But having a child is a big life change."

"Elodie, you are right. Being a father hadn't exactly crossed my mind lately. But that papa-bear internal-instinct bullshit is legit. So here I am."

At last, I crack, my jaw tense and the corner of my mouth stretching. "It is real," I assure him, voice low. "That's why I'm mama bear right now."

We offer each other a comforting look.

Inside of me blooms what I can relate to. "I get it."

One flick and his eyes dart straight into me. "We have a lot to unpack, eh."

"We do," I agree.

Another waiter arrives with a few dishes of food to share. A tossed salad, breadsticks, ravioli, and a slice of tiramisu.

I frown, but at the same time, I try to fight a grin. "Feeding an army?"

He chuckles as we are left alone again. "I figured we might be here a while and might need fuel for our discussion."

"Smart."

He leans back and shows little interest in food; he studies

me up and down, and I begin to feel self-conscious. "How is the cousin who married your prom date?"

"Filing for divorce," I say blandly. "How is your dad, who told you to be reckless? I'm not sure he would have suggested an unexpected pregnancy as part of his advice, but still." I lift a shoulder.

Hayes bites the inside of his cheek, and I must have said something because a shade of vulnerability appears. "He passed, actually. A heart attack. Last year."

Sympathy fills me. I touch my chest. "I'm sorry to hear." He spoke about him a few times that night; they were close.

He begins to smile faintly to himself. "Maybe that's why I'm jumping in? Something to do with that. Not having a father anymore. He was a good man, humble, and did his best to give me opportunities. If I can give Lola opportunities, I will. He for sure influenced me to ensure family comes first."

I slide around the circular booth to be close enough to comfort him, and I consider touching his arm. "Sounds like it."

My fingers give in and imprint on his arm, my thumb stroking that spot between his expensive watch and his elbow. That feeling that my body hasn't forgotten, the thrill of being around someone I'm attracted to, with not a care in the world. Hayes pats the top of my hand in appreciation of the comfort.

"You still smell of coconut," he mentions faintly. Wow. He remembers a lot, apparently.

The memories of the island come back. At times, we ignored everything but that moment. Except it's different this time when reality hits. We are now two people responsible for a child. I wouldn't change it for the world, but this is by no means easy.

"So tell me, Mr. Self-Made Billionaire, how did it all come to be?" I smile.

He grabs his glass. "Not much to say. I had a scholarship for a private high school—"

"Superstar swimmer. I remember."

"Yeah. With my grades, I got into one of the best universities on the east coast, and after that, I just found luck with the right companies to take a chance on. I'm used to tech, but Julian managed to persuade me. Operations can be applied to any company. Here I am. A change."

"A challenge, maybe, too. Shipments are not algorithms."

"But running departments can be the same. Improving internal day-to-day running is essential for any company."

I shrug my shoulders. "Fair enough."

"You? How did you end up at Haven Crossroads?"

"Typical story. Graduated from college here in the state. By chance, Olivia in HR is also from Everhope, although she was a few years ahead of me in school. Anyhow, she helped me join the graduate program, and I worked my way up. I would like to think I'm doing alright. Even when I accidentally got pregnant, I kept going—proving I'm capable, even if it sometimes feels like I need to defend my success. But I digress."

Something in his mind is stewing, but he isn't sharing his thoughts. "What do you want to do now?" he comments more than asks.

"Attack the salad first." He squints at me, and I grin. "Not like there is a bigger issue at hand," I joke.

He chuckles under his breath at my ability to add humor to this situation.

"Only meeting my daughter for the first time," he responds lightheartedly.

I let our touch go and quirk my lips out, considering the approach. "This weekend?"

"Sooner." He's obstinate, but his voice is calm.

"After work, I pick her up from daycare, but she can be crabby. We get home, have dinner, bathtime, then bed by seven… for her, not me." His eyes turn bold, and he must be thinking something else because he has a droll smile. "Not that my bedtime matters or anything."

"No. Not at all." He sounds unconvinced. "But leave work early."

"I'd need to talk to Foster." Hayes glances away awkwardly, and my internal radar flashes. "What did you do?" I nearly grit my teeth.

"You can leave early. I might have already…"

I grumble to myself, then remember to stay calm. "You've got to be kidding me."

"I was with Julian, who already knows, obviously. It made sense. We have a few optics in the office to figure out, you and me."

Giving him a stern look with my finger pointed at him, I issue my warning. "Do not mess with my job. I can only imagine what people in the office will think. I'm not the woman who sleeps around to do well in her career." I huff a breath of exhaustion.

"I won't. And who cares? You were working at Haven before I even joined. People will find out, though. You're going to have to find a way to wrap your head around it."

"Lola won't be a secret, I know. Plus, her daycare probably already has theories, so thanks for that," I say sarcastically, and it makes him have a boyish, cocky look that is appealing, to be honest.

I really do see that he isn't trying to be vicious… today, at least. Last weekend was rough.

He lightly touches my shoulder. "Please…" he begs delicately. "Can I see her this afternoon?"

Work has already gone out the door, and logic dictates that Lola will be in better spirits in the afternoon.

"I really want this before the announcement. I'll be able to think more clearly," he implores.

"It's not about you," I point out, but then my face tightens because he has already lost enough time with her. A little more than two years, and more if we're counting the pregnancy. He's persistent, and at some point I need to test the waters to see him interact with Lola. Maybe he'll change his mind about his role as a dad. I doubt it, and that's probably what weighs me down. This is all real, he's here in my life now and with full intention to stay. I need to take steps to help me figure out how to handle my new reality.

"Okay. How about 4pm?"

His eyes light up with agreement.

It took three minutes for us to agree that neither one of us seemed to have an appetite. We asked for the food to be packed up.

For now, nerves made us full enough.

———

IT's best that I pick up Lola and head straight home to ensure everything at home is ready by 4pm. Hence, I'm at my desk in my office and closing down for the day. My office is most definitely not a corner office. It's small but still has a large window with a view of the skyline.

Blair, my colleague, who spends her lunchtimes eating salad and redoing her makeup, stalls mid-pass by my door. "Have you heard?"

Glancing up as I zip my purse, I see her with her dark pink nails holding her routine afternoon bottle of sparkling water. "What?"

"People saw Hayes Callahan around the office this morning. For sure, they are announcing tomorrow that he's the new COO. How lucky are we? Have you seen him? Heard he's single, too."

I stall as I'm about to swing the strap of my purse over my shoulder. "Maybe." Something is brewing inside me. Concern for what the office will think, the reminder that even at work, Hayes and I will cross paths, and a bit of possessiveness that Blair needs to keep her claws away from him. Because yes, I've seen him, and my body hasn't forgotten him, either.

"Hopefully. Anyhow, where are you heading? I saw that our one-on-one has changed times." She spots the paper doggy bags. "Whoa, did you go out for lunch to that new spot? Heard they book out for weeks."

I continue my quest to leave. "Yeah, sorry. Lola is sick, and I need to take her home," I lie and choose to bypass the answer about the restaurant.

"Oh, hope the little squirt feels better."

"Thanks," I say and speed past her. I cruise through the hallway and straight to the corner office, where Foster's door is open. I'm lucky that we have a good rapport, so this only feels 75% awkward instead of 100%.

Knocking softly on the door pane, he glances up from his desk only to do a double take. His crooked smile appears strained.

"Sorry to disappear, but I need to go."

"*Yeah*. No worries." He appears equal parts understanding and in an awkward position.

I roll my eyes because I don't need to explain further. Because Hayes already went above me to tell him I'm taking off. "I will sort something out so this doesn't become a thing. Just need to establish some…" How do I phrase this correctly, but I give up. "Foster, this is…" I try again, only to blow out a raspberry and quickly glance to the sky for a miracle.

"A little crazy," he supplies.

"Yeah," I agree.

"Go. See you tomorrow." He reassures me with a sympathetic expression on his face.

But as I turn to leave, I stop mid-pivot and look back at him. "Can I ask you something not office-related?"

"Always."

The last 72 hours have already been spinning enough that I might as well get it all out. "You know Hayes better than I do. Even if he isn't, can you just tell me he's a good guy? I need to hear that."

Foster's mouth stretches into a warm, closed smile. "No need to lie to you. He's a good guy. Stubborn but a good guy."

I breathe easy and let it be.

———

TWO HOURS LATER, my heart is racing. Lola woke from her afternoon nap a while ago. I fixed her pigtails, and now she's happily playing with her tea set, completely oblivious to how the doorman phoning to announce Hayes's arrival is life-changing.

I'm lucky, we live in a nice building, though by no means extravagant. Our two-bedroom apartment is in a new and secure building. Probably not even a quarter the size of Hayes's new place, but we have enough space for us, and the building's elevator has been a gift that keeps on giving for the stroller hassle.

I scanned the living room and spent a solid 20 minutes cleaning up. I'm not sure Hayes would be judgmental, but I want to ensure he has the right impression. Simply, that Lola and I are fine.

Walking to the door, I shake my hands, attempting to rid myself of nervous energy, but it fails. Slowly I open the door, waiting for him to appear from the elevator, and the moment he does, my body jolts.

Hayes holds a bouquet of peach-colored roses in one hand and a stuffed bunny with a pink balloon.

I race to him and start to claw the balloon. "You have to get rid of that."

He is completely perplexed at what the hell is happening. "What? Why?"

I yank the balloon down by its string and begin untying it. "Lola is petrified of balloons."

He scoffs a laugh. "Balloons? A two-year-old is scared of balloons?"

"Yes." I quickly push the loose balloon into the trash can near the elevator, hurry back to him, smile with relief, and wipe my hands. "Good."

Hayes continues to stare at me, bewildered. "My child is scared of balloons?"

I shrug before I usher him along into my apartment. "Weird, I know. It's a work in progress."

Closing the door behind us, he turns to me, and I step forward to square his shoulders with my hands. "Okay." We both breathe together, then I turned puzzled. "What's the bouquet of roses for?"

"Well, after the bad impression I made for our reunion, I felt compelled to show you I'm not a demanding ass… most of the time. I thought—"

I cut right in and shake my head. "Oh, Hayes. Hayes, Hayes, Hayes," I tut. "Flowers do not win me over and make up for the last 72 hours and your demeanor." But I'd be lying if I tried to deny that I don't have butterflies right now. He just pulled a Prince Charming move, and for a split second, I remember the man I met on the island.

"A guy can try," he replies in defeat. He notices the side table next to the coats hung on the wall and a basket with Lola's unicorn rainboots sticking out. He tosses the flowers on the table and continues to hold the bunny.

"Ready?" I ask.

He smiles. It isn't nervous. Nor scared. It's excited. "No. Are you?" He continues to grin.

"No."

"Then we should probably do this while we are completely overconfident," he teases.

I agree with a half-smile, and I turn him around and give him a little push in the direction of the living room. But the touch causes us both to still because there's a spark that travels between us, and I feel a tiny jump in my chest. He briefly turns his head slightly to the side as though he wants to look at me to check that I felt it, too, before he continues his journey forward.

When we enter the living room, Lola is completely lost in her tea set.

"Look, we have a visitor," I attempt to grab her attention, and her head perks up. She instantly notices that Hayes is next to me. Lola doesn't seem sure what to do or say, but her eyes notice the bunny, and suddenly her focus is lasered.

Hayes looks down to see what has her attention, then zips his eyes back up, smiling in the process. He shakes the stuffed toy. "Got you something. I heard Bagel could use a friend."

My hand clenches my heart. What a perfect gift to give. He remembered what I mentioned. It's also completely cute when the handsome man next to you wants to be sweet with a little girl with pigtails, warily staring at him.

"It's okay, Hayes is a fr…" I stop mid-sentence. She's at that funny age that I'm not sure what she will or will not remember; she is also resilient. "A special guy."

Hayes gives me a quick glance that is a little hard on the edges, but he returns all focus on Lola, who now totters slowly her way to us, still unsure. He crouches down and holds out the bunny.

"She can be a little shy and not say much," I assure him as she hides behind my leg but peeks around.

They stare at one another eye to eye, and I notice that Hayes might be choking up because I see the bob in his throat as he swallows. Lola accepts the stuffed toy but then hands it back to him.

Chuckling, I'm watching the scene unfold. "That's a good sign. She must like you if she's sharing."

He grins at her. "Thank you." Hayes looks up to check in with me. "I kind of wish the store had bigger emotional support rabbits."

Lola waddles away to grab Bagel from the sofa and returns to Hayes and hands it to him.

"Ah, a bunny family," he notes.

Lola nods fervently and smiles, showing her gap-toothed grin.

"Not going to say hi?" I ask her.

She looks at me, then back to Hayes, then me again. "Hi," she says matter-of-factly, and it causes Hayes and me to chuckle.

"It's okay, she needs time." Hayes stands up as Lola continues to stare at him in awe.

"Better be nice. Otherwise, I'm not sure teddy cookies

and mac n' cheese are on the menu, missy," I playfully tell her.

"Banana?"

I bring my finger to my chin. "Hmm. A negotiator."

"Like her fath…" Hayes stops himself.

The mood suddenly thickens, but Lola has no idea and totters back to her toys on the floor.

"Yeah. Like him," I rasp to myself.

"She doesn't want ravioli?" he asks, as I have a lot of leftovers that I brought home.

I pat my hand on his shoulder. "*Yeah,* given a choice between fancy ravioli or bear noodles with cheese, what do you think will win?"

A wide grin spreads on his face. "Solid point."

"But we can have the ravioli left from lunch. Am I assuming you're staying for dinner? I mean, if you…"

"Yeah." He only watches Lola. "I would like that a lot. I need to meet the leadership team for drinks, but that's not until later."

Lola continues to stare at him, completely bewildered as she holds both bunnies close, and she sits on her knees next to her tea set.

But my daughter isn't afraid, nervous, or shy.

There's a connection.

No doubt about it.

She just knows.

He isn't a stranger who walked in. The man looking on with so much interest and love that I already see is her father.

Hayes takes the plunge and cautiously approaches her before joining her on the floor. She glances at me, and I nod assurance to her, and she looks at Hayes.

And when they begin to play with the teacups and stuffed

animals, flutters inside me warn me that this is the image of a family that could break me, or we could all be exactly where we've always belonged.

5

___

HAYES

___

"She goes to sleep that easily?" I wonder. When I hear Elodie patter back into the living room, where I've been perusing the wall of photos of Elodie and Lola, I unstuff my hands from my pockets and bring my gaze to her.

She smiles angelically. "Normally not but having a visitor over after a day of daycare can drain some energy."

"All she did was stare at me," I deadpan, and it causes her to hiccup a chuckle.

I did my best attempting to play with the bunnies with Lola, but she just kept hugging them and looking at me with curiosity. At dinner, we were in a deadlock, and she kept filling her mouth with food with that cute little spoon, but her eyes never drifted away from me. A multi-tasker, I guess. And when Elodie told her that it was time to go to bed, Lola gave me a little wave and continued her long appraisal of me as her mother towed her away.

I took a peek into Lola's room once she had her pajamas on. There were unicorns everywhere. Even if it was a giraffe, bear, or whale, they all had unicorn horns. I waved good night to her when Elodie set her in the crib, then let them be. She mentioned that Lola is moving to a bed; she was going to do it in the next few weeks. I make a note of it in my head for my place because these little practical things keep trickling into my brain.

I've looked over the rest of the home. Everything here exudes love.

How the hell am I going to fit into this picture? I don't know.

"Well, she announced her other bunny is called Berry. That's something. You're new and interesting. Plus…" Elodie seems hesitant to say what she's thinking. "I don't know. Kids are more intuitive than we think. She's aware that you are not just a friend stopping by. Who exactly, not sure. But it's just… different. I haven't seen her like this before, but she's happy."

Our eyes meet, and we both understand how profound this is.

I've been going crazy for the last two hours. I'm stuck on seeing Elodie, the way her smile still radiates with no tropical sun needed, or how she bellows out short laughs when she finds something amusing, and then there is the fact that every time we connect through glances, my pulse picks up. She's still beautiful, caring, and motherhood suits her. I got lost until Lola's little squeals would grab me and remind me of reality. I'm not here to remember the way Elodie tastes or the softness of her lips. I'm here because we have a daughter.

The little girl who only knows how to do adorable things. It's instant, a bond already forming. I feel it in my bones. Why else would Lola only be calm when I'm in the room? She watched me with interest, I think. I'm not the best reader of toddlers, yet.

Tilting my head in the direction of the kitchen, I suggest that we head there, and Elodie follows. We ate at the counter that divides the living room making small talk, and she was quick to collect the plates. But not to clean; she needs to occupy herself to avoid recognizing that the air is shifting around us.

I pick up Lola's plate and have to half-smile to myself. Smooshed banana remains on the pink plastic plate. "She's a good eater."

"Yeah, but breakfast is her jam. We could make that a three-course meal, and she still wouldn't want it to end." She sets the items in the sink, and I follow her lead.

"We'll have to do breakfast then," I casually mention, but it just opened up a door to a whole other conversation, and I sense it.

Elodie turns around to lean against the edge of the sink. She crosses her arms and sighs. I mimic her movements, and we are next to one another as we both look forward.

She nudges my shoulder with her own. "How does it feel? Meeting her?"

Instantly, I smile. "A mix between over the moon and on the edge of a cliff. She's special. I'd like to think she has some of my attributes."

"I know. It's been kind of hard to escape you when she has your resemblance."

Suddenly, I feel slightly numb with another thought. "Did you want to escape me?"

Gingerly, she shakes her head. "No. It was just hard not knowing where you were."

I'm trying to imagine her position; it's a bit of a struggle when I'm jealous of all the time she had with Lola.

"I'm here now," I whisper to myself.

But she heard me. "What is it that you want, Hayes?"

Elodie saying my name in any tone stokes fire in me. Both the good and the bad. "More of this. I get that we can't just tell her who I am, but I'm not going to wait long to do it, either."

In the corner of my eye, I see her nod once slowly as she listens. "Have you told your family?"

My lips quirk. "Not yet. Well, my mom will be thrilled. She might go a little overboard. That's bound to happen when her only child becomes a dad, I guess. I'm not getting younger, either. Plus, since my dad died, she's been trying to find ways to fill her time. I try to talk with her at least once a week and ensure she is taken care of. Her spirits will lift. What better way than a grandchild? Be afraid that she'll consider moving to Illinois."

Elodie continues to listen attentively. "She's on the east coast, right?"

"Yeah, Boston." My mother is a character, insists on going to the gym several times a week even at seventy, and she's done her best to stay in good spirits since my dad passed unexpectedly. I should fly out to see her more often. "Your parents are going to murder me, aren't they?"

"Nah." She waves me off. "They are good honest people. Your money is nothing to them. My dad just retired after years as a manager at an agriculture company near Everhope, and it gave us an upbringing that we count our blessings for. To be honest, nobody in Everhope is struggling."

"Reminds me of my family. My dad worked hard, and my mom was a teacher." We grew up similarly in a way, and I would like to think that it means we grew up with similar values. A smile tickles my mouth. "You're avoiding the main question of how they took the news."

"I mean, they weren't over the moon when I told them I was pregnant and the dad wasn't in the picture. I mean…"

She raises one hand above her head. "My brother is serving his country." She lowers her other hand to show a difference in scale. "Their daughter accidentally became pregnant, with no man in her life," she quips before turning serious. "But I've explained to them how this all came to be… after my dad's favorite hockey team won a game and he'd had a few beers, of course. To lighten the blow." She isn't joking.

She continues, "They dote on Lola. It worked out. They are aware you re-entered the picture and are giving us space until I'm ready for you to meet them. They don't blame you. Even if they did, would you care?"

Scratching the back of my neck and crossing one ankle over the other, I have to highlight the obvious about me. "People don't scare me, Elodie. But out of principle and respect, then maybe. It's the honorable thing to do, to stand by a woman when you get her pregnant."

She hums a sound. "It's commendable but has to be for the right reasons, Hayes. Not because of the way we were raised or think it is supposed to be."

I have to chuckle. "I'm not sure my mom from Boston with a strong Irish Catholic background would agree. She still sometimes goes to confession. I'm already anticipating her second sentence, which will be about marriage."

One look and Elodie seems petrified.

Shrugging, I have to calm her, even though a part of me considered the option. "I'm not suggesting that, unless that's what you would have expected from day one had I been there at the beginning."

She shakes her head fervently side to side. "No. My parents have an amazing marriage, and it's because they married for the right reasons. Not because of a sense of obligation."

"Still, I've gone crazy the last few days because I can't

pinpoint so many aspects of how to go down this road. Honorable and responsible keep coming to mind."

Immediately, she scoffs and steps forward. "This isn't about the honorable *thing*. You don't need to get close or suggest all of these documents if it's out of obligation."

She moves to leave my orbit, but I'm quick to touch her wrist and prevent her from going. "Obligation and wanting to provide are almost the same. I *want* to get to know Lola, and I *want* to provide."

She eases, but my hand is still on her arm, and my fingers feel glued to her. Touching her could become a vice. I just can't let the magnetic force between us go. She doesn't step back, either.

"Uhm." Her voice is delicate, and her fingers feather over the back of my hand glued to her wrist. "You mentioned your dad passing. You spoke about him a lot on the island. What do you think his reaction would've been?"

It stings that he isn't around. It's the memory of him that has helped remind me to soften around Elodie and Lola. I slip my gaze away from her as I reflect. "Nobody expects to see someone at breakfast, then never again when everything seems to be going well. I'm grateful that I was in town when it happened. We had lunch the day before, he and I, after he met with his broker." I smile somberly to myself. "We were talking stocks. You and he might have gotten along. Numbers and all."

"He sounds like a good man."

"He was. I've been wondering what he would think of all of this. He was a little traditional in some ways and not in others. I guess it's unpredictable where his opinions would lie. I think he would've laughed and passed me a cigar."

She smiles sympathetically. "I could envision you

accepting it, even though I guess you don't really smoke cigars, do you?"

"No. Occasionally at a wedding."

Silence grows between us.

"When do you want to see her again?" she asks softly.

"Later in the week? I'm slammed for the next three days with the COO announcement. Doesn't mean I don't expect updates or photos."

Her face begins to bloom with a changed mood, and I think it's because of my request. "I can do that," she promises.

I run my hand up and squeeze her arm, and the fingers of my other hand wrap around her opposite arm, caressing to soothe her and to drive my senses wild. "As for the office…" I know it's on her mind. "This week, we don't say anything, except HR should probably know before they hear it on the grapevine. It will help give us a breather to figure it out."

She fights a laugh that seems desperate to escape. "A breather? You? I'm not sure that's possible, I've quickly learned."

Glancing away, I drag my gaze back and smirk to myself. "I guess you know me well, but we barely know one another at all."

Quiet surrounds us, and her eyes narrow. "Is it crazy that I'm well aware that I'm not familiar enough with you, yet I'm not sure it feels that way?"

Ahh, our connection. She feels it too.

"Well, I guess we haven't been able to stop and actually talk as two people who thought they would never see one another after an amazing night, and then here we are. We've been occupied with other topics."

"With the product of that amazing night," she quips.

I haven't let her go or broken our gaze; we are trapped in a moment that we don't want to end. "We probably need to address something else in this whole equation, which is—"

"Co-parenting." She cuts me right off, and my chest tightens because apparently, I hate that word.

"Never want to talk about…" I drawl, hoping she would finish the sentence.

Her hands wrap around my wrists to remove my touch from her, but she glances down and doesn't let me loose. "My head is spinning already."

"So, exploring…" Why am I dragging us down this hole? I'm smarter than this. But I need to poke around the option for both her and me. We have to figure out what we remember of one another from our night together, if the traces of carefree us are still there. We were good together.

I'm captivated. By Elodie. Our spark is still strong, and it will circle in my head until I have an answer. It's dangerous considering we have a child in the mix, but I'm not a man who backs down.

"Hayes," she purrs, giving me a warning, and the corner of her mouth tugs. She can read my mind, and she's the responsible one right now. Hence, why she isn't letting me utter the words.

"Okay." For now.

At last, she lets me go, and I comprehend that not even a finger-painted blob on a paper on the fridge can distract me from the obvious. I'm a hot-blooded man who is forever bound to this woman, and I need Elodie on the table. Not only *on* the table, but also the option of whether we are worth investing in.

With her back to me, she stands behind the opposite counter and grabs a kitchen towel. "Slow."

The way she says it has me trying to understand what she

means. I would say it's about Lola, but I'm not entirely convinced.

We might go around in circles right now broaching the topic, and I believe we've had enough for today, especially considering how the day started with Elodie not very pleased with me.

One glance at my watch, and I can't stretch these minutes any longer, and we both could use the space from one another. "I should head out."

"Yeah, of course, Mr. Successful has places to be. I'll walk you out."

Following her, we walk painfully slowly. If we had all the hours of the day, I think I would actually be staying. We'd open a bottle of wine and talk about everything under the moon. Similar to the island, except this time, elements of our future would creep into the conversation. No matter what happens, we're bound for life through Lola. And truthfully, without her, finding one another again would've led us to the very same conversation. I've been hoping to see her again for a long time. At times, I worried it was an obsession in my head of fantasies.

When we stop at the front hall, we square off to each other. It's a dangerous move, but I reach out and swipe a lock of her hair behind her shoulder, and my thumb grazes just under her jaw. I stay an extra second and keep her entrapped.

"I might have a career, Elodie, but I still have to be successful at the dad thing. And if there is something else I want, then I need to find a way to succeed at that," I rasp, and that's my warning with my eyes spearing into hers.

Her lips part slightly, but no words come out.

And that's a good thing because we might be heading down a road worth discovery, and I don't need the protest.

Although that would just fuel my persistence.

"Good night, Elodie." That's all I leave her with.

————

THE NEXT MORNING, I wait while the entire company gathers in the auditorium for presentations. A couple hundred people sit, and a small section of media stands to the side as everyone grows quiet.

I've barely slept, but this isn't my first rodeo with the lack of sleep; I have a job to do, a routine. After Elodie's, I met the leadership team for drinks, where we discussed strategy for the next two weeks of onboarding. I'm lucky that Charles, who is retiring and whose role I'm taking, will bring me up to speed. But talk turned personal, admittedly. The men around me are colleagues, but out of office, they're friends.

Naturally, conversation drifted to Elodie. I couldn't help but ask Julian for all the tidbits that I doubt Elodie would share. I'm an ass, or simply the elements of possessiveness are creeping in, but I had to know if Elodie has dated at all since the island, and Julian confirmed she hadn't, according to Savannah. He also shared that she played a major role in ensuring Savannah didn't throw his ass to the curb, and for that, he owes her for life. He didn't surprise me when he listed all of her qualities. A dry sense of humor, a strong work ethic, and a preference for low-key outings when without Lola. She has a sitter who comes every once in a while so she can enjoy happy hour drinks with Savannah. Everything checks out with the woman I met at a bar.

But the revelation that tugged at me was when he told me that Elodie would become quiet whenever the topic of Lola's father came up. As though she would get lost in a memory. Nonetheless, and I can't fault Julian, but his alliance is with Savannah, which means he's protective of Elodie. It all equates to the warning that I had better not misstep and hurt her.

Standing off-stage, I watch as Julian approaches the podium with that grin that is honest yet ridiculously cocky. I still haven't figured out if half the company fears him or worships him.

"Today is an important day for Haven Crossroads. We are having a great year, with record numbers and staff who put their all into the company. I'm grateful to you all, and for your patience, as everyone has anxiously waited for the announcement of our new COO. Sometimes great ones need to retire." He looks off to his side and outstretches his hand to Charles, the man about to embark on the chapter of his life that involves grandkids and golf. He smiles in appreciation as the room claps.

When the appreciation wears off, Julian continues. "We will forever remember his contributions and, on a personal level, his profound impact on growing the company with me. I know everybody has patiently been waiting to hear who will be named our new Chief of Operations, a role key to our strategy for success. A role that ensures we run smoothly across all departments. Our patience has paid off."

My heart begins to quicken. I'm confident in speeches, but this time, eyes are not only on me, but everyone in the company is already forming opinions from this moment on.

"We have just the man to hit the ground running. You're familiar with him. A visionary who has launched many startups into billion-dollar companies. We're entering a new era where we continue to grow, and to help us get there, I'm pleased to announce Hayes Callahan as our new COO." As the room erupts in applause, Julian angles his body to the side to indicate for me to join him on the stage. "Ladies and gentlemen, your new COO."

As I walk out, flashes from cameras flicker in the corner of my eye. I hate to say we're doing this, the cliché announcement, but we are. I'm in a sharp suit that says I'm career-driven, paired with cufflinks worth more than any intern's salary. Perhaps I appear to be a man who can be fair or ruthless, it's up to the audience's interpretation. I have a strong grin that is returned by Julian as we shake hands and pause for the cameras quickly for the golden photo before he steps away to offer me the podium.

"Thank you," I tell him as the claps simmer down back to quiet, the last sounds of cameras tapering down. I'm not a man who needs to rehearse in the mirror for such events, but right now, I kind of wish I did.

A fucking magnet draws my attention. Even under the bright stage lights, my eyes zip straight to a speck in a room of hundreds to spot the woman who has had a life with my daughter for two years, plus another nine months in the womb. Nobody would notice the brief pause when my eyes slide to her, and her upper lip twitches in response, because her attention is on me with intensity no different from that of middle management and up, who are probably sizing me up, debating my weaknesses and strengths. Except that Elodie's attention is on a personal level. She's my weakness that others haven't yet figured out.

The connection that nobody will be able to match, no matter how much they claw their way up the corporate ladder. Elodie is the woman who, out of the office, will be tied to me forever.

I nearly lose my focus, but I'm quick to bring my attention back to the middle of the room and fix my smile. "It's a privilege to join Haven Crossroads. I'm ready to start at full speed…"

I deliver the expected acceptance speech to loud applause and a standing ovation.

I'm a man driven by excellence, always willing to go the extra mile.

Even when my dad passed, I kept moving.

But now? For the first time ever, I'm distracted.

And that's a real fucking problem.

6

ELODIE

The last thing I ever wanted was to end up in the head of HR's office due to my personal relationships, yet here I am.

But I'm smart, and it is important to do things by the book, especially with Hayes's high-profile role. HR also has a policy of confidentiality, so I'm not too worried about office gossip.

For a second, I admire Olivia's nude pump heels with her light brown pantsuit. She has fashion sense, and it offers a brief distraction from my nerves. And even though Olivia is from Everhope and we are familiar with one another out of the office, who loves waking up to an email from HR? Not me. Even though it was expected.

"This doesn't need to be a long meeting," Olivia says as she sits in her chair, while Hayes and I sit on opposite ends of the sofa in her office meeting area.

"Short and to the point is the best way to do this." Hayes doesn't seem too concerned. He's already fixed his suit as though he will stand to leave any second, as though he can control the time and narrative of this meeting.

Me? I'm not the one who is only one step down from the CEO. I have a long way to go. Even though Haven Crossroads is family-friendly, it doesn't slip my mind that there must be people in the office who judge me for being a single mom. I've had to prove my worth more than others, sometimes. Now *poof.* Hayes enters the picture, and I'm sure they will form theories of favoritism as to how I've excelled in my role.

"Standard procedure," she says, sensing Hayes's lack of interest. Olivia's eyes fix on me. She shifts in her seat with a small smile. "I understand the… dynamics of your lives." Olivia is trying to be tactful.

"I believe we are disclosing our…" How do I label this? I'm mirroring her communication style now. "Relationship as co-parents."

Hayes clears his throat and gives me a strong glare through side-eye before he turns his attention to Olivia and offers her a more neutral smile. "We have a personal relationship for obvious reasons."

Really? That's his label for us? Just ring a bell, let everyone guess what we are.

"We're here because of formality. Technically, as long as you both disclose your… connection," her voice is a little uneven, "then you have done what is needed."

"We are disclosing it to ensure there are no issues. Foster is my manager. Hayes and I are in different departments. I will barely cross paths with Hayes, and we will avoid being seen together in the office," I assure her.

"Well, that might be a step too far. Being seen together in the office will be happening." Hayes smirks. "On a professional level, of course."

Olivia's eyes travel between us. "Professional it will be," she reiterates and gawks at him. "Obviously, it would be hypocritical for Julian to ban office relationships. But let's not use Julian and Savannah as the standard."

"Oh, I will." Hayes grins, probably because he can only guess they lacked professionalism at times when she was Julian's assistant.

"No." I shake my head. "No, he won't. Savannah left after they got together. I'm staying. I'm happy here, it has great benefits for Lola, and I enjoy working with numbers in finance."

She gives me a soft smile. "I know. Your employee reviews sing your praises." She spreads her hands up as she lifts her shoulders. "All I can say is you've disclosed, and Hayes will never be able to sign off on any project that you are involved in. And discretion is key for you two." She lowers her arms. "It helps ensure colleagues are put in a comfortable position."

He raises his brows, and Olivia grimaces at her choice of words. We all let it slide. Hayes stands, brushing his hands down the front of his suit jacket before buttoning it.

"It's been a pleasure. Formality is now complete."

"Sure. I'll send you both a document to sign to confirm we discussed the topic." She gets up and walks back to her desk.

I release a breath I've been holding. Relief. Finally, it's over.

"There is one more thing since I have you both here."

"Sure," I reply.

"Also for consideration down the line, you might need to chat with payroll. For tax reasons and such, it is necessary to ensure that Lola is a dependent on the correct parental health insurance and that family leave coordination is in place for both of you. Those kinds of things." She says it so easily, but my body tightens, and I bite my lip. Olivia notices my tension. "Just standard when both legal guardians or parents work here… something to think about."

"Perfect. Have payroll reach out." Hayes is eager.

Swallowing back my mixed emotions, I'm not sure what I'm feeling. I'm in limbo because he is Lola's father, yet he isn't legally her father. He's assuming, even though the papers haven't been signed yet. But he is very correct; he will have to be. It's his right. That means there are many implications for our dynamic. Thanks, tax man.

"Thanks, Olivia," I say as I leave.

I'm hoping he'll wait for me to leave first, but halfway down the hall, I know Hayes has already ditched his promise to keep his distance in the office—confirmed when he treads close behind me toward the elevator.

I sigh in frustration when I step inside the elevator, and he follows. When the door closes, I don't look at him.

"She's right, you know."

"About the distance in the office? Yeah. Well done for not following that rule ten seconds in," I reply dryly and look forward at the elevator buttons.

He grabs my arm softly and encourages me to look in his direction. He pins his gaze on me, persistence tinged with a shade of sensitivity. "The other part. The legal parent and dependent factor. Lola's birth certificate?"

"It makes sense to add your name to it."

"Something is bothering you." I don't think I've heard his voice this way. It's softer, more concerned.

My heart pounds—tears threaten, but why? Everything is hitting at once. "Nothing. I'm just processing." It's the safest thing I can say. But it bothers me too much, and I turn to him and huff a breath. "Please take it seriously at the office. The professional factor. I'm not you. I'm still building a career under unusual circumstances at my age. I have years to go.

Respect that, because the idea of being pushed away or judged all because of you won't help us."

He goes mute, and his eyes draw a line up and down my body, although he is pondering my words. It must register with him. I'm being logical. He steps forward and touches my elbow, merely a feathering touch. But it's enough to make my heart race even faster. My eyes land on his chest because I don't dare peer up. Having him close makes my brain go haywire. "Okay, Elodie." He's resolute in tone, pure sincerity glinting in his eyes.

"Thank you." I'm uncomfortable under the weight of his stare. I feel heavy and too rooted to the floor, unable to leave his orbit.

"We'll keep work and our parenting separate. Anything else bothering you?"

I shake my head, even if it is a lie.

He doesn't seem to believe me but is reluctant to pursue. "Okay. Well, we'll get the fine print sorted."

My eyes drift back to the door as the elevator slows at my floor. "Sure." Because either way, that step is coming, so we might as well get it out of the way. I'm a responsible person when it comes to Lola, and I owe it to her to ensure she has the best opportunities, and Hayes is part of that equation.

Relief floods me the instant the doors slide open. I can't get out fast enough.

———

"NEVER? REALLY?" Savannah doubts me as she stirs her coffee.

We're sitting at Beans, the coffee shop with decent coffee at the bottom of the building, where anybody from the public can go. I've been catching her up to speed and have calmed down. In the end, nobody said anything wrong during the HR meeting yesterday. It was simply fact and procedure. It was bound to happen, and now it is out of the way. Savannah, although supportive, has now broached the topic I was hoping to avoid.

I set my chicken salad sandwich down on the plate. "I'm not just going to slide back into his bed," I remind her. If I didn't have Lola to think about, then the answer would be quite different if I'm honest.

"Whoa there, tiger. I wasn't talking about that. Good to know someone's mind is in the gutter, though." She smiles and brings her mug to her lips for a quick sip. "I was actually talking about exploring the option of a romance. That sometimes involves other things, in case you need a refresher. Maybe dinner or flowers. A kiss, *then* the good stuff that your mind is clearly thinking about."

It's only natural—chemistry doesn't always just switch off because a relationship changes. Especially when his cologne still lingers at my place as a reminder. But we share a daughter; nothing is simple.

"Hmm. Okay."

Lines form on my forehead. "What do you mean, okay?"

She lifts a shoulder. "I think when it cools between you two about how to navigate Lola, then you both most definitely are going to be investigating something else. If Hayes is like Julian, and from what I know, he is, you have a persistent man in your life now, so congratulations."

Grumbling to myself, I pray inside that she's wrong. Can't I have it easy for once? Must my life be complicated?

"I can't get twisted into..." I twirl my hands in the air, "whatever it could be. My priority is Lola."

"Who deserves to be happy, including her parents being

together if the option presents itself?" Savannah preambles the suggestion and smiles contritely.

Rolling my eyes, I rake my fingers through my hair. "Why must you drag me into this conversation, my dear best friend?"

"Because someone needs to say it out loud, the obvious question everyone is wondering. Most of all, you, and that is you and Hayes, Hayes and you."

Shaking my head, I crack a smile because her annoyance is warranted. Admittedly too, the mere picture in my mind of that scenario isn't a negative thought. I glance at my phone, which is lying on the table on silent, noticing the screen flash as a message from Hayes appears. We've had contact about Lola over the last few days, but not much else.

HAYES

These are the kind of updates that daycare sends?

I snort when he forwards a screenshot from the app showing Lola's day at daycare: naps, food, playtime, activities, and photos. Today's update wasn't exactly spellbinding —songs at 9am, apple and crackers for a morning snack, a quick 11am nap.

ME

Yep. Also, how many diaper changes, too.

I'm surprised to see the dots moving in our chat. I thought he would be in a meeting. His schedule is filled to the brim.

HAYES

Riveting. Are you okay if my assistant contacts you about ordering some items?

PAs at our company sign NDAs, and whatever is going on

in Hayes's life, she probably already knows. But still, me having to handle her?

???

HAYES

She can help me arrange things while I'm in meetings. It's for Lola's room at my place.

My stomach sinks. We haven't gone into every detail yet. I feel like I'm always scrambling to catch up, but he's always twelve steps ahead. I can see what's on the list of establishing a co-parenting relationship, but it's like he moves at record speed, barely giving me a moment to brace myself.

Oh. I mean, we can talk about that.

I don't even get a chance to finish writing because another message comes in.

A unicorn rug? And she needs a crib that will become a bed soon, right? I'll get pool toys and floaties so we can go swimming. I would love to teach her to swim.

He types so quickly. I can't help but smile. A few days ago, this would have unsettled me. But now, even though I'm still jittery, I know him a little bit better and the way he reacts. No matter his mood, he's sincere. I'm also truly happy for Lola, even if she doesn't know yet.

Regardless, I finish writing my original message.

Right. You're really thinking about this. We can talk about it next time we meet.

> Sure. But my assistant will be in touch if that's okay with you. Need to kid-proof my new place, too.

> Okay.

"Earth to Elodie." Savannah waves her hand in front of my face, snapping her fingers until I blink and focus on her again. "Whoa, you just exited Earth's orbit and took a trip around space. Was that Hayes lighting up your phone?"

What is happening to me? Heat rushes to my cheeks, giddiness bubbling up. Am I really charmed by him asking how to make things work for Lola at his place? It's adorable —if only he didn't rush everything like we're sprinting through life.

My friend looks at me with a wry smile. "It must have crossed your mind a million times what it would be like if you crossed paths with him again, and now you have. Thank your lucky stars that it's a guy who is invested, easy on the eyes, and probably might push your buttons. I get it. You don't want to do anything to jeopardize Lola, but if you ever had a connection with Hayes, then you shouldn't ignore it, either."

Picking up a pickle and turning it over in my hand with no intention of eating it, I bite back the urge to blurt out that she's right. Instead, I say, "I'll think about it, okay?"

She grins. "Great. We need to go for drinks soon. De-stress you a little."

"I could use an espresso martini," I admit.

"It's settled then."

When my phone lights up again, I'm a little disappointed that it isn't Hayes. Instead, it's an email from Hayes's lawyer. With one read of the opening line, my entire mood drops.

Holding my phone out to Savannah, screen facing her,

tension coils in my jaw. I can't let my guard slip, not even for a second. "See?"

I hate the shape of a circle.

Because that's what is happening in my life right now.

———

HAYES CLOSES the back door of the dark, expensive car, only for me to rush and open it.

"Oh no, you don't," I say and slide into the back with him, slamming the door behind me.

He scoots to the next seat, eyes squinting in surprise as I hijack his ride. I didn't want to wait, and his schedule made this my only chance to see him today.

"What are you doing here?"

"We need to talk." I'm back to my hard-as-nails tone because I have no fuzzy feelings right now.

"Sir, this is a loading zone only. We have to move," the driver in the front calls out.

With my eyes arrowing straight into Hayes's, he doesn't give the man a glimpse because Hayes grasps my adamancy. "It's fine. Circle the block or something."

As the car begins to move, my nostrils flare. I want to be angry, but the feeling won't come. Why can't I just let myself be furious? I grip the seat, waiting for the anger, but it just fizzles. Probably because I'm aware the calm-and-collected approach is best.

"Where's Lola?"

"Savannah picked her up and is bringing her home. I asked your assistant where you'd be, and she mentioned you had business drinks to attend."

His face remains stoic, as though he won't falter from whatever I throw his way. "To what do I owe the pleasure then?" Something sizzles behind that sentence, the lift of his mouth too devious.

"I still received the papers from your lawyer. And no, it isn't just the correction of the birth certificate."

He sighs and looks away. "It's nothing big—just papers for Lola's trust and a co-parenting outline. We don't need to sign now, just something to consider. The trust isn't about custody. It ensures she can go to college and have financial stability. It's fair."

Crossing my arms, I debate with myself whether I'm satisfied with his answer. "Other than the birth certificate, can't we just leave any documents out of the equation at this moment? Even if they are just to review? I thought we were on the same page about that."

Hayes drags his hand across his jaw, and I notice the stubble after a long day of work. It's sexy and tempting to touch. But I need to think straight right now.

Without warning, I slide across the back and straight into Hayes as the car takes a sharp corner. Neither one of us bothered with seatbelts because we were stuck in our standoff. I touch his arm to brace myself, and the combination of his smell and the firmness of his arm begins to play tricks on me, especially when we're flush together, and he peers down at me. Our breaths meet in the small distance between us, it would only take a small tip of my chin for our mouths to meet.

A shot of electricity threatens me again, we can't avoid it.

"I agree until I don't," he whispers.

I yank myself back. This man melts my guard, but I won't forget why I need it. My composure wobbles, just for a second.

"Don't threaten me, Hayes."

He grabs my wrist and tugs, a reassuring smirk curling on

his mouth. "I'm not. We're going to have to learn to make concessions with each other. You got the documents because I asked my lawyer *before* we spoke at lunch on Monday. I figured that it could still be good to read them. I hope we can work it out on our own, but if things go south, then yeah, I have rights too."

"That explanation didn't end so well."

He flexes his jaw as he replays the words in his head. "I'm keeping my word on what we agreed. I'm sorry if it came across a little… brash," he apologizes sincerely.

I study his face, searching for anything dishonest. "You mean it? No more lawyer games for now?" My hope is fragile, but I want to believe him.

His thumb circles along my wrist; it's soothing and far too delicate and sensitive for my body. "Promise."

"Good. I don't want us to yo-yo back and forth about everything. Nor do you want to wear down my patience. I'm also going to hold you accountable and call you out when you're being an ass." I raise my brows with my gentle warning.

The corner of his lips lift. "I'm getting that gist."

Lifting my chin, I give him one last appraisal to confirm that I feel confident with his answer. "We were going smoothly again. From this moment forward, no more surprises to set us back," I confirm.

"Agreed."

"Okay."

Silence finds us, but our eyes remain locked.

He grins, smoothly shifting topics. "Come for dinner Saturday? You and Lola?"

Gosh, the man has smolder. It's hypnotizing, and right now it's directed at me. I need to wrap my head around demanding-Hayes who quickly turns tender when it involves Lola, but it also feels like his request isn't just for her.

I stare at him, stuck in his magic. Then it hits me—we have steps to take. "Okay," I croak.

"Are you going to keep saying okay? I can add that you both can stay over." Now he's just being cheeky.

I point at him. "Hold it together, Hayes."

He places his hand on his heart. "I am. It's an innocent invite. You can check Lola's room, and there's a guest room if you want it."

Now he's just flirting.

"I need to get out of here before this conversation goes south again."

Somehow, that doesn't really stop the innuendo.

He continues to smirk, his tongue sliding along the inside of his cheek before he leans toward the front. "You can return to the office," he tells the driver.

"Please," I add, flippant.

It's a short drive, and at the end, that man's eyes meet mine, and I leave this world. He must know that.

I exit the car, and I don't look back.

But I feel his heavy eyes on me.

And now I'm wondering what the weekend will bring.

HAYES

My heart is beating fast as Elodie leans down and, with careful fingers, unbuttons Lola's coat. They're in my hallway to join me for the afternoon. Spending time with Lola is important, and Elodie agrees, but I also sense she wants to inspect where our daughter will be spending some of her time. Lola, with part of her hair up in a ponytail on the top of her head, glances up at me with curiosity as Elodie unclasps the last button. Lola timidly stares at me. That's a promising start.

Elodie slowly stands up, and the air thickens between us. The situation is delicate.

"Come on. I'll show you around." I wave to them to follow me.

Elodie takes Lola's hand. They trail into the large, open living room. The ceilings are high, and the windows stretch from floor to ceiling. It makes the place seem bright.

I hear Elodie begin to chuckle, and I glance at her.

"Brave. A cream-colored sofa. You clearly haven't spent much time around kids."

I scratch the back of my head, realizing my error. "No

snacks on the couch then," I say, already picturing crumbs on the cushions.

Elodie continues to beam as she shakes her head back and forth. "Wrong answer. How will she enter a daze of watching cartoons while snacking? It's your moment of silence to regain your sanity."

Grinning, I appreciate her lighthearted judgment. "Speaking of snacks, would you like one after the tour?"

Lola appears shy yet smiles as she clasps Elodie's hand. Snack is apparently a trigger word.

I crouch down to her level. She snuggles onto Elodie's leg. "I have a banana, crackers, yogurt pouches, and grapes." At Elodie's soft throat-clearing, I glance up. "Cut in half, of course." Her smile returns.

"Cookie?" Lola's eyes light up.

I remember what Elodie told me once about Lola's favorite foods. "Blueberry bagels."

She stares up at Elodie with a wide smile. Standing, I've achieved a step in winning her over, and I grin proudly.

"The way to her heart," Elodie casually mentions.

Inside, I beg a higher power that it's true.

I continue to walk, and they follow behind me. Elodie pauses to set Lola's little backpack down on the side table along the wall. I'm not entirely sure what the contents are, but I'll assume something to play with.

But it's not needed. "I have toys," I blurt out. "You didn't need to bring any."

"Oh? Okay." Elodie continues to smile.

I head straight to the built-in shelves near the television and open the bottom cupboard to reveal toys. It doesn't take long to hear little feet running toward me, and when I see Lola's expression, then I believe all humans in the room are absent to her. Elodie stands next to me, watching the scene unfold.

Lola is quick to check out the new boxes of toys: crayons and coloring books catch her attention first. She also explores Play-Doh, wood puzzles, toy animals, and whatever else my assistant crammed in there.

"Wow, okay. That's a success," I remark as Lola already drags out a puzzle.

"Lola, ask first," Elodie reminds her. I'm thankful that Elodie is raising Lola to be kind and have manners.

Little blue eyes look up at me. "Puzzles now?"

"Please," Elodie whispers.

"Please," Lola adds.

My grin grows to the extreme. "Of course. Play away."

She flops down onto her bottom and gets to work.

We both watch her ignore the world around her, and I feel Elodie bump into my arm. "Nice play, Hayes. Snacks and toys."

"Yeah? Thanks." We glance at one another, and I'm grateful that in terms of our daughter, we are more and more on the same page. "I can show you the rest of the place."

"Depends on how big this place is. I don't want to leave her alone. Safety, a new place, and all. It takes two seconds for her curiosity to turn into an adventure."

I didn't think about that. "You can have a wander if you want. I can stay with her."

Elodie's eyes blaze open. "Really? Just letting me loose to explore?" She seems surprised.

I shrug "Why not? You're going to be here a lot."

"Logical." Her mouth slides back and forth, and she considers as she studies Lola for a long second. "Okay. But let's take a few minutes for her to get used to you."

I nod in agreement, and for the next ten minutes, we all

play on the floor with Elodie next to me. Elodie gives me a glance as the cue that she is going to escape.

"Have fun." I touch her shoulder.

"I'll be right back, Lola. I'm just down the hall. You okay with that?" Lola nods as she continues her quest of discovering the toys.

I can't help noticing how Elodie flutters her eyelashes, still trying to adjust to all of this, but after a few seconds, she walks away.

For the next few minutes, Lola and I break out the small wooden train set. Admittedly, that was a selfish purchase I asked my assistant to arrange. I loved having a train when I was a kid. My dad and I would spend hours playing together. It's a fond memory. Even as an adult, when I walk by toy stores and see one in the window, I always stop to peek. Now it's a reminder to me how I want to be a hands-on father like my own was. I want to share the experience with Lola who is clearly a pink princess and unicorn girl, but maybe I can win her over with the train.

My daughter's shyness remained but eased by the minute, and we still managed to play together on the floor. I've learned her favorite sentence is "train go," and she's excellent at sharing.

I barely hear Elodie return to the living room, but the feeling of eyes on me weighs heavily, and when I look up, I see that she is watching us with a peculiar look. She's calm but lost in thought.

"How is it?" I ask.

"You two seem to be best friends." She avoids answering. "I was just admiring you two for a second."

Handing Lola the caboose piece, I stand up and lightly touch Elodie's elbow, guiding her to step a few feet away from our daughter. "We seem to be getting along. I'm relieved," I say.

"You gave her a palace." Her voice is monotoned. I lift a brow, trying to catch up. "You set up her bedroom. It has a tent with stars, a library of books, a bed, a crib, and a sofa. I'm very confident her closet is well-stocked. Did I mention the giant stuffed bunny on a rocking horse?"

Is she angry? I can't for the life of me read her right now. "Is it a bad thing…?" My voice drags.

The beautiful smile of hers begins to draw on her face. "It's overboard, but it's… perfect."

I pretend to wipe my forehead. "Phew, you had me worried there."

"I'm not sure she'll ever want to live at my place again," she says. Her sarcasm fades; the undermining hits too hard. Soon, Lola will split time. The idea of all of us living together is an event in itself, if it happens.

"I remember you mentioned that she is soon moving out of a crib to a bed. Oh, and there's the guest room. The sofa in Lola's room also turns into a bed if you want to stay." She smiles in appreciation. It gives me the sign that I can make her laugh or test the waters. "Also, my room. In case you didn't check it out. Did you check it out?" I tease her, but I'm aware that I'm digging for clues to where her mind is when it comes to the two of us on a romantic level.

She shoves me as she grins. "Don't. Don't drag us there." She rolls one shoulder back and avoids looking at me. "But maybe I did take a peek," she mumbles.

"Oh yeah?" I smirk cheekily.

"I should see everywhere in the home where Lola will be. Inspection and all."

"Sure," I pretend to believe her.

We both return our focus to our daughter, who seems

content. "We won't show her the room yet, okay? Small steps."

"I get that." I comply because we do see eye to eye on some things.

"And how in the world did you arrange all of this?"

"My assistant."

The way Elodie hums sounds like suspicion to some, but she works at the same company and knows who my assistant is. "They gave you the assistant who's married with a kid in college, right?" she asks, double-checking.

Smirking to myself, I enjoy hearing her maybe having a little moment of jealousy. "Yep. Why? Would it be a problem if I had someone else?" I'm riling her. It's easy to do, we have banter.

"Of course not." She sounds unconvincing.

"Sure. Anyhow, should we head to the kitchen?"

"Bagels!" Lola shoots up, clearly having heard a trigger word that is apparently "kitchen."

Elodie and I look at one another and just laugh.

———

AFTER EATING, Lola fell asleep on the opposite sofa, curled up under the knitted blanket Elodie brought and with her two stuffed bunnies tucked under her arms. Elodie and I sit on the other sofa, talking quietly and holding glasses of wine.

The blanket intrigues me, though I'm unsure why. "It's a beautiful blanket. Did your mom knit it?"

She smiles shyly. "This is where you are going to discover that I am such a nerd who deals with numbers and has a hobby of knitting." She buries her face in her hands as though she's embarrassed yet finds it funny.

My eyes grow, and my grin hurts as I learn the fact. "I am

trying to imagine you just sitting there and stitching away. I wasn't expecting this to be your thing."

"Well, you have swimming, and I have knitting. I haven't had time lately, but when I was pregnant, there were days when I didn't want to get out of bed, and I was bored. Figured I would make something for my dau—" She stops herself and smacks her lips together. "Our daughter, I mean," she corrects herself. It's going to take a while for her to get it into her head that she now shares parenthood.

"She'll cherish it forever. I had a quilt growing up from my grandma, it's probably still in a box somewhere."

"I'm sure your mom has it stored away for you. I also make Lola little dresses sometimes. I sew, too. Anyhow, have you enjoyed your first week at Haven Crossroads?" she pries. Her bare feet are tucked under her knees as she sits comfortably, resting against the back of the sofa.

I finish my sip of expensive French wine. "Yeah, everyone has their head in the game. Connecting with the leadership team was never going to be an issue. My schedule is already full. I'll have to visit our London office soon, among other places. Dinners, and more dinners—if in doubt, there's always another added to my calendar. I'm happy to have a low-key day off." I chortle, swirling my wine. "Well, low-key is a stretch. Kind of a big deal, since I'm getting to know my daughter."

"So far so good."

The gentle features of her face, accompanied by her subtle smile, calm me. Our eyes catch, and for the millionth time, they hold, no words needed. Sometimes I wonder what she is keeping inside her head, while other times, I'm able to read her as if it's second nature.

She narrows her eyes at me, and her head tilts slightly. "I've learned something about you this week."

"What might that be?" I'm intrigued.

"Although I met you as a man with persuasiveness, I didn't expect you to be someone who enjoys power." She sets her glass down.

Smirking at her observation, I find it slightly humorous when someone forms opinions about me. "How so?"

Elodie laughs under her breath. "The way you walked into the news with only your way as the option, the way you walk around the office very self-aware that people admire you, and the way you look at me feels somewhat possessive, to be honest."

My hand slides a little above her knee, a move that probably confirms everything she just said. "True. I tend to lead the way. And of course I'm possessive of you. You're the mother of my child."

Her breath hitches from my choice of words as our eyes remain fixed on one another.

I continue. "You can't be surprised by that." Inching closer to her, she remains still. "You're a great mom, Elodie. I see it. I don't deny it. How you cut her food, teach her manners, or tuck her in for a nap. The little things. But I'm here now. You're going to have to let me in on all of that."

Her fingers find my wrist, and the tips begin to feather my skin in strokes as her eyes dip down to watch. "I am, trust me."

"Good. Now enjoy your wine," I order.

She begins to grin again. "I don't often drink around her. I save it all for my after-work drinks with Savannah, and sometimes another friend, Sutton. When I can get a sitter, of course. I try to avoid department drinks and keep those connections to birthday cake in the staff room. Out of work, I just need my time to disconnect, away from mom life and work."

"I still find it a little funny that you are a numbers kind of girl. On the island, I got the sense your job would be something smart, but it's unexpected. I just didn't think it would be in finance and at Haven."

"Small world, right? I guess I also need to see your merman skills in the pool one day. Let's see if you live up to all the talk you gave."

Chuckling, I'm riding the flow of this conversation. "I would love to teach Lola to swim and to prove you wrong. Obviously, you'll need to be in a swimsuit too." I flash my eyes at her.

"Slipping that in, are you?"

"Innocent until proven guilty."

The room grows completely still again, and we both focus on where our fingers are finding a home. I stroke the side of her thigh but keep it innocent. Her own hand begins to travel up my arm. Our touches are light, grazing, and still overload my senses.

"You shouldn't be attracted to me if it's only because I'm the mother of your child," she warns me.

"It's not that. Wasn't I attracted to you years ago? Have I not thought about you since then? Lola maybe adds an extra factor, but she isn't the reason. I could ask you the same thing."

She grimaces. "I knew you were going to throw that back at me. And truthfully… it's the same."

"We're aligned then."

But she presses her lips together and thinks for a second. "Actually, it's kind of different. Since then, you got to imagine me as the woman you met. I've thought of you, always have. I just had to think of you knowing you are also Lola's father. It's an extra connection or gravitation. Does that make sense? I need to separate attraction because of us or attraction because of the way we are connected."

It makes sense, but I don't enjoy the complication of her thought process.

She diverts her gaze away. However, I'm too far gone. I need to open Pandora's box. I'm a man who accepts challenges.

Fuck it.

"Elodie."

Our eyes meet. Are they conveying a dare? Doesn't matter. I'm confident with my choice.

Leaning in, our space begins to close. She doesn't back away. Instead, her hand begins to tighten around my arm, as though she needs to hang on, as she doesn't intend to flee. With her eyes wide and searching, I bring my hand beneath her chin, hooking a finger to tip up her chin. I need to do this carefully because the magnitude of how we feel physically with one another has consequences. My lips meet hers. Slow, steady, and familiarity is there. I don't need longer to figure it out. It's already proven. All because I want more. My hand floats down to rest on her waist, and as our kiss continues, the palm of her hand meets my chest, her lips seeking more pressure from mine.

I want to take more, but I'm aware that this is to explore our curiosity. One more angle, then a feathery chase of her lips as we gather a new breath, and I feel the static energy between us.

The moment she pulls away, I take satisfaction in the way she keeps her eyes closed, still soaking in our kiss, remembering. When her eyes flicker open, I greet her with a smirk that informs her that I've been proven right. A few days ago, she warned me about co-parenting only, but I'm not going to let her call the shots. Not now that it's blatantly obvious that our physical connection has never been broken with time.

I don't want to be the man who holds legal documents over Elodie's head to get what I want, but a part of me could resort to that. I'm struggling to keep the business part of me separate from my private life on this one, but it's a challenge because I'm infatuated with this woman on a romantic and physical level. Scorching the earth has never been my play, but right now, I'm a man who has no intention of letting her run away. Exploring what could be between us isn't just for Lola, it's for us. That's not being selfish, and even if it was, I don't think I'd give a damn.

Elodie silently curses to herself as she unglues our lips. "We can't do this with Lola in the room," she whispers.

She has a point. It's careless on our part, but by no means an error or mistake. I let the moment between us stretch, still tied together purely by our pull.

Until she backs up to safety, and our space returns.

She brings her fingers to pinch the bridge of her nose to cope with the fact that she just gave in to me. "This is not what was supposed to happen today," she reminds herself, but I see the tiny smile struggling to hide.

"Get used to it, Elodie. I don't think I listen to you so well."

She throws me a glare. "*Yeah*, point proven by your comment earlier about your need to always have it your way."

Am I giving her a sly smirk? Probably. "Learn to enjoy it."

She nibbles the corner of her lip and chuffs a deep chuckle to herself. "Great." Moving her body, she grabs her wine from the side and takes a long drink.

"How much left of her nap?" I slide my vision to Lola, who is sound asleep.

"Maybe twenty minutes more."

"When she wakes up?" I ask firmly, and she knows what I mean.

Elodie glances down into her half-empty white wine. It's the longest pause in conversation in my life. "Yes."

I sigh in relief because not telling Lola who I am was beginning to wear me down, but now we're going to do it. "Good. I'll let you lead the conversation," I assure her, and I stretch my arm along the back of the sofa to touch her shoulder. At first, it's a gesture of comfort, but I'd be lying if it wasn't selfish. Having her near yet not being able to touch her doesn't make sense to me.

"I'm not sure I'll say the right thing, but I might just talk in her language and use two words." She scoffs a laugh.

"Safe bet."

We talked more about life, and I avoided making her blush again. Thirty minutes later, after Lola stirred awake and she was fully up with a snack in her belly, we all sat on the floor. She already started pouring tea from the set, and I'm grateful I found the off button on the pot because that song was going to annoy me.

Elodie and I feel one another's nerves, and my heart thumps hard.

"Thank you for the tea." Elodie raises her little teacup to our daughter.

I pretend to sip my tea while I wait for Elodie to take the plunge.

She grabs Lola's attention through eye contact. "Lola. Daddy." Elodie points to me. Our daughter doesn't get it. "Daddy, Lola." She points again.

"Daddy." I attempt to help, and my hand lands on my heart.

She swings her gaze between us. She says nothing and begins to play again.

It's not that I'm disappointed that this didn't turn into a big event for us, but maybe I am. On the other hand, my daughter seems kind of chill.

"She's two," Elodie reminds me. "Pink toys always win the conversation." She attempts to make me smile.

And when I look at Lola, happily comfortable, then I smile too.

My mom answers the video call in good spirits, it seems, as I sit in the back of the car for an early-morning meeting out of the office.

"Hi, Mom," I greet her. It's early, but since she's on the east coast, she's an hour ahead, and she normally eats breakfast around now. Morning calls are not unusual for us.

"Morning. How are things? I haven't heard from you since before you moved. How did it go? I can imagine unpacking will be a pain." She's sitting in the living room with a mug of coffee in one hand and the phone in the other.

My heart races because I'm about to share the life-changing news. "Yeah, sorry. Something has kind of happened. I have news."

Her morning smile disappears with concern. "What do you mean? Is everything okay? Were you at the doctor's or something?"

Quickly, I shake my head. "Nothing like that. I'm fine. I discovered something pretty big. As in I have a daughter."

Her entire face turns to shock. "What?"

"I have a daughter," I reiterate, and I smile as well. "She's two years old, and her name is Lola."

She sets her coffee down to cover her mouth, which is in a wide O. "You're a dad?"

I nod. "Yeah."

"And the mother?" She sounds indifferent.

"Her name is Elodie. We met on vacation, and it was a one-time kind of thing, then." Because now I'm not so sure anymore what the future will bring.

"How do you know Lola is yours? She could be after your money."

My eyes grow as I tip my head to the side. "No. She isn't. Hasn't even asked for a cent. It's also a small world because she's Julian's fiancée's best friend and works at my office. She wasn't trying to keep her from me, either. We never exchanged…" Not sure now is the time to admit to my mother, even as a grown man, that I had a nameless one-night stand. "Adults make mistakes. I'm guilty, too. Let it go. She's in my life now."

"She kept your daughter from you." My mother sounds protective, yet I'm concerned that she might not let it go.

"Not exactly like that. I need you to close that topic and trust me."

She doesn't seem to agree. "But you'll marry her then."

I scoff a laugh. "It doesn't always work like that."

"It's what your father would say to do."

My chest pings at the memory of him. She's right, too. My brain spirals and questions if I should consider it more and really put the option on the table for Elodie. But I already know she would laugh.

"Plus, you're both adults who should be settling down by now. Why is she still single at her age? Isn't that cause for concern?"

Yikes, I don't recall my mom ever being this judgmental. "First off, take it down a notch. And Elodie is young, she doesn't exactly have a clock ticking."

"How young?"

"Ten years younger than me."

She chuffs a laugh. "How did you two meet?"

"When I was down in Puerto Rico a few years ago."

"Oh my gosh, so she's a spring-breaker?"

My jaw drops. I've never seen her so worked up. "No! Simmer down. Elodie comes from a small town here in Illinois and works hard. She's recently been promoted to manager. A great mother, too. You two will hit it off."

"Fine. If she is all of those things, then consider being together and get married. We didn't send you to Catholic mass growing up for nothing."

"I'm not sure tradition is for me." It's partly a lie, but there is a piece of me eager to go buy a damn ring.

My mother hums a sound of perhaps disapproval, but then she calms, the moment stretches, and her features lighten. "I have a granddaughter?"

"Yeah. You'll see a resemblance."

Now she's beaming, and I'm relieved our conversation is back in the right direction. "I was getting worried that I might have to wait forever. You're pushing your late thirties. When can I meet her?"

My chest tightens as I take a deep breath, my mind flooded with apprehension. "Soon. Just not yet. I only just met her. We're going to need some time to adjust and get to know one another. I'll send you photos, though."

She sighs. "Fair enough. You can only hold me off for so long, though."

"I figured." I grin and grab my tie, which is lying on the seat next to me. "Listen, we can talk more about it later. I've got to run. There is a minor crisis at the office, and I need to jump into it."

"Of course."

We say our goodbyes, and it's good to know that she will have joy in her life again. It's not often we talk about my dad's absence, but it's fresh enough in our heads, as it's only been a year. Lola is a gift in a way. Unexpected, but she will bring a little extra happiness to my mom. My elation at the thought is ruined when the driver informs me we are approaching the restaurant for the breakfast meeting.

———

Two hours later, Foster and I exit the car after our ride from the restaurant and step onto the busy sidewalk. It was an early-morning breakfast meeting at the crack of dawn because he has a plane to catch at ten.

"That was excruciating. Now we have to cram a leadership meeting into ten minutes, all because someone in our Miami office fucked up some numbers," he complains.

Rightfully so, there was a miscalculation in import tax that ran into the seven figures.

"Everything is fixable, remember that," I encourage, even if I'm going to get dragged into this headache too.

Entering the bustling building, people are in line for elevators, and the escalators are full. To my right at Beans, it's busy too.

Foster and I head straight to the elevator reserved for the top floors, and luckily, we don't have to face a line since the top floors indicate seniority and not many people get that privilege, so we have space and fewer members of staff.

He jabs his finger into the buttons, and we both look up to see the light moving above the doors.

A strange sensation tugs at my leg. Confused, I frown.

"You have a kid at your feet," Foster flatly points out.

Looking down, I see Lola, and I'm quick to crouch down level with her.

Elodie is hot on her trail. "Sorry, she just sprang free from my hand on our way to daycare." She lets out a long exhale. "She's been a fun one this morning." I sense the sarcasm.

"Has she now?"

Lola pulls on my suit pants.

"Why, hello there."

Elodie steps forward. "She kept asking about you last night. Well, more why did our friend have her favorite toys."

"At least you remember me, even if it is for my toys." I grin.

Lola stares at me with neutrality and hugs her bunnies. "Dada."

For a moment, I freeze, disbelief rippling through me as if time pauses.

"What did you say?"

"Dada," she coos. Simply but confident.

She did.

She uttered the word.

To me.

Glancing quickly up, Elodie seems taken aback, almost misty-eyed as she smiles affectionately at her daughter. "I guess she was listening the other day."

I can only smile.

I'm officially a dad now.

ELODIE

Savannah throws a humorous glare over her shoulder at me for being on my phone. She's standing in a white lace dress on a pedestal in the bridal shop. We've been here for two hours, and I'm getting antsy, to be honest.

Four of the five dresses she has tried on could be perfect for her special day. I've been watching with a mixture of excitement for her, secret envy, and nerves.

How Hayes and I have managed to avoid any mention of our kiss, I'm not sure how, but kudos to us. My mind is taking the brunt of twisted thoughts about it instead.

Sitting on the side between her aunt Bea and Sutton, we've been watching her in complete giddiness while we sip champagne. Aunt Bea came up from Everhope and is staying with Savannah, and Sutton is in town from Baltimore, although she is looking to move back. We all grew up together on the same street, although she was a few years ahead of us at school.

I bury my phone back into my bag. "I know, I lose points

for the maid-of-honor duties," I admit, and bring the rim of the champagne flute to my mouth for a sip.

"Uh-oh, Elodie might be fired from her wedding duties," Sutton jokes, twisting her honey-brown hair into a bun on top of her head. She grins at me, and the laughter grows.

"Nah, it's okay. She has her reasons," Savannah assures me. "Any updates?"

I shake my head. "I'm not crazy. Am I?" It's the first time Hayes is taking care of Lola alone. I'm not sure how it'll go. Maybe she was a little weary at first but then relaxed. "It should be okay, right?" I glance around, hoping for reassurance.

He was back and forth all week on business trips, and we have had a few chances to all be together for an hour here or there, the three of us. Now he's back and wants to see Lola for a longer period. When I mentioned that I had a sitter for Lola while I went dress shopping, he was quick to jump in. No sitter was needed, and this would be a little stepping stone for him to be alone with her for a full day. He's with her now at my place after I spent a solid hour explaining everything and checking his diaper-changing skills, plus ensuring that Lola was comfortable with him before I left.

Savannah's older aunt touches my knee. "It's only a few hours. They will be fine."

"Look at the bright side, you are now guaranteed a date to Savannah's big day." Sutton nudges my arm with her own. She's always positive and bubbly. It's surprising, as I don't meet many lawyers who are.

Savannah turns to look in the mirror while a store attendant continues to fluff the skirt of the dress. "Very true. The maid of honor and the best man, no need for a plus-one at all. *Except* our Elodie only wants to co-parent." She is teasing me now.

When Aunt Bea snorts a laugh, I look at her, brows knitted. "How is that funny?" I ask, my voice half-teasing, half-puzzled.

"Co-parenting can be the only way sometimes. But in this case? Dear, I've watched you grow up. I've watched you become a mom. I haven't seen you with Lola's dad, but I've seen pictures of him. Plus, Julian and Savannah were talking about you and him at breakfast when I woke up. I'm not sure your idea will work."

I dart my gaze to Savannah via the mirror, trying to hide my embarrassment. "You were talking about me at breakfast?" I question, almost disbelieving.

Savannah pretends to check the sleeve of her dress. "I mean, you might have come up in conversation while Julian and I were drinking coffee. We didn't realize that Aunt Bea was awake."

Aunt Bea looks at her niece with a knowing smile. "Let's not lie, Savannah. It was a full-fledged conversation. It can't be surprising to Elodie that the man wants to try." Her tone is gentle but clear.

That's not unanticipated to me, but the fact that he's been talking about it with Julian is a little more confronting. From what I've learned about Hayes so far, it suggests he has plans. He gets what he wants, after all.

I swing my gaze between everyone in the room, and no matter what I could say to justify the situation, they have all formed their shared opinion already. "Can we not have this conversation right now?"

"Then we won't. We've just highlighted that we might be rooting for the chance… and in the long run, you have a guaranteed wedding date who happens to be the father of your daughter," Sutton cheekily smiles but then her smile wilts slightly. "Besides, even if you're not together in that way, then I'm sure you two will be good friends. Probably would even be one another's platonic dates, anyhow."

"The wedding isn't until the summer," I remind us all. Oh gosh, the idea that maybe we could be something by then, or maybe not at all and he has some gorgeous blonde on his arm, is causing chaos inside of me. "My love life is no longer the topic of discussion today. Instead, I will shift focus to Sutton, who is lacking in that department."

She's about to protest, but my phone pings, and everyone quiets while I dig out my phone, and with one tap, I'm greeted with a selfie of Lola sitting in her highchair, eating a cut-up waffle and fruit, and Hayes is standing behind her, bent down, while he holds his arm up to use the phone. She has a wide smile.

HAYES:

They were out of blueberry bagels at the bakery. I negotiated her down to waffles with fruit.

I feel everything inside of me burst into complete elation. They're doing fine and seem happy. My cheeks rise from the smile that keeps pulling on my mouth. Both ladies on my side lean in to peek.

"See? All is well." Aunt Bea squeezes my arm and smiles, too.

"It is. I think he's kind of a natural at this," I say, because it's becoming obvious.

Then my mind slips into another tunnel in my mind. The one where I wonder what he could be like, as a boyfriend or a man who maybe one day finds me here trying on dresses, too. The curiosity is a little more overbearing today than it has been in recent weeks. Wedding dresses are confronting apparently.

Savannah clears her throat to bring all of our attention back to her. "You can calm down. It's not like he's insisted you both get married for the sake of tradition. He's taking his time, which, if he works at Haven Crossroads and is a friend of Julian's, then it normally equates to that he's plotting something, but hey, we have champagne, and I need to pick a dress. So, shall we?"

Chuckling to myself, I agree with her plan. "Is this the one?"

She repositions her body in the mirror to gain a new angle. "I mean, it's a snug fit but feels comfortable."

"Really? We can see almost everything under the lace," Sutton deadpans.

I wince because that was brutal, though a true review. The dress is lace from the waist up, with nothing underneath; her breasts are barely covered. Still, the details make it classy, and it's long-sleeved.

"Maybe we can check just one more," her aunt suggests, and it's clear she hates the dress.

Setting my champagne flute onto the side table, I quickly grab a throat lozenge from my purse pocket. I've been feeling a sore throat coming on all day. I watch as Savannah spins around and heads back into the dressing room with the attendant holding the train of the dress.

She's having a big wedding. I never pictured her wanting that, but marriage is a compromise. Her fiancé owns a billion-dollar company; everyone wants an invite. He already bought a house in Everhope for Savannah so they can have their quiet weekends. I try to recall my own wedding dreams but draw a blank. Maybe they vanished when I had Lola. My life has reversed. Now a man has entered my life, and with him, possibilities.

But first, we would need to date.

And to date, I would need to agree.

To agree, I would have to give a sign.

A sign that I'm debating whether I want to make.

Yet, every day, I'm getting closer to throwing in the towel and saying okay.

ELODIE

E ntering my apartment, I hear the television softly on with a hockey game. Slowly, I place my purse on the side table and remove my coat. It's past seven, and I wanted to see Lola, but I think I missed her.

When I reach the living room, Hayes gives me a smile that is far too sexy for sitting comfortably on the sofa.

"She's asleep?"

He scoots over to make room for me on the couch. "Yeah, went down about 15 minutes ago. I'm not sure who's more exhausted, her or me. That hour between morning nap and lunchtime was brutal. Does she always have that much energy then?"

I laugh as I grab a throw pillow and sit down. "Yeah. But we're moving toward one nap a day and also potty training."

"Okay, remind me to study all of that."

"A shame the weather wasn't great, otherwise you could have gone to the playground."

"It's okay, we went to that coffee place around the corner next to the bakery. They have a kids' corner and a shit load of caffeine for me."

My smile hurts. "So you survived?"

He blows out an exhausting breath. "I did. We had to leave when a kid brought in a balloon."

I laugh. "We really need to figure out why she hates balloons."

"No kidding. Just one glance and she was clinging to my leg with a cry that was as good as a scream."

"I'm sure you saved her."

"I did." He timidly brushes it off. "I'm hoping next time that I'm with her to take her swimming."

"I think she would like that. Speaking of which, I got you a present." I walk to the side table in the living room and open a drawer, grabbing the item, then I return to the sofa and flop down, stretching my arm out for him to accept the gift.

Instantly his smile is ear-to-ear as he examines it. "A giant unicorn floaty. I'm not sure this matches the aesthetic of the building pool. But she'll love it."

"Admittedly, she hasn't been in a pool enough."

"Well, I'm here now."

Yeah, he is. It doesn't faze me.

"How were the champagne and dresses? Kind of thought you would arrive home a little tipsy."

I scratch the back of my head. "It was an option on the table. However, my throat hurts a little, and champagne can do things to one's brain, opening a Pandora's box of potential life choices."

"Anything you want to share? And I'll get you a tea." He's already standing before I can answer.

"You don't have to—"

He interrupts. "It's not a problem, and I already know that you won't share the mixed messages in your head that are probably 99% due to me." He winks.

Blushing, heat rises to my cheeks. I clench my jaw, torn between mortification that he can read me so easily and irritation at how transparent I am around him.

Regardless, I let him make tea while I change into yoga pants. Returning, I grab the throw blanket and snuggle into the pillows as Hayes comes back with two cups of tea.

"I'm not sure who's more tired, you or me. I've been blinded by white dresses. Nine. That's how many dresses she tried on." I accept the mug of tea and hold it close, taking in the warmth and the smell of lemon and another ingredient. "What is this?"

"Ginger and turmeric. You had a hidden tea box in the back of your cupboard. The recipe for health. Sometimes I have it when I'm traveling and need a boost."

"Smart." I take a long drink and let the warm liquid slide down my throat, already easing the scratchiness of my voice. "It's nice. So what else is new after your day with Lola?"

He sets his mug on the coffee table, and it kind of pinches me in a good way that he is making himself at home here. "My mom is desperate to visit."

"Funnily enough, my parents have continued to subtly mention how they want to meet you." I grimace.

"Why don't we just knock it all out at once?"

My eyes grow wide at his suggestion. "You mean all of our parents in one room at the same time? Brave."

He chuckles, and that smooth grin of his appears. "Why not? Everyone is aware of the facts. Lola will simmer everyone down, no point putting ourselves through it all twice. Besides, my mom is thrilled, and I assume your parents are…"

"They are protective. They haven't met you, so they're cautious but also happy for Lola." I haven't really spoken to them much at all in relation to Hayes. They've always respected my wish not to press me on Lola's father, and they aren't changing that behavior now that he's in the picture. They know I'll tell them about any important updates in my own time.

"I like a challenge. Should I tell her to come in a few weeks? I think it would be good for her. It's my dad's birthday then, and I have a feeling she might need to be cheered up."

I reach for his arm instinctively, my touch gentle but sure —the kind of gesture that only comes from real care and understanding. "I get that. I can only imagine how hard it was for her. You, too."

These are the things I need to hear. Although he has passed, there is still contentment to be brought to Hayes.

It grows quiet for a beat, and his mind seems to drift before it returns. "Anyway," he begins. Perhaps his father's passing is more raw for him than I thought. "Shall we agree that we can see all of our parents in a few weeks?"

"Yeah, that gives us a little more time to fit into one another's lives." My eyes squeeze closed when I recognize that my sentence is up for interpretation. Opening them, I see Hayes already thinking two steps ahead, with that grin still perfectly pasted. "I don't mean *us*, I mean Lola and parental us."

He casually picks up his tea for another sip, his self-satisfied smirk staying put. "Careful, Elodie, honesty always seeps through," he taunts.

I rub my temples as I grow frustrated with myself for being unable to hold it together. It's easy to crumble even slightly around this man. "Can we just focus on… I don't know, preschool lists or something?"

"Random topic, but okay, I'll play along. I guess she starts that soon?"

"Next year, but right now I'm on the waiting list for one. It's super hard to get a spot, and it will cost a fortune, but it's perfect for her and near the office, too."

Hayes gives me a stern look that feels like a reminder. "Money isn't an issue."

Shaking my head, I'm not doing well at picking topics right now. I don't want to argue. "Okay." That's all I reply. "Anyhow, I feel a headache coming on." It's only half a lie.

It causes Hayes to sink further into the cushion and throw his arm over the back of the couch. "I'll stay for a while then in case Lola wakes. You need your rest if you have a headache."

Nervously, I smile, because he's on to me. I'm digging myself into a hole. "Fine. Let's just get it out in the open. We kissed."

"I'm aware." He's confident and doesn't seem concerned that this could lead to an uncomfortable conversation.

"It's not exactly smart of us," I say, and it feels scratchier in my throat.

"Is it?" he challenges.

For a fraction of a second, our eyes meet, and I'm wondering if there is any way out of this circle, because he won't be bringing logic to the situation. Inside, I wrestle with myself because I'm exhausted from fighting it. I give up in defeat.

"Maybe not." I look away from him, hoping his heated eyes on me won't feel like daggers of a man who is winning.

"It's pretty intelligent of us, if you ask me." He really is easy breezy about this. "No point in ignoring our chemistry. Lola having two parents together is only a small piece of it.

We're allowed to be selfish in life. Just so happens it comes down to you and me."

Licking my lips, I carefully bring my gaze to meet his eyes that don't blink; instead, they are resolute. "I'm *perhaps* getting closer to agreeing." Hayes doesn't respond and seems to be waiting patiently for me to say more. "You kind of scare me."

He seems taken aback by my revelation. "How so?"

The corner of my mouth curves into a delicate smile. "You're impossible. Stubborn. And do things only when it's guaranteed you'll win. That's a lot to soak in. Especially if I'm the target."

"Oh, you are most definitely the target." The swelter in his voice is sexy, and the message is clear. If I let him in, then it won't be casual. He won't allow it.

I've debated with myself about whether I should be with a man who is dominating as my type of partner. But once I was able to stand my ground with him on the Lola front, I began to see that everything he does is very attractive and causes flutters of excitement inside me.

His smooth smirk is trying to persuade me right now.

I crack a smile and playfully shoo his arm. "Your message is clear, and maybe you will wear me down, but not tonight."

"Sweetheart, I wasn't aiming for tonight." He begins to adjust the blanket on me, and I'm not sure where his mind is. "You're not feeling too well. I hear it in your voice."

"You mean mentally?"

He laughs. "No. I meant your voice is turning hoarse. You need sleep. Want me to stay in case Lola wakes?"

"Now someone is brazen," I tease him, and my voice does sound scraped.

He can only smile, and I feel his strong arm pull me, encouraging me to lie down. Studying him, he isn't a man with a hidden agenda right now. He genuinely wants to take care of me.

"You were watching a hockey game before. We can finish it if you want?"

Hayes seems pleased with my suggestion. "Good. It was only the end of the first when you arrived home."

"Then I ruined it."

He chuckles as he drags my feet onto his lap. "You were the first-intermission entertainment."

"Ah, I have a purpose then."

He bobbles his head side to side as he grabs the remote. "Something like that."

We watched the end of the second, had a snack at the second intermission, and somewhere in the third, I felt myself begin to doze off. The man has this magical move where he low-key, under-the-radar, strokes my calf through the blanket with one hand, and his other hand massages my feet. So natural. So calming. Soothing enough to cause me to doze off completely.

I'm positive I had fallen asleep when, in my dream, I sighed and said, "If it were easy, you would have me."

Because in my dream, he whispered as he brushed hair away from my face. "It's only a matter of time until you're mine."

MONDAY MORNING, I'm sitting in Foster's office for a catch-up on the latest for the team. He leans back in his chair with the Chicago skyline on full display. It's a clear blue sky, but it still has the chill to the air that people from Illinois have learned to distinguish.

"We have only five of the 150 invoices still open, and I'm

chasing them with claws. That's a win considering last month we had nine," I explain as I scan over my tablet.

"Measly numbers."

I hum in doubt. "Except one of those invoices is from Everest, and they still owe us 1.2 million for the logistics of their plexiglass to Sweden. You're going to have to speak to someone because they haven't paid for their goods, yet they are on a freighter somewhere off the coast of Scotland right now. Can't exactly throw it all into the sea."

Foster blows out a breath. "Let me cross-department check what can be done. Anyhow, are you still sure that you don't want to attend the conference out in Houston?"

He asked me a few months ago if I wanted to attend a conference for logistics companies. Every department is sending someone. "My answer is the same. I don't want to leave Lola for more than a few days, and besides, there are people on the team who would relish the opportunity."

Foster stands and turns to get a better view of the outside. "You're the manager. A bit more senior. Truthfully, the attendance would also boost your chance for another promotion. If I can't convince you with that, then I'm not sure what to do. I'm not the type to strong-arm you and say it's a job requirement because I'm not that kind of man… well, not today. I'll move on from that topic."

"Thank you."

"Getting all geared up for the monthlies?"

The one-on-ones with team members are meetings that I enjoy. A time to review things and check on improvement points. "Sure. I don't mind them."

"At least someone on this floor loves them."

A knock on his office door draws our attention to see who it is.

Nerves kick in when it's revealed to be Hayes. My chest

is pounding because I'm not sure what to expect. This is the first time we've crossed paths professionally. Sure, in the office building or that HR meeting, but not during the workday on our respective floors. Hayes, in a gray three-piece suit, is not good for humanity; it weakens us all. Or just me.

His eyes hold mine for a mere second longer than needed before he shoots his gaze to Foster. "We have that meeting in ten, want me to come back?"

"Nah, it's okay." Foster waves me off. "Elodie and I were just finishing." He grabs his phone off his desk and begins to walk toward the door, and I stand as well. "Just give me three. I'm starving, and somebody brought Polish pastries in today."

"Doesn't your assistant bring you that stuff?" Hayes asks, bemused.

"Normally, but she's away sick for the day. Another reason that I deserve the extra carbs. I don't have someone to organize me," Foster complains as he leaves his office, not taking much notice of who he left behind.

I'm relieved that Foster continued on as though the company's most awkward pair isn't taking up residence in his office. But we're all professionals, right?

Except Hayes is now staring at me, giving me the predatory once-over that heats up my middle and brings pain to my clit. He takes a few steps farther into the room. The charcoal of his suit makes his eyes extra intense, deep as a sea.

"Elodie," he states.

"Yes?"

The corner of his mouth twitches. Does he take pleasure in this run-in? I want to keep our work and personal lives separate.

"There are drinks later. Leadership, perhaps, a representative from every department. I'm looking into some expansion projects and need insight from everyone. I prefer to get out of the office to have a more open conversation. The sitter is already taken care of. Meet me downstairs at a quarter to six and we can ride together, that would be grand." He's being cocky.

Wait, what? I flutter my eyes, trying to comprehend what he just said. "Excuse me?"

"You heard me. Drinks, be on time." He stuffs his hands into his pockets as he towers over me.

"Why isn't it a question?"

"Because it's not. I already arranged the usual sitter for Lola."

My jaw drops. "You what?"

He remains cool as a cucumber. "I know. I thought through all of the logistics, didn't I?" He's boldly proud.

"You can't just order me to go with you." I step closer to him, wanting to stand off.

"It's work."

Shaking my head, I'm going in all directions. "Still, everyone in the office will form theories about us."

"Why? We're just two professionals." His face remains stoic.

Remembering that I still have a job to do, yet our lives are entwined, I'm wrestling with myself about how to swallow the connection to remain professional. "Fine," I bite out.

Our attention flies to Foster, who returns with a napkin and a powdered pastry. His eyes travel between us. "Thought I could avoid this with you two, but I guess not," he casually mentions before he bites into his food and proceeds to head to his desk. At least, he doesn't appear too fazed.

"I was just leaving." I begin to walk away, but Hayes gently stops me by touching my elbow.

"Just remember, Elodie. It's only a matter of time," Hayes mentions.

Instantly, my eyes blaze open, and my lips part from shock.

Damn it, I wasn't dreaming.

Which also means he heard me.

Ignoring him and straightening my shoulders, I choose not to reply, and I leave.

I'm slightly riled when I get to my desk.

Blair appears the moment I manage to sit behind my desk.

"What's up with you and Hayes Callahan? I was on my way back from the restroom, and I saw you both." I'm not sure if she wants intel or is genuinely curious. I'm choosing option one.

I fix a smile. "Nothing. He had a meeting with Foster and asked about which floor has the best coffee," I lied.

Lines form on her forehead, as it isn't the answer she was expecting. "Wow, he can be pleasant. I've been hearing from people that he's a little scary."

Yeah, I know.

"Yeah? Is that what's on the grapevine?"

She nods. "People on his floor find him a little intense, but somebody else said he just has a steely exterior and is actually a nice guy. Just, well, don't give him subpar work, otherwise he will let you know."

"That's what people are saying?"

"Yep. See ya later." She walks away.

Quickly, I unlock my computer screen and check my phone next to my keyboard. I notice a new email from the preschool.

Opening it, it takes one word to see that Lola now has a spot at the best preschool. Made possible by Mr. Demanding Drinks himself. I'm not even going to complain because it's all for our daughter. It's also a reminder of how much he wants to provide and care for her. But I mentioned the school very briefly, and less than forty-eight hours later, he made magic happen. It probably only took one call. Hayes always gets what he wants.

And I want to feel what it's like on the other end when he finally has his win.

Me.

ELODIE

Walking into Jupiter, I inhale a sharp breath as I begin to unzip my coat. The room is filled with the noise of people talking while indulging in an after-work drink. The location is prime, which is why it attracts many from nearby offices. Later, it turns into a dinner spot. The warehouse vibe with hanging lightbulbs sets the tone for sophisticated yet trendy. It also radiates a glow off people's faces. In some cases, their moody glare, too.

When I notice Hayes in the corner, his shirt sleeves rolled up, his expensive watch on display, and his blazer ditched, it seems he has already daggered his eyes into me. He can't be happy, as I'm a little late due to an email that had to go out to chase a client's billing. I sent him a message, but why else does his gaze seem heavy on me right now?

I'm wearing the same clothes as I did earlier, just might have popped a button and gone for a darker shade of lipstick. Approaching the table, I feel his eyes dragging me closer until our contact breaks when Matt from compliance and Jody from logistics look up with smiles. Both are a bit older than I am and have been at the company longer. At least, this set-up wasn't a ruse. A legitimate meeting.

But I do notice their drinks are nearly empty.

"Hey, Elodie, survive the email crisis?" Matt asks with a smile as he makes space for me at the high-top table. He's always friendly and is recently engaged to his girlfriend, whom he met in college. That fact is important; otherwise, I'm not sure Hayes would be so relaxed. I have the feeling he has become possessive of me.

"All fine," I say, and hang my coat on the back of the chair.

"I'm about to leave. I have a 7AM client call tomorrow and still need to catch the train to the suburbs," Jody explains as she quickly takes one last sip of her drink, which seems to be a gin and tonic.

A waitress quickly pauses next to me, and I order the same, and she buzzes away. I also make a mental note to double-check the bar that one particular bartender isn't working tonight. He gave me his number a while back. I did nothing with it, as I wasn't into the dating scene then. The last thing I would want to add to the night is seeing Hayes overreact about it, because I think he must feel this sense of possessiveness. I feel it, too, when it comes to him, and I'm not sure I'm entitled to it.

I sit down to join them, across from Hayes. "Downer's Grove, right?" I ask Jody.

"Yeah, it's an easy ride, though. But I want to see my husband quickly before he heads into his night shift."

Hayes leans in. "You mentioned he's a doctor, right?"

Jody beams a smile, clearly proud. "Yeah. A pediatrician here in the city. Finally finished his residency and all of that. We're actually thinking of moving closer because of his work. But with his hours and the car, he can fly into the city if there's no traffic. Plus, we get more house for our money, space and parks, all that."

"I totally get that. I'm from a small town, and the value of a good park is underestimated," I agree.

Matt grabs his coat and stands, confusing me. I'm losing Jody—him, too? "Leaving already?"

"I also have that meeting invite for the 7AM call. I'm hoping my manager emails to say we don't need to be in the office and can video call, but I'm not feeling that lucky. Better call it an early night."

"Completely fine. We've spoken enough, and you both have given me some great insights for the upcoming project," Hayes assures them with an easy smile. A façade where that smile conveys to them that he is relaxed and relatable, but to me, he's calculated.

I bite my lip, growing a little frustrated. It would have been nice to bounce ideas off others and see Hayes's approach to work—does he listen, offer constructive feedback, encourage others? Instead, my suspicion that this was all a plan has been proven correct.

"Definitely consider applying for the coaching program. Really home in on your strengths for personal development." Hayes does sound genuine.

Jody zips up her coat and seems happy. "Thanks. I didn't think about the program until we talked about it. It's on my mind now."

"Thanks for the talk. Sorry to dash," Matt says.

"You'll both be okay getting home?" Hayes double-checks.

Jody nods her head. "Yeah, Matt and I are both heading to the station, so we can walk together."

"Alright, otherwise I can arrange a ride," Hayes offers.

"No need," Matt confirms, glancing at me. "Good luck discussing work. He's not that bad—promise," he teases.

I keep a false smile fixed while resisting the urge to roll my eyes. "I'm sure. Have a good night," I tell Matt and Jody as the waitress approaches and quickly sets my glass down.

We all say goodbye, and they leave. I watch them disappear into the crowd by the door before turning my sharp gaze to Hayes. "They don't have a 7AM meeting, do they?"

He smirks to himself as he brings his whiskey to his lips. "In about a half-hour, when they get a notification that the meeting has been canceled, they won't."

A match inside of me has been lit. "Manipulation with a side of control—great. What the hell?"

"Funny. Two years ago, you didn't want to get away from me at a bar. Now you don't want to come near me in a bar."

His logic requires a long sip of my gin and tonic with lime. "It's messier now—an HR field day. Untangling the sides of us as co-parents and colleagues is uncharted territory. Still, I'm sure this isn't the way to handle it."

Is he even listening or just waiting to reply?

"You know there isn't a difference. You look exactly the same as the last time we met in a bar. That's… inconvenient for my self-control."

I scoff, a bitter chuckle slipping out. My tongue glides over my teeth. This is pointless. "If you wanted me alone, why this? We've met outside the office before."

He tsks at me, and it's filled with sin. It's attractive if I'm being honest with myself. Very. "When Lola is around, then yeah, all is well. But the moment we're alone, you and I, then you want to run. This is me trying to figure out the best approach with you non-Lola related. My patience is a peculiar kind, it tests waters until I have the answer. However, I am a man of my word, and you're here. So let's talk business."

I lift my nose, trying to inspect his sincerity. I'm convinced enough. "Okay."

"You refused to go to the conference. Why? Foster has asked twice."

My eyes lift because this is the topic he's bringing up, and his tone is a mix of concern and curiosity. "You've been talking with him about my career?" I accuse him.

"No. He brought it up."

"That has nothing to do with your project."

"Doesn't matter. Answer me."

Sighing, I clutch my drink but don't sip. "I don't like leaving Lola. My parents could stay, but I've never been out of state without her. The spot at the conference should go to someone less worried—even if it affects my job. Lola matters more."

Hayes nods his head as he listens patiently. "I thought you might say that. However, you might have to take the leap once. I'm also in the picture. Puzzling our schedules around each other is part of how things are going to have to go."

"I'm aware." I'm getting a little agitated. "But let's leave her out of this, Hayes. I also don't appreciate you talking with Foster about me in the office. Can we just focus on work right now?"

He smiles almost affectionately. "Okay. As I said to the others, we must improve efficiency and workflow between departments. More cross-department meetings are a good idea. Clients face many obstacles from the company, but communication could be smoother—more central."

I continue. "Finance knows nothing about crate sizes or cargo routes that avoid the Bermuda Triangle, and we don't need to. We communicate in numbers, often with a client contact who also lacks logistics knowledge. Finance should be kept separate, and the client should have a single point of contact for other issues. Invoicing often requires someone authorized to approve payment."

"I'm aware. Just thought I would run an idea or two by you, so here we are."

I snort. "Are we? Because it seems the work-related discussion's already done."

That suave grin appears. "You may be right."

Taking a long drink, I debate whether I should just close up this evening and leave. Alas, I am not so smart. My eyes flick up to meet his. Even though the room is loud, it feels silent right now. Hayes enters my bubble by switching seats so he's next to me. The presence of his body is magnetizing near my own.

And truthfully, when the responsibilities of being a mom and work slip out of my mind and I'm with him, then I'm reminded. The way he has the ability to make me feel secure enough to be spontaneous. I'm a woman who runs life by the book, except on the island, that click between us was instant, new to me, and it unlocked a side of me that I didn't know I have but had been waiting for a time to come out. It did then. And I'm having déjà vu all over again.

"Isn't it crazy how our lives were always so close, yet we never crossed paths?" I wonder, almost fondly.

"I have been thinking about that lately."

I smile wryly and meet his gaze. "You could drive anyone crazy."

He licks his lips, amused. "Do share."

"In a suit, you're all sharp edges. Out of one, you let a few walls drop."

His long finger brushes my wrist as I grip my glass on the

table. "Which version do you want tonight?" His words slip out, slow and heated.

Feeling my cheeks warm, I recognize that my body is reacting to him. In truth, both versions of him have the ability to suck me in. "That's a dangerous thing to ask," I rasp with honesty. Either way, he's intriguing, and either way, I'm well aware that deep down, he is the same man I have always shared a strong sexual attraction with.

It took only a few hours on an island to end up spending a night with him. A few weeks have passed since I first saw him again, and though the chemistry is still strong, I've hesitated to act on it, even though his signals have been clear that he's open to it.

"Let me tell you a theory I have," he begins and taps my wrist. I swallow a single nerve because there is a high chance he will be spot-on. "You have two sides, too. One is when you have a backbone to level with me. The other hesitates and you fight with yourself, and it shows. Elodie, you give everything for our daughter. You do all the right things. Work, home, and being a good friend. But you don't ever do something for yourself."

"Of course I—"

"Uh-uh, let me finish. You overthink and end up stopping yourself from enjoying life. You are still allowed to do that, you know."

"Don't be ridiculous," I attempt to protest, even though he is blatantly right. The words catch when I feel him slide his hand onto my thigh under the table. My resolve for the evening begins to crumble, and from the way his eyes flick up to meet mine, he probably already knows it.

"We're doing this. You know it too. Neither of us can let go of the idea. A chance or just reliving a memory."

I remain mute.

"Elodie, we've kissed. You felt something too." He leans in, his mouth close to my ear, and the space between us shrinks. "If I'm wrong, then tell me now; otherwise, I'll make a damn vow that I won't relent until you explore it," he threatens with a whisper, and it feels like a taunt, too. A persuasive, makes-my-center-weak taunt.

I try to focus on taking a deep breath to regain composure, but it doesn't do much. Turning my head slightly, our faces are far too close for public. Our sewn-together eyes send a clear message that we are both trapped in a circle.

"Excuse me." My voice is collected. I swing my legs to the side and hop down from the chair. I walk in the direction of the bathroom, and I feel his attention still on me.

This is my life today. I need to flee to the bathroom to throw water on my face because Hayes does all the right things to make a woman melt.

The moment the door to the bathroom closes behind me, I lunge to the sleek and modern sink and turn the faucet on. It seems that I'm all alone, as the two stalls are open. After a quick splash, I pat my face dry with the nearby cloth hand towels, then toss it into the wicker laundry basket under the sink. Pulling a tube of lipstick out of my pocket, I lean over the sink to apply. The shade is called *Dangerously Red,* and it couldn't be more fitting.

Especially when I'm not sure this is a red-flag moment at all.

Because when the door swings open, Hayes appears. He closes the door and pauses when he is about to flip the lock. I freeze with my lipstick still held up and stare at him through the mirror.

"A bit pointless. It will only be coming off. Don't you think? You didn't answer me about exploring our chemistry. Last chance, Elodie. Otherwise, I'm locking this."

All I have to do is say it. Remind him of this bad idea.

But now? Mr. Theory of My Life has a point and already used the key to unlock the part of me that is freeing.

I do everything for everyone else. I overthink responsibility, to the point that I deny myself possibilities. Of course I share the same thought as him. It isn't even a thought, it's a feeling that I want to either remember or hope with him. All of these things push and pull at me, and at some point, I'm going to break.

And that time has come.

His eyes remain pinned on me, and my heart races because I'm going to do something for me. "You're right," I rasp weakly.

He clicks the lock and begins to walk my way with swagger; he's hunting, and it's for me.

I toss my lipstick and hear the sound of it landing somewhere in the sink.

I wouldn't know because I'm too quick to meet him halfway and allow our lips to slam together.

12

ELODIE

I t's the way that I want it. Hayes's kisses are anything but soft. And because we are both equally kissing like starved people, then I'm not sure who is more desperate for the other. One thing doesn't make sense to me, though. He makes my heart race, but I somehow feel calm with him in this moment.

We've kissed already since he's been back, but this has more reverence.

His tongue strokes mine with insistence as I fist his blazer to hang on. Then things only escalate. It's one angle in one kiss, then a new angle in another. His hands cradle my head, and I'm giving zero signs that I'm going to pull away.

All because I desperately want this. He's occupied my mind non-stop, and he has the key to open every single door inside me.

Our kisses become hurried and unmeasured, and there is no stopping. Sometimes logic and curiosity collide. I'm not going to make logic out of this right now. Sometimes we need to see how far we'll go and test limits, even if it is something wild.

My world begins to spin as we move.

He's leading us back, and we nearly tumble into a bath-room stall.

I yelp, and he chuckles under his breath. We slam the door for extra precaution and find ourselves in a very close space. At last, our eyes lock for a quick, quiet confirmation that this is what we're doing.

"You remember, don't you? The way it was. You and me. The connection didn't stop," he rasps with his fingers clasping the back of my neck.

I slowly nod the truth before we kiss harshly. I can't say that what's transpiring is a profound moment other than giving in. But it is most definitely a memory that will chase us for years to come. Hayes seems to bring out that side of me. I never would have done what I did on the island, and letting us transpire in this setting also seems like I'm pushing boundaries.

But it's safe. Because it's him.

"Fuck, Elodie. Your mouth looks really good swollen from my kiss." His voice is husky.

"Then don't stop," I beg.

He must sense the need in my voice, because one step and he has me trapped between the wall and his body. My dress gives him zero obstacles, and with one touch, he's hiking up my dress, taking my leg with him until it's wrapped around his thigh. A shiver runs through me from anticipation as he slides his fingers along my inner thigh, straight to my drenched lace panties. For a second, I'm thankful that we have a fabric barrier because I'm in sensory overload.

I'm craving his touch, and adrenaline shoots through me that Hayes is about to touch me intimately.

I gasp tightly as his fingers slip under the fabric and we

touch skin to skin. His other hand rests over my head against the wall.

"Is this the way you've always been around me? The way you will always be?" His tone is firm and adamant that I answer only one way.

It doesn't matter because it's the truth. "Yes," I rasp.

His sinful smirk appears as our gaze holds, and his finger flicks my clit.

"Thought so."

I'm burning up, and his eyes on me only add to it. I whimper when two fingers intrude inside me. My hands splay at my sides on the wall to hang on for balance.

"You've been waiting for me, haven't you?" Another pump inside me. "Since we saw one another again. You've been waiting for me to touch you." With purpose, he slows his movement, a finger inside me and his thumb on my clit.

I'm searching his eyes for his thoughts, but all I see is realization. "Yes," I barely whisper as my breath is heavy.

"Good. Because I've been waiting a hell of a lot longer than that."

His remark causes me to light up inside. For a second, something more intense is happening in this moment that has nothing to do with being physical. It's the reminder that even after we left that island, we both occupied one another's minds.

And that just sends us into a spiral.

Our mouths meet for a kiss that is messy yet feels far too good. His fingers drive up to yank down my panties, and my fingers begin to fumble with his belt. In the process, my thumb brushes against his hard stomach muscles.

I pull down his boxer briefs and pants to mid-thigh as he pulls out a condom from his pocket easily.

I simper a laugh. "You came prepared. You always carry those around like that?"

His mouth finds my neck for a quick nip as he sheaths himself. "Only when I'm around you."

"And you stalk me to a bathroom," I tease him.

"You're snarky today."

I hum a blissful sound right before my body tightens as I feel his tip about to enter, and it's pure anticipation. He invites my leg to wrap around his waist, and he parts my legs slightly wider. I'm hyperaware of his strength to keep me anchored and his dominance to lead us.

One of his hands remains on my thigh, and his other fingers burrow deep into my hair. I'm completely at his mercy.

My moan is quieted by him kissing me as he enters me. Hayes reads my body and goes slow the first few pumps before he works up to going deeper and slightly rougher. Every kiss erasing my thoughts, every thrust sending me close to a ledge. I feel completely full from his solid length, and the sound of his grunts drowns out my anticipation.

We're already too deep into what is transpiring between us.

I'm greedy and try to take more, and I roll my hips and tighten my thighs around him. My head spins as he continues to hit me against that spot deep within. Our breathing is labored as we work together. We don't have time to prolong this.

That will be for another time.

The fact that it is already my expectation is a flag. One that I push to the side because I'm too lost in this bliss. It does something extra to me to know this man wants me this much, and I can't help but keep him on a line because I want him.

Here we are, tightly wound and fucking in a bathroom.

He murmurs something into my skin below my ear. I can't make it out, but it feels like praise. His body, his cock, and his commanding lips all have me anchored to earth, even if I feel like I'm floating. Our eyes catch as he slows but takes me as deep as he can. His force. Our breathing is music, and I feel his pulse matching mine. He captures my mouth, our lips meet, but not for a kiss; my moan escapes into his mouth as I hold onto his shoulders.

I'm barely hanging on, and when he begins to shatter, so do I.

It's all a blur as every nerve-ending releases from the ache that had me crazed for him to touch.

My body is numb as he gently sets me down, and my eyes flutter to adjust to the light. He's panting as he zips up his pants.

"So this is what you wanted?" I whisper, because the truth is that I just succumbed to his chase. The one that I believe I've wanted.

He helps me adjust my dress while our eyes hold. "It's a bonus, but there are still many other ways and places where I can take you."

I turn away and leave the stall with him trailing behind. My first view in the mirror shows a wanton woman, flushed, and completely over her head. Yet elated in every way. I walk to the sink and place my hands on the counter to gather myself and cool down.

"Is it what you wanted?" I hear him say, and my gaze snaps from the mirror to Hayes, who gives his shirt one last straightening before he sets his hand on the handle of the door to the ladies' room.

I'm not sure how to lighten the mood to point out the setting of choice for where we had sex, or admit vulnerability that I'm completely captivated by him and every second has been exhilarating and somehow right.

My answer is simply a subtle, wry smile.

"Thought so." His look is smug before he unlocks the door and leaves me be.

———

With luck, the sitter had already gotten Lola down to sleep for the night. I flop down onto my mattress and stare up at the ceiling. My body is still buzzing. The last time I had sex was when we created Lola. And sex in a public bathroom? Yeah, that's never happened before, nor was it on my Elodie-lives-reckless list. But that's Hayes. He brings out another side of me.

I'm torn between grumbling with myself and letting my giddy smile break out.

The sound of my phone alerting me to a text message breaks my train of thought. I roll onto my belly and pick up my phone. One swipe of my screen and the smile wins. I can imagine Hayes's satisfied grin as he wrote the text. Sighing, I flip like a pancake to my back, unsure if I'll sleep or not. It's either awake because of my thoughts or sound asleep because of my physical exhaustion. I read the text once more.

HAYES

Next time I'd prefer a bed, but I appreciate how resourceful we can be. Get some sleep. You'll need your strength if you plan on resisting me tomorrow.

13

ELODIE

B eans is buzzing as everyone arrives at work for the day, so we opt to find a spot outside the entrance in the main lobby, halfway to the elevators. We are out of the way and have a wall to lean against.

"Thanks for the quick coffee," I tell Savannah and hold up my to-go cup in cheers.

"No problem. It's sometimes nice to return to my old stomping ground from my assistant days." She smiles as she straightens the lid on her coffee.

I got in early, which gives me a few extra minutes to get a listening ear. It only took thirty seconds for me to burst out my news, and she instantly stated she needed coffee for this. An extra shot, too.

I didn't sleep last night. I kept thinking about Hayes and what we did. On one hand, it feels good to be spontaneous again, and it feels safe because I've only ever been spontaneous with him. But now I'm not 100% sure the next play, if any.

"So, you haven't seen him yet this morning?"

I finish my sip of coffee. "No. That isn't unusual, though.

He hasn't had Lola spend the night yet, and he gets daycare updates. He normally tries to see her during a break or lunch, just not too often so he doesn't disrupt the routine. But he also has many morning and lunchtime meetings. I'm not sure his fridge at home even has anything other than yogurt cups with animals printed on them and a few protein shakes."

"You do have a glow. Good for you. You satisfied your curiosity, too. Right?" She wants to beam a smile but is keeping it in check so it doesn't come off as teasing me. I think she might have been shipping Hayes and me since she put two and two together about Lola.

I tilt my head to the side, trying to hide a blushing smile. It comes far too naturally. "The attraction is still there, that's clear. He seems to be on a path of pursuit, too. He's great with Lola." I list everything, and it's all positive.

Savannah takes another drink and asks, "What's the problem then?"

Pressing my lips together, I stare at my best friend before admitting a simple fact. "It's not him. It's me."

Savannah nearly sputters her coffee as she breaks out in laughter. "Really? That's the explanation you are going to use? That cliché? In your case, it's also a lie."

"Not exactly," I sigh. "I just choose not to articulate the reasons why it's me. Which is that it feels like it could all be too good to be true. I also haven't dated in, like, years. I keep reminding myself to be cautious. I'm not 100% sure who is driving this ship, you know? One second, I think he's letting me go at my own pace. Other times, he is frustratingly on a chase with his rules and actions, and if it wasn't for my head spinning, then it is hot as hell, to be honest."

"Listen, I don't know him so well. Julian does. From what I've heard, Hayes is a good guy."

"Yeah, I keep hearing that…" I reflect and glance into the

new swarm of people arriving through the revolving doors. "Now I have the issue of what the hell to say or do now that we were intimate. Do I pretend nothing happened? Do I address it and set new boundaries? Or just say fuck it. Either of those options involves a bucket of nerves."

"Hmm," she ponders.

Both of our eyes drift to the side as Hayes approaches us. Cologne strong, charcoal suit finely pressed, his eyes landing right on me. My heart quickens because he's near, and flashbacks of last night hit me. A question of the future, him, it all morphs together in a single second.

"Morning, ladies." His grin is a crime.

"Hey there," Savannah greets him, the best actress in the world, showing no signs that she is privy to the last 24 hours of my life.

"Morning," I say and avert his gaze.

"My afternoon has been reshuffled. I would like to pick up Lola early, and I'll bring her back before her bedtime." I'm still not used to puzzling schedules, and it must read on my face. "Concessions. Co-parenting," he reminds me.

I put all events between us aside, because this is about Lola. That's maybe a good sign that I can compartmentalize. "Sure. She'll like that." I make the mistake of slipping my gaze back to him, where his eyes with a glint arrow straight into me. The flicker inside me doesn't dampen, it's even almost as exhilarating as last night.

In my peripheral view, I notice Savannah looking between us, a sly smile curving on her mouth.

"Well, I'll leave you both. I have places to be, and I'm sure you two have a lot to talk about." His face remains neutral, but the subtle tick of his cheek is there. "Have a good morning, ladies." He turns and struts away with such confidence that the crowd parts.

The feeling of a hand on my arm brings my attention back to Savannah, who is grinning.

"Ooh, this is fun. Let me think… You two probably need an icebreaker to get you both over the hurdle of morning-after conversations. Might need to be an external force."

"That would be a miracle," I deadpan. I'm good with confrontation. I've done it many times since Hayes entered the picture. But when it comes to him and me on a romantic level, my talent goes out the door.

"Like, other than the leadership team, *nobody* at the office realizes you two are together… I mean, that he's Lola's father?"

"Well, daycare and HR know. But they can't say anything. The company is strict about NDAs and privacy, especially when it comes to kids. We mostly avoid each other. Or at least, I asked for that boundary. I don't think anyone notices."

She continues to think. Sometimes, when your best friend knows your thoughts and fears inside out and they appear to be conspiring, you should be worried.

But I have bigger fish to fry right now.

———

BLAIR CONTINUES to inspect me even as I just closed my tablet after our one-on-one meeting that has now wrapped up. Throughout the whole meeting, she seemed to lose focus on our discussion. She has talent and is a team player but needs a bit more attention to detail. I always give compliments, then suggestions, then more compliments. The perfect sandwich method.

But right now? The roles seemed reversed.

"Elodie, can I be honest? Off the record?"

These meetings are for open conversation. I'm her superior who wants to listen, and compared to others, I feel I'm more approachable and easy to talk to. "Absolutely." I smile.

Blair hesitates. "How do I say this?" She seems to be struggling.

"Just say it. No need to overthink it."

She shrugs. "Okay. Well, Alexis saw you at Jupiter last night."

A bolt hits me with slight fear. I do my best not to appear like a deer in headlights. I maintain my polite smile with a struggle. "And?"

"You were with Hayes."

My smile is still strained, but I'm going to keep pushing forward. I still have half a day at the office to get through. "A few people from work were there. We had a meeting."

Blair asks, "Alone?" in a doubtful tone.

"Well, some had to leave early, and I was late."

"I hope I'm not overstepping, but there is a rumor."

My brows raise as more fear flows through me. "Oh?"

"She said you were quite close together. Is there something going on?"

Maybe my nose flares as I grip my chair, a bit tired. "Nah. It was just work."

She nods softly. "Yeah, I thought so." She doesn't sound completely convinced but seems to let it go when her smile reappears. "Well, thanks for the feedback. I'd better get back to data input. I am not looking forward to an internal audit." She blows out a big breath theatrically.

"Who does?"

She stands and leaves, giving me a few seconds to collect myself. Exiting the meeting room, I begin to feel relief trickle inside me. Everybody is busy at their desks. When I turn the corner to my office, I can't help but instantly smile. There are white roses.

I should be angry. This is the last thing I need right now. With rumors, my mind struggling with life decisions, and blurring lines on the professional front.

I walk to my desk and lift the card, chuckling. I should have known.

Savannah and I have always had a funny game. Betting on things in the office or things happening in Everhope. We would send things back and forth to whoever won. Cakes or flowers. I just didn't realize we had an ongoing bet.

The card reads: *These could be from someone else if you choose.*

I snort a laugh to myself. Of course. Her interference would help me focus.

There's a knock on my open door, and I peer up to see Blair. "Sorry, I forgot to ask one thing about the paid tariff for Europe." I notice quickly how her eyes draw a line straight to the flowers. "Ooh, someone has an admirer."

"Nah, it's only—"

I'm interrupted by a masculine voice behind Blair. "Who the hell is sending you flowers?" Hayes stands in the doorway, fury filling his eyes.

Blair's eyes widen as she steps aside. Hayes, his face stone, seems too tense to step farther into my office.

"It's none of your business," I say defensively. *Shit.* That is not going to help this situation. Not when I have a man completely possessed in front of me and probably half of the office listening right now. Riling him up is my mistake.

"It is my business. You're the mother of *my* daughter."

In that moment, it feels like the world stops. Blair's jaw drops, and the office is so quiet I can hear the sound of the coffee machine a distance away.

I drop the card onto my desk, bring my hand to my hip, and my face hardens with anger. "Blair, can you give us a minute. And by all means, fuel that gossip train as Hayes is Lola's father," I tell her flippantly.

Blair still seems in shock, which is fair enough, as she has just witnessed an office secret pop. She nods nervously before fleeing.

Hayes ignores her and steps into the office, carelessly closing the door behind him. "Answer me."

Shaking my head in disbelief, I'm furious. "First off, they're from Savannah, so calm it down." He instantly sighs in relief. I clench my hanging fists in the air, pushing back every ounce of wanting to shout. "Bravo, Hayes. The whole office now knows."

He thinks for a few ticks, hopefully realizing what his slip-up has just done. Instead, I get, "I don't care. I have no problem with people knowing that Lola is mine."

Continuing to struggle, I roll my eyes and now resort to clawing my hair. "Indeed, we were not going to hide our connection forever. We were just waiting for the appropriate time but remaining *professional* in the office." I smack my lips together. "Not sure this was the way."

Hayes winces. "You're right." He pinches the bridge of his nose and glances away, then drives his gaze straight back to me. "No. You're not right. I'm sorry it happened like this. But I'm not going to apologize for not waiting any longer."

"You said you would respect my work boundaries. I'm not in a position to snap my fingers and demand my team sings my praises. I don't get that privilege like you do in your career," I scold him. I notice the remorse appearing on his face, and I drop down onto my chair, giving up. He has every right to be proud and open about Lola. We do have company parties for bringing your family to meet Santa or the Easter

Bunny. It wouldn't be fair for him to stand back and just watch us. I've been holding the big reveal back, so afraid of optics. Somebody was going to break early. It just happened to be him. Nor is it surprising.

"Would you be thrilled if you saw me with flowers for someone that isn't you?" he calmly challenges.

Sighing, he just hit the nail on the head. "No, I wouldn't be thrilled," I admit, deflated. In fact, I hate the mere thought. Is it crazy that I feel a sense of possessiveness all because we have a connection that nobody else could have and I would be jealous if that were to change by being with someone else.

He crosses his arms, tilting his head in several angles as he inspects me. "We agree on something else again. You're exactly where you are meant to be, Elodie. You just don't say it out loud, even though you know it, too. It's happening." He moves to tower over me with both hands planted on my desk. "You and me, in case you need clarity, but you're already fully aware."

I feel my throat dry, and I'm filled with that sensation of blood running extra fast inside me. It's easy for me to say he's right. But this isn't the place, nor do I want him to get the impression that I give in so easily to agree to everything. Instead, I tamp down my anger and resort to humor. "You know it would be easier if you did send me flowers. Then I could throw these at you right now. But they're from Savannah, and I won't ruin them, so you're saved… but either way, I don't think I would. You're safe. Because your points are valid… very."

"Good. Now, other than my moment a minute ago, I do have restraint, so getting you on the desk isn't going to happen," he replies.

"Oh, the shock and horror," I reply flatly.

"I'll see you when I drop Lola off, okay?"

"Yes. I'm still a little rattled, though, from your outburst."

It only causes him to smirk as he slowly leaves, taking all of the tension and insanity of the scene with him. Now I just have to deal with my team.

Rolling my shoulders back, I decide there is no time like the present to rip this bandage off. Everybody knows about Lola, and nobody has ever asked about her dad, and I never brought him up. The office does establish boundaries, unless you're Hayes, which means people tend not to press about life out of the office if they get the hint not to. My time has run out, as it's now public knowledge.

Straightening my blouse, I walk out of my office with my head held high. I already see my team congregating in the corner by the coffee machine. The moment they spot me, they pretend to be unaware.

"It's fine. I'm sure you heard." I pause for a second. "The whole floor, perhaps," I quip. "So I will get this out once. I'm connected to Hayes, he's Lola's dad, and no, I am not working here because of him. I already worked here before we ever met, and my promotion was long before he even joined the company. Say whatever you want, but I'm always open with my team. No further questions?" They look at me blankly, and I paste on a bright smile. "Good. Now, I heard someone brought chocolate chip cookies today."

Hayes with Lola. Check. Office knowledge. Check. Attraction. Yep, also check.

I'm taking the next step.

Guess my list is about to be complete.

HAYES

S hifting on the seat along the conference table, the chair swivels slightly. I listen to Easton, our head of marketing. I'm secretly relieved that he is the last of the leadership team to give an update in our weekly meeting. I'm finding a rhythm here, which is good. In the last few minutes, he has reminded us of the charity endeavors the company is partaking in, and his relief at handing off the holiday gift baskets project to the HR department is obvious. He was quite grumbly, feeling that his department needed to remind HR that they don't handle measly projects for staff children. I don't know Easton too well, but well enough.

"I'm fearing your mood comes with the holiday season," Julian deadpans.

Easton shrugs. "It's a fair opinion. My tolerance for HR and recruitment sometimes wears thin. Yes, recruitment and marketing go hand in hand, as we want to appeal to candidates and lists in the media for being the best company to work for. I would say 99.9% of all our events involve marketing. But do you know what doesn't?"

"Holiday baskets with candy for the little kids of the

staff," I mundanely finish his sentence that we have heard him ranting about all meeting.

"Exactly." He tosses his pen onto the table.

Olivia from HR rolls her eyes. "Way to be a team player. Now, if you will excuse me, I have a department meeting in five." She stands, looking sharp in her dark pantsuit.

"Sure, run along, Olive." He smirks cockily.

"If you call me that one more—" She stops herself and opts for a glare as she leaves.

Foster snorts a laugh. "Tradition. Easton pisses off HR."

"Let's be thankful that Ned from Digital is sick today. On that note, I think we are all set, unless anybody has anything to add?" Julian asks as he closes his laptop. We all shake our heads. "Good. I'm hungry. Pass me one of those snacks."

There is a perk to executive meetings: the food is always way above par, and I could use some energy. Elodie is taking it all purely by occupying my mind.

Last night was unexpected. I've been on the pursuit, but did I think that it would end with me inside of her in a bath-room stall? No. Not in that setting. Truth be told, it gives me a few directions to choose from in my head. I'm just trying to figure out what's fair to both of us.

We all grab a small plate and some food, and the tone is set to leave business out the door for a few minutes. We need a break.

"How is it going with Elodie? Since the big scene earlier." Foster isn't asking, he's stirring the pot while he enjoys a chicken salad sandwich.

"So let me get this straight. You lost your cool due to flowers? Yep, that's totally my fiancée's doing. Apologies." Julian smirks to himself with a hint of pride.

Foster rumbles a chuckle under his breath. "Elodie handled it like a pro. That's why I have her on the team. She's feisty when a client is late paying an invoice, even by a day. Imagine what she was like with this crazy guy over here." He hikes a thumb my way.

"At least it's in the open. What now?" Easton wonders as he pours a new bottle of sparkling water into his glass.

"Stop it. Leave the man alone. They need to figure it out without our opinions," Julian warns.

My brow rises from curiosity. "What might those opinions be?"

Foster's face contorts, debating what to say. "Focus on your daughter."

"Really? Nothing else?"

"I mean, no need to rush into it all in one go. You have practicalities to work out, and maybe the shock or adrenaline of your new situation will crash at some point. Make sure everything is for the right reason. Even if slow doesn't exist in your vocabulary," he clarifies.

Is that what I'm doing? Because attraction will always be there, whether we go slow or not. I've already acted on it. Our ship is already sailing. But an outsider is reminding me that maybe I could be thinking irrationally.

"True. Slow doesn't mean more isn't going to happen. You just need to take smaller steps," Easton voices.

I look around the table, a little disappointed they aren't urging me to go for it.

"Or he can go all in from the get-go. Hayes isn't one to wait patiently. Besides, 'Elodie is on the same wavelength, it just takes longer for the fog in her brain to clear'… end quote from Savannah," Julian teases. "No, but seriously. There is something there. Don't listen to us. Err on the side of caution, sure. But everybody has their own pace."

I smile in appreciation. "Thanks. I needed to hear that.

I've kind of been setting our speed. I think Elodie finally grasps that."

"Well, that's good then." Foster continues to listen.

"Except, maybe I'm just wearing her down." I'm not sure that's a good thing either, but I can't control myself around her. There is only one vision of the future for her. "Either way, Lola comes first, and I will see Elodie tonight."

"Awkward child handovers?" Easton throws a chip into his mouth.

I chuckle to myself. "Thankfully not. I'm getting the hang of the dad thing, and most of the time, Elodie is there, too."

That's the hard part. Our attention is rightfully on our daughter, but the relationship between Elodie and me still lingers when all three of us are together. Every time I catch Elodie's gaze, we both acknowledge it. At some point, it's impossible not to keep our boundary around Lola when we both want to break it. Just crossing over that line is approached differently between us.

"It will work out, and if not, remember HR prepared a nice holiday basket of candy for you to bring to them," Easton says sarcastically.

My phone buzzes on the table and I swipe the screen, I see a message in the daycare app. It seems they couldn't reach Elodie, and it feels good to be the next on their contact list. It seems that Lola isn't feeling well, which isn't so great. I've been warned that kids get sick a lot, and normally it's just a cold. Right now? I'm entering new territory, a type of worry and a new protective shield.

The events of last night have to be put aside. I guess this is where co-parenting comes into play. I send her a quick message.

ME:

I think you're in a meeting. Daycare says
Lola isn't feeling great. Since I was going to
pick her up in an hour anyway, I will go now
and bring her to my place. See you soon.

LOLA LOOKS at me with wide eyes as I sit on the edge of the sofa and stare at her peculiarly. I set her up on my couch with a blanket and her stuffed animals. When I picked her up from daycare, she walked straight to me and wrapped around my leg while one of the carers explained that Lola was warm but no fever, she just didn't seem like her energetic self. One look at her and I sensed it too. In the car ride back, she just hugged her bunny and sucked her thumb.

At first, I was a little scared that she was still shy with me. It's only been a few times that we've had one-on-one time. But it quickly became apparent that she just isn't herself.

"That family of dogs show?" I ask, holding the remote, and continue studying her. She seems drowsy, so my guess is I only have to endure a few minutes of cartoons, though admittedly the theme song has been stuck in my head for days.

She nods her head in answer. "Juice."

"Ah, little majesty is demanding drinks and snacks now." That's a good sign.

But I wince when I see spots on her skin, and she looks at me, bewildered in response as I stare at her. I'm not sure why I didn't notice in the car, or maybe because they hadn't yet appeared on her skin. Instantly, I think of chickenpox. Of course, on my watch and in the early weeks of forming a bond with my daughter, I get hit with not just a cold-sick Lola, but chickenpox-sick Lola.

"Be right back with your juice. Cookie?"

She shrugs. Yeah, that is not a typical answer.

I frantically type away on my phone to research as I make my way to the kitchen off the living room. Thankfully, the other week, Elodie gave me every emergency number she had. I thought she was overdoing it, but now I understand why, and I have the pediatrician's number. It's a quick call because it is plain and simple. Lola has had her first vaccine, but it isn't fully effective, and her next isn't until she's four. I'm already making a list of things that I'll need as I grab a juice box. There is one question that I need answered, though.

Calling my mom feels slightly nerve-wracking. I know how much she wants to meet Lola, but I said to give it time. Yet, I'm still reaching out to her for advice.

To my surprise, she answers after three rings. I figured she might be at her Friday-afternoon book club or something.

"There's my son. I haven't heard from you in a while, not that I'm counting or anything." I can hear her smile on the other end.

"Sorry. New job and all."

"Mmhmm, I'm aware and waiting."

I set her on speaker and place my phone on the counter so I can search for cookies or crackers in the cupboard. "Listen, I appreciate the patience, and I promise you will meet Lola. I would love to talk, but I don't really have time right now. I called to ask if I had chickenpox when I was younger."

"Oh." Her mood changes. "Does she have chickenpox? You did. It was normal then, as they didn't have the vaccine yet."

"The pediatrician's office said there is still a chance

before the second dose. Not common but possible. It should be mild, fortunately. She doesn't have a fever."

"That's reassuring. I gave up counting how many spots you had, but they did go away quite fast. You weren't itchy like others. Oats are your new friend."

I'm relieved it's safe for me to be with Lola. "Thanks. I'm kind of getting thrown into the deep end here."

"Parenthood," she points out.

"I'll see if she wants to eat."

I snap up a box of mini cookies. The housekeeper has instructions to ensure the cupboard is filled with options for when Lola visits. I'm about to open the pack of dinosaur cookies, but I pause when my mom speaks up.

"No sugary foods. That's never good for inflammation."

Like a hot potato, I drop the cookies. "I'll water down her juice, and crackers it is."

"Perfect."

For a moment, I reflect on how it's a new situation for our dynamic. Me seeking her advice on parenting. It might take a little getting used to. "Thanks. I'll text later. I need to get back to Lola."

"Of course, I love you."

"Yeah, yeah, yeah. No need to get sappy," I tease her. "Love ya, too." Then I hang up.

A little while later, the doorman lets me know that Elodie is here, and I'm already waiting for her by my open front door. She exits the elevator, and I'm already impressed that she seems calm and collected.

"I'm still salty over your flower outburst, but we have something more important to deal with. What's wrong?"

She is intent on crossing the threshold into my penthouse, but I throw my palm up to stop her from entering.

"Hold up there, sweetheart. We have a situation."

Now panic begins to set in, and wrinkles form on her forehead. "What?" She's already trying to peek over my shoulder, and all we hear is the television on.

I grimace. "We got home, and spots started to appear. I already phoned the pediatrician. What are the chances you've had chickenpox?"

Her jaw drops. "No," she gasps, but seems unsurprised. "I knew there was a chance after one of the other daycare kids had it."

"Call me a doctor, but are you sure you've had it or the shot before?"

"Yeah, I have. Wait, I think I have. I'm sure my parents mentioned." She seems to be doubting herself.

"I'm positive that if you haven't, then this is a no-enter zone for you, so you may want to double-check."

She pushes me to the side. "I don't care."

But I grab her wrist and reel her back to me and give her a pointed stare. "Elodie, adults getting chickenpox is danger-ous. Let's not put you at risk. It's the last thing we need. Listen to me as the older and wiser one. Can't you call your mom and ask?"

She seems annoyed but then wrestles with herself because she grasps that I'm right. "Yeah."

I smile softly in reassurance. "I've asked downstairs to send someone for that oatmeal bath stuff, and apparently there is some spray. It should be here soon. You can call your mom and go check downstairs," I suggest.

Elodie blows out a long breath. "You're right." She still attempts to get a view and stands on her tiptoes. "Is she crying a lot?"

"She's doing well, actually. Just watching cartoons with Bagel and Berry."

She mopes back into the hallway. "Wait, how did you know all of the things to get?"

"The internet. It's called the internet," I wryly reply, and she gives me the tiniest of smiles before she heads to the elevator.

I return to the living room to see Lola now sleeping. Switching off the television, I kneel down, sit on the edge of the couch, and tuck the blanket around her and her animals. Watching her is one of my favorite pastimes. She always has this tiny snore. I hope all of her dreams are good ones.

Five minutes later, I hear the faint click of the front door, and soon after, Elodie appears in the living room carrying a bag. She stalls and a half-smile shades her face as she looks on at the scene.

"All in the clear then?" I say in a low voice.

Her free hand comes to her heart. "Thank goodness, yeah. She's sleeping?"

I nod. "Out like a light."

She holds up the bag as she approaches us. "Your list… I'm positive new coloring books weren't a necessity." She leans down and grabs a few throw pillows, carefully placing them around Lola. I now understand that she is creating an extra safety area on the already giant sofa. The back of her fingers very faintly feather Lola's cheeks before swiping her hair to her side. "She isn't too warm," she whispers.

"A little more than normal, no?"

"Mmhmm. Come on," she tells me and indicates with her head. When we reach the kitchen area of my open-plan living room, her steps slow, and she spins to perch on the opposite kitchen counter. Her eyes flick up to meet mine as her lips purse.

"What's first on the agenda? Oat bath?" I ask.

"When she wakes, I'll take her home." She means it harmlessly, but I don't like it.

I take a few calculated steps closer to her. Enough distance between us, but not enough to be free from danger. "No," I inform her firmly.

Elodie seems taken aback. "No?"

"It makes zero sense to move her right now. She has her own room here."

Her lips roll in, and she glances to the side, away from my daggered eyes on her. "She hasn't slept over yet, her room is new, too." It's almost inaudible. She is internally weighing her options.

But I have only one option to choose from. "You are sleeping over, too."

Her eyes nearly bug out. "What?"

I light a dim half-smirk. "It's probably comfortable for you to stay and will help Lola get used to being here more."

She bobbles her head side to side and crosses her arms low on her stomach. "Bu—"

I'm quick to interrupt her. "It's not an option, Elodie. I've made the decision already."

"So you *demand* it." Her eyes are set on me, and she's irritated.

"I'm allowed to make demands, Elodie. Considering I missed…" I catch myself speaking in a hard tone, and I don't finish the sentence. Now isn't the time to throw jabs. Elodie keeps her lips tightly closed, and her struggle proves it. Taking a deep breath, I reset myself. "Still, you are not leaving."

"I don't have any of her clothes here."

Snickering a sound, I remind her of what she already knows. "Really? Have you seen her room?"

Her eyes divert away from me. "Fair point," she

mumbles, but then livens when she seems to have another idea. "I don't have my things." I find it cute the reasons she comes up with. I figured it out fast. She couldn't give a rat's ass about logistics; she's trying to avoid a situation. One that I'm more than happy to address. A few strides and I'm right in front of her, making a point to brush against her body as I reach into the cabinet above her to grab a glass for a drink I don't even want.

"I'm positive lacking clothes is not a problem," I taunt. That electrical current between us causes my body to react, my heartbeat quickens slightly, the urge to touch her is strong, and a feeling swells that I want her here, with no escape.

She smiles contritely at me. "Cute."

I place the glass on the counter and lean my hip against the edge, angling toward Elodie, watching her. It's fun. "I have clothes you can borrow."

"Now I'm staying and wearing your shirts." There is a hint of amusement there.

"I'll send someone to some stores so you can have things as well."

"What a millionaire thing to say. One click." She snaps her fingers. "And the problem is solved with money," she teases me, because so far, I've had no indication that she cares about my bank account. Her smile begins to fade. "But… you're right." She's serious and turns to face me. "It's best to let her rest."

"Good." We get lost for a few seconds in a stare-off. "There are clean sheets on my bed too."

I give her points for keeping a straight face. "That's very presumptuous of you, especially when I know there are bedroom options."

"Uhm, I'm not sure there are."

She cackles a sound and gently shakes her head.

"Shocker. You're not giving up," she replies dryly yet the smile is there.

Smugness swells with a smirk. "I'll order in some dinner. It could be a long night."

Her eyes grow bold, and I chuckle. "I mean with Lola. The chickenpox," I remind her.

She bats her lashes. "Oh, right, yeah."

"So I'm ordering in Chinese for dinner? Opening a bottle of white?"

"Now, I'm having dinner with you, and apparently sleeping in your bed." She points a finger at me in warning. "Not yet answered."

She rubs her face and makes a sound in frustration, but the moment her hands fall away, I see a small smile. "Twenty-four hours. That's all it's been."

"For what?"

"Let me see. In the span of 24 hours, I've had sex with you in a bathroom stall, experienced your outburst over flowers, our daughter gets chickenpox, and now I'm staying here."

My head lolls to the side, and my tongue pushes inside my cheek while I absorb the day that will definitely go down in our history book. I've driven us right into all of those scenarios, and never break a good habit.

"So, that's a yes to eggrolls?"

●
15
────

HAYES

────

Elodie passes me a towel as she closes the door of Lola's room, keeping it ajar.

"Let's get this in the laundry. You do know how to use a washing machine, right?" Elodie whispers, teasing.

When Lola woke up on the couch, we brought her straight to the bathtub in the bathroom next to her room. I prepared the bath, threw in some bath toys, and let Elodie bathe Lola while I retrieved fresh pajamas. Then, like clockwork, we helped one another dress her and got her settled into her new crib. At first, I was concerned that I might be wrong and that Lola would be more comfortable in her own room at Elodie's. But one look at her room here, with her eyes displaying awe, and I was eased. She gave me a little hug good night, and I left the rest to Elodie.

"Yes, I know how to use a washing machine," I mock her as we walk back toward the living room.

She playfully pinches my arm in response. "Not sure it helps but let's just keep throwing things into the machine that she has touched a lot. We need to be strategic with timing for

Bagel and Berry, otherwise we will have a meltdown on our hands."

"Solid thinking. I'll take this to the laundry room, and someone is coming up with our food."

"Okay."

With everything happening with Lola, Elodie was saved during our earlier conversation. If we're responsible enough, we need to address what happened last night. When I re-enter the living area a minute later, I pause when I see Elodie oblivious that I'm watching her take cartons out of a bag and place them on the dining table. She moves as though she lives here. Pointing that out might be a little too much right now. We have enough to deal with.

Except it's far too easy to tease her and cause her cheeks to flush red.

"When is it you get on the table for my dinner?"

She stops mid-carton, her jaw goes slack, and she tilts her head to the side. Slowly, I approach her with a satisfied smirk on my face.

She chuckles cynically. "Taking us there already?"

I slide right onto the chair at the end of the table and continue to watch her. "What could you possibly mean?"

She rolls her eyes at my antics and continues with the last box. "Smart thinking, by the way, that you put the sofa bed in Lola's room. I don't want her alone during the night, and it is the perfect and safe place for me to be." Her pointed look is searing as she smiles and plops herself onto a chair.

"I only aim to please."

"Just pass me the fried rice, will ya?"

I get to work on digging in and setting items on my plate. Truth be told, I'm hungry. As much as Elodie is a constant breeze in my head, the focus on Lola was too prevailing. But now it's our time.

Elodie's moan when she takes a bite of her sesame beef should be a crime. "This is so good. How did you find this place?"

"Easton recommended it two weeks ago, and I've had it once. Now I'm sold and shall not speak of any other establishment."

"Good. This is a winner. Unless I get food poisoning, then the score may go down," she jokes.

I cut into my egg roll. "Then you might be staying here forever if you get sick, too."

She slows her bite and lifts her gaze to study me but says nothing.

"Your thoughts are running, Elodie. Don't think too hard. It was a joke."

Her body eases, and her sight returns to her plate, except she begins to play with her food. "Since this is the longest 24 hours, then we might as well lay it all out on the table."

My imagination gives me a millisecond of the thought of her and me, which is why I say, "On the table is officially a banned phrase for the rest of the night."

It causes her to grin. "Agreed. Can we just focus on dinner?"

"Agreed." I smile.

We enjoyed our food and chatted about Everhope. I guess I'll be returning to that small town quite a bit. I'm curious, as it sounds like Elodie had a close-knit and well-grounded upbringing in the little town in a world away from the buzz and gloom of city life. After a while, our conversation lulls and an awkward silence settles between us.

She begins to voice, "About last—"

I stop her from finishing her sentence. "Let me make this easy for you." Taking hold of my chair, I lift it slightly and scoot closer to Elodie, ensuring that space evaporates between us. Our eyes latch, and the sly little lift of the corner of her mouth indicates to me that she is expecting me to say anything. "We fucked. Hard. It was good. We needed a release. Sex. Why? Because our attraction never went away, and it sure as hell isn't going to. I never wanted to fight it, and you've given up on attempting to."

"That isn't necessarily a good thing."

Well, that's a start. She acknowledges there is something.

"You can hide behind Lola all you want, but it won't change reality." She briefly shifts her gaze away, then aims it right back at me and continues to listen. "Answer me why you really gave in last night."

"I-I… Spontaneity isn't me… except with you. It's an exhilarating feeling." She doesn't sound confident with her answer. Her entire body goes slack. "No. It is, and it's more. I'm aware of the possible road we can take."

My face remains steadfast, and internally, one part wants me to ask, and the other part begs me not to. "Getting you to take the turn is driving me crazy, you know?"

She forms a subtle crooked smile as her fingers fly to my hand on the table, and they swirl unorganized patterns near my palm. My response is to let my other hand do the same to her arm.

"How about we go on a date?" I suggest.

Elodie scoffs a laugh. "You mean one where you don't manipulate your way into getting me alone?"

I have to chuckle to myself. "Exactly. I'll pick you up at a designated time, go for dinner, and see where the night takes us." She's considering, which is a start. "Envisioning me showing up with flowers at your door like a perfect gentle-man?" No response. "Or I can just send flowers to your office until you say yes," I threaten, smiling.

That gets me a response, and her face becomes animated. "Don't you dare," she humorously warns me with a stern eye.

I hold my hands up in surrender. "I promise." Although tempting, it is probably best that we don't draw more attention to ourselves in the office.

"You know…" She abandons our touch and me by getting up and walking to the floor-to-ceiling window, hugging herself and watching the city at night. "I've learned very quickly that you keep your promises."

I join her by the window. "We're getting to know one another, but some things we already intuitively know."

She nods without looking at me, her gaze fixed on the city. "Kind of like being around you without Lola is a completely different world. More intense."

I take a deep breath. "That's what is driving you crazy?"

Her head sharply turns to me. "Yes."

I can work with this. Taking a step forward, I let our magnetic force do the rest of the work, and it doesn't take much. My fingers begin on the curve of her shoulders and slowly move to the base of her neck. "You enjoy it?"

"Admittedly, yes to that too."

My mouth begins to curve into a satisfied smirk. My palms engulf her neck, with the intent of moving farther up. I lead her back against the window. "So if I kiss you right now?" I whisper.

Her mouth ticks, a smile she can't quite commit to, but her eyes glint with an invitation.

One that I take. She presses against the window, her hanging arm flat against the glass, and our fingers intertwine while my other hand holds her jaw and tips up her mouth.

My lips slam down on hers as my hand settles at her waist, and the way she leans into me feels as though she's been waiting for this all night. For a second, I consider slowing to kiss her only for a taste. The plan fails when her fingers twist the front of my shirt and our kiss deepens. Are we desperate for each other? Because there is no indication that this is slowing down.

Until the sound of Lola beginning to work up into a cry breaks us apart, albeit with a struggle to unlatch. The city lights glow behind Elodie's face as we part. One look at one another and we don't need words to communicate, we both beeline it to Lola's room.

We turn the lamp's soft light on, and it's obvious.

Yep, a cheetah has competition on the spot front.

She is standing up, hands gripping the air, and Elodie rushes to pick her up, while I stand back to give them a bit of space.

"I know," Elodie coos. "Itchy?"

She just cries.

Elodie feels her forehead. "No fever. Must just be bothered by the spots, they're blistering."

I wince. "Baby pain reliever?"

"Yeah. Also, her sippy cup with water. I forgot that."

"Da."

"What's that?" Elodie holds our daughter close.

Lola reaches her arm out in my direction. "Dada."

It takes Elodie a moment to digest what Lola is doing. "You want Daddy?"

Lola nods.

I'm not sure Elodie wants to smile or cry. Her lips tremble, and she blinks rapidly, torn between laughter and tears. My own heart aches and swells, flooded with a fierce, unexpected joy.

"Oh. You want to be held by Daddy?" Elodie seems to double-check more out of disbelief.

Lola nods again.

Elodie walks to me and hands off Lola straight into my arms. "I've been demoted." She sounds defeated, but there is enough lightness in the undertone that I'm positive that she won't go cry in the kitchen. "I'll get the things. Just rock her a bit."

"Sure." I don't even watch Elodie mope away. I keep my daughter close and walk around the room. We check out stuffed animals, and when she seems that her eyes are droopy again, I lie on the sofa bed.

When Elodie returned, we gave Lola medicine and a fresh set of pajamas. Still, Lola cried, and I seemed to be her calming answer.

Not sure when, but I fell asleep with her on my chest, and when I wake, it's already six in the morning. No Elodie in sight. I carefully set Lola back in her bed and then explore down the hall. Checking the guestroom and finding no sign of Elodie, I assume she's probably gone to get more supplies. That gives me an opportunity for a quick shower.

But the moment I open the door to my bedroom, I have to half-smile because she didn't go anywhere other than my bed, where she is now sleeping under the covers. I should let her rest, but I'm far too intrigued that she chose my room as her sleeping spot.

"Well, well, well. Look what I found in my bed," I whisper to myself with my eyes set on the view.

I lean against the door pane, cross my arms and ankles, and watch her peacefully in her slumber. I feel my smirk creep up at the view.

Because she is exactly where she should be.

16

ELODIE

My body begins to move as I struggle to open my heavy eyelids. Stretching out my body, I groan before my eyes give in to the light. Gosh, this bed is heavenly.

Wait.

I nearly shoot up as I remember that I'm in Hayes's bed. Glancing over, I see that his side of the bed hasn't been slept in. Not a single wrinkle on his pillow. Maybe that means he has no clue I was ever in here because he was always with Lola. Highly doubtful. I do have logical reasons for being here, I'm just not entirely convinced they are the real reasons.

I stretch my arms high into the air as I leave the bed. I'm in yoga pants and a shirt that I changed into last night, because Hayes arranged for a delivery from a store near here. A surprise was he had a bag of knitting supplies delivered since it could be a long weekend and maybe he thinks I need to calm myself. I'm sure I look disheveled, and I'm scared to look in a mirror. I'll figure it out later and see what supplies are waiting for me in the guest bathroom. Instead, I opt for a messy bun, the solid choice for people to figure out if you are just being lazy or aiming for cute. But I want to hurry and check on Lola.

I comb my fingers through my hair as I walk into the hall and slow my pace to her bedroom next door, but the door is wide open, and the curtains are already drawn to reveal a cloudy morning. She must have already woken up, and Hayes is with her. I left them last night when she fell asleep with him. I'm not sure if she was squeezing Hayes or her bunnies more; either way, my heart was getting squeezed between them purely by the scene.

On my approach to the living area, it doesn't take long to figure out they're in the kitchen. I smell something peculiar. It's not eggs, but it's not sweet either. I'm not sure it's breakfast.

The moment I turn the corner, words lodge in my throat. If my body wasn't fully awake yet, well, now it is.

Hayes is at the stove in sweatpants and no shirt. The guy has lines, and the V under his belly button, heading straight down, leaves little to the imagination. But I'm more of an arm gal, and his toned arms are perfect for wrapping around things. Not overdone but still convey that he's strong.

He glances up from a pot, and that boyish grin is already making me lightheaded. As I swallow, I move my body along. "Morning."

"Sleep well?" The way he asks is a taunt, proven by his sly smirk.

Walking to Lola in her highchair, happily eating a cut-up bagel, I get this over with. "Your room is closest to Lola's so I could hear her. Who cares? You weren't using your bed anyhow," I defended without giving him a look.

"Did I say anything?" he says, playing coy.

I throw him a glare over my shoulder, and I see that he's

bringing a cup of coffee to his lips. Turning back to Lola, I smile.

"How are you feeling today, missy?"

"Itchy," she says, and she doesn't sound great, but at least her bagel is getting attention. That's a good sign.

I kiss the top of her head and leave her to grab coffee. Hayes beats me to it and is already at the machine making me a cup before I make it to the finish line. I'm grateful because the machine seems confusing. I stand next to him and watch, making mental notes for next time. But the problem with this situation is that we are too close to one another. His closeness means my body is floating, but there's a tightness between my legs, and my heart races too.

"You know I could point out that you slept in my bed because you feel it's the right place to be."

"Coffee," I flatly reply.

"It's good to know that you picked a side of the bed. For future reference and all."

The sound of the machine grinding covers me when I snort a laugh at his morning antics. "Our daughter only wanted you last night. I might as well enjoy sleep."

He turns halfway with that suave look that weakens me. "Nothing to do with you feeling safe in my bed?" he asks softly before the machine stops right on cue. "Or were you waiting for me?"

My jaw slackens from this circle of taunts that should make me blush because I am the one who voluntarily went to his room. Glancing real quick at Lola, who is staring at her strawberry, debating if it should be eaten, I return to stare at the smug man who is a natural pro at being a dad.

I'm going to stand my ground. "Look, you may have been inside me less than 48 hours ago," I say in a hushed tone.

His jaw drops, and his eyes blaze, thoroughly entertained.

"Elodie, what a dirty little mouth you have, and it isn't even 8AM." He hands me my coffee.

I roll my eyes. "Hayes, we are damn good about focusing on Lola when she's around." I splay my arm out in the direction of our daughter. "Guess who is around. And while you're at it, put on a damn shirt. I can't handle it."

His chuckle doesn't help the situation, nor does his little salute to me. "Your wish is my command." He walks away and sweeps his shirt off the counter, then pulls it back on.

It's in that moment I realize that minus the pox, this is what Saturday morning with him and Lola feels like. It's cozy is the first thing that comes to mind. It feels normal, too. And for a speck of a second, it's a glimpse of the future if I want it.

I inspect our daughter from afar. "She seems to have multiplied in spots. Some aren't looking pretty. We're probably going to need to change her sheets again from all the lotion."

"I have extra sets of everything. So, no chance of you trying to find an excuse to go home." Hayes casually sips his coffee while stirring the pot.

A mind reader and apparently a cook. "What is that?"

"Chicken soup made from scratch."

Blinking my eyes a few times, I wasn't expecting him to say that. "Homemade? You just happened to have a spare chicken lying around? And *you* cook? And match the recipe choice with the sick occasion?"

The corner of his mouth snags up. "I had a delivery for the ingredients, and yes, I do cook. My mom's recipe that she sent me. I only got to have it when I was sick growing up. Figured I would give this a try. Throw in some ABC-shaped pasta and hope it passes Lola's test, right?"

Taking a quick sip of my coffee as I rest against the counter, the wheels begin to turn in my head about one aspect of our new dynamic. "We can only hold off our parents for so long."

"I'm aware. The clock is almost up on my end, to be honest. My mom's about to lose it."

I set my mug down and take a deep breath. "My parents, too. The holidays are coming up. Plus, you have your travel calendar for work."

"Thanksgiving. It has to be. It's already tough on my mom since my dad passed. They loved the holidays. She still probably does, it's just not the same. But there is Lola, and I think—"

"Of course, it's fine. A good idea," I encourage.

Appreciation floods his face. "I'll let her know. If you hear shrieking from Boston, then you'll know why."

I smile at him. "My parents will be…"

He shakes his head. "Just do it. Let's just take this all in one go."

"Thanksgiving." I smile awkwardly, and he nods in agreement.

The beginning of a cry grabs our attention, and we see Lola's chin quiver as she builds up into tears. "Itchy. Ow." She begins to scratch.

Hayes and I rush to her, and both wince when we notice various spots in different stages of the virus.

"Let me find the spray stuff," he mentions and begins to scan the kitchen counters.

"Mommy." Her hands get grabby in the air.

I scoop Lola out of the highchair and hold her close to me and begin to stroke her hair. "I know. It's not fun, is it? We'll put on some fresh jams and read a book, okay?" My words fall on deaf ears as she only cries.

Hayes frantically returns with two bottles in hand. "It's going to be a long day, isn't it?"

"Very. Coffee and little sleep. Just the way we wanted to spend our Saturday," I say and hold Lola closer to my body as I sway.

But something in Hayes's face tells me that he isn't complaining at all. This is where he wants to be.

———

THE ENTIRE DAY was a constant team effort to spray, spread cream, and freshen Lola's clothing and sheets. Luckily, she ate, which meant I could devour my own food that Hayes had delivered. He quickly learned that nuggets are a magical food group in themselves for Lola, and I needed salad with fries on the side. But finally, we got her down for what I believe will be a few hours of actual sleep.

We both carefully tiptoe out of her room with the night-light projecting stars on the ceiling. Leaving the door open, we get one last look at her tucked in and now asleep. I nudge Hayes's shoulder to encourage him to let her be, and I'm not sure who leads the way, but I go into his room next door and leave the door open in case Lola makes noise.

Collapsing onto his bed with a mutual loud sigh, we stare at the ceiling as I feel the toll of the day has taken on my body.

"I think she might be getting a little better," he comments. "Hopefully."

I hear him shift, and in the corner of my eye, I see that he rolled toward me on his side with his head propped by his arm. "You're amazing, Elodie. For doing all of this."

"You helped. Remember? I have competition on the cuddles-when-sick front."

He cracks a soft smile. "I mean, who knows how many times you've done this in the last two years, and alone."

Moving, I roll to my side to meet his gaze. "I would do it all again. But I also have friends and family."

"Still."

I quirk my lips to the side. I don't particularly want to go down the guilt route that we share. For him, probably, that he wasn't there for it all. And for me, the feeling that I kept her from him, even if it wasn't my intention.

Changing topics is my solution. "Lookie here." I pat the mattress. "I'm back in your bed."

His lips press, aware of what I'm doing, but his growing smirk also shows me that he won't let go of the obvious, either. "Where you should be."

"Is that so?" I smile to myself. "Someone is a little confident."

"Someone knows we're both sleep-deprived, and as you already experienced this mattress once, then it's logical you would return."

"Nothing related to *whose* bed this is?"

His long finger combs a loose lock of my hair behind my ear, purposefully gentle to cause that sensitive sensation to wave down my body. "It's you pointing it out, not me. I'm playing the gentleman card."

I roll my eyes theatrically. "Smooth."

"I know, right?"

A calm silence finds us as our eye contact remains strong. His thumb feathers circles where my jawline meets my ear.

"Elodie, I'm still trying to figure you out. In the first few days, as I tried to navigate our situation, once I found out about Lola, I saw the angry, upset side of you. But I have never seen you sad. I just realized that. There are many sides of you that I have yet to learn. I hope I never have to see you sad."

"I can be sad." I was when I couldn't tell him about Lola,

but I don't want us to dwell on it right now. "Just don't be the one to do it," I warn him.

"I don't intend to be." His tone is serious. "I was only trying to point out that you are mostly an upbeat person, and that's what I remembered about you. You struck me that day on the island as someone who would always find a positive. Remember when you saw the waiter drop an entire pitcher of iced tea on somebody and you said at least they don't need to worry about the heat anymore, or their ugly shirt."

I laugh with a wide grin. "You remember that?"

"It's the little things about you. Kind of hard to forget."

Reflecting for a few seconds, I recall all the moments I remember. They've been living rent-free in my head. "You hate eating ice cream in cones, some weird phobia."

"It's not a phobia, per se. It's more adults eating ice cream in a cone lacks sophistication unless—"

"They use a spoon," I finish his sentence.

"I'm sure you can agree if you think about it." I stare at him blankly, and my arm gravitates to rest over his. "I also tried hard to forget the way you would talk, then suddenly be asleep. Your mouth twitched when your eyes closed."

"You noticed? We only had a few short naps all night."

"I did. It will forever be crazy that we were so close yet so far. I don't even think we made it the full six degrees of separation, more like what, two?"

My eyes grow. "Some would say it's fate. I just think it's a dark joke on us."

"Agreed."

"We are accepting it, though, right? I'm trying not to dwell, but it hurts," I admit.

He kisses my forehead gently. "I know. That's why I think I might be a little grumpy at the office. It reminds me."

I snort a laugh. "You, grumpy? Hmm, can't say that I've

heard a rumor that you are scary, no-nonsense, wears nice suits, but stay out of his way if I'm involved. Like that, the rumor would just be crazy. It's not like I would hear it by chance from a group congregating next to the coffee machine, eating somebody's birthday chocolate chip cookies."

His face contorts. "I need to work on it, don't I?" I see a shade of pride in how people perceive him.

I shrug. "Maybe."

He sighs. "Elodie, Elodie, Elodie… what am I going to do with you?"

"I'm not sure. But I see the special parent-fatigue spell taking over you." We're both tired.

He tries to cover his yawn. "If you won't let me go down on you right now, then we should get some sleep." He's only half joking.

I chuckle until it simmers down, and I realize that I never answered him yesterday, and I can easily answer, too.

"Hayes."

"Yeah."

"I'll go on that date with you." I smile.

"Smart choice. Now come here." He pulls me close, my cheek resting against his chest, and we both close our eyes to sleep in one another's arms.

17

ELODIE

"The recruiter has some great offers, including Haven Crossroads." Sutton tosses her phone on the mattress and watches me fret over clothes. "They probably assume it's an easier transition since I'm moving back to the state."

I peruse my earrings as I listen. "It could also be because you were promoted in the last two years. Working in legal isn't easy. I would love it if you moved back, and even more if you worked at the same company as me. I think you want to, as well. Why else would you be out here for interviews?"

She presses her lips together and takes a tick to think. "True. I mean, it could be because of Olivia in HR and her influence," she ponders. "Sorry this is a quick stop. I have to catch a flight back. Happy I could be of service, though. Nothing like watching your friend being a nervous wreck because some gorgeous man is taking her on a date."

Checking the mirror, I see her smirk to herself in the reflection. "I'm not ner—" She gives me the warning scowl not to finish my lie. "Fine. Ooh, if you move back, then I can totally set you up with someone."

"Up for consideration, but no diverting. I guess this isn't your usual date, considering you both share a daughter. Still, he'd better bring his A-game to woo you."

Grabbing my lipstick from the dresser, I pause as one thought comes to mind. "I have zero doubt with Hayes in that department. He's someone who goes all in. I've learned that quickly. I'm just curious what romance is to him."

"I don't know, but thankfully, Savannah is watching Lola so your date can turn into breakfast." Hayes picked Lola up and brought her to Julian and Savannah's place.

"Only if he impresses me," I joke. Deep down, I'm very aware of how this night is going to end. It would have to be a colossal disaster for it not to. I step into the middle of my room and smooth my dress. "What do we think?"

Sutton's eyes blaze open with a smile on her face. "Love it. Black, tight, yet classy. Ditch a sweater so he has no choice but to give you his blazer."

"Uh. One, we don't know that he's wearing a blazer, and two, it's November in Chicago, so I will take a pass on the lack of sweater."

She shrugs. "Logic wins. Seriously, no hints? He hasn't said anything about where he's taking you?"

I shake my head. "Since the chickenpox fiasco weekend, he has been super busy and had a business trip. Our contact has been about Lola, with the occasional flirty text thrown in. I'm not sure if keeping it all under wraps was intentional from Hayes or simply that work has been chaotic."

"Both explanations are fair." She claps her hands together like a little penguin. We share an elated look until hers simmers down. "Elodie."

"Yeah?"

"I don't want to dampen the mood, but I'm your friend and I also work in law. Just... be careful. Friends who work in family law have shared stories how things can get out of hand. Don't be blindsided or put in a position where arguments happen. Not saying that's going to happen. Nothing about the guy says red flag. But I care about you, so all I'm saying is go at your own pace."

Wow. That's a mood killer, even if from a place of concern and love. I only consider it for a second and send it to a corner of my brain. "Thanks, but it will be okay."

Sutton's assurance returns across her face. "Good." Her smile grows wide. "I am so excited for you. I really wish I could hide to watch him pick you up, but I need to head to the airport." She stands and begins to gather her purse and phone.

"If you decide to take a job here, then we won't have to worry about airports." I give her a knowing look.

"Yeah, and I'll also have to deal with my parents telling me to come home every weekend for dinner. Speaking of which, how are your parents coping?"

My shoulders sag, and I blow out a breath as I return to my dresser. "They haven't met Hayes yet."

Sutton laughs. "Take photos of that first meeting. Lola will want to see someday."

"They're meeting at Thanksgiving."

She looks at me as though I'm crazy. "You two are brave, but at least united in bravery." Her phone beeps, and she checks real quick. "My ride will be here in five." She comes to give me a hug, and it's tight. "I guess I don't even need to tell you to send an SOS text if needed. You're with Hayes. You put on the new lingerie, right?" She's double-checking considering she brought me the gift.

I shake my head, amused. "Yes, thanks for the, uh, thoughtful lace."

"It was a joint effort. Savannah was in on it, too."

I walk by her side as we head to my front door. "Thanks

for stopping by. Sorry, we couldn't meet somewhere for a coffee or something, I just didn't have a lot of time today."

"This is ten times better. You'll have a great night. I know it."

"It's odd to feel calm yet nervous at the same time. It feels unusual but makes sense, too," I admit.

"Probably because it's right. Enjoy it, Elodie. You deserve it." She smiles. "Have fun."

One last hug, and she's gone.

———

THE MOMENT I open the door, deep red roses nearly hide Hayes from view where he stands in the hallway. Instantly, I form a giant smile.

"Last time I showed up at your door with flowers, you didn't want them. I'm hoping my luck has changed," he explains and steps to the side as he hands me the bouquet. His shirt is fresh, a dark blue with the top two buttons undone. This is Hayes's out-of-a-suit-yet-still-formal outfit. Either way, his eyes stand out.

"Debatable." I catch Hayes eyeing me up and down.

He whistles through his teeth. "Wow. That's, uh, a dress." He swipes his thumb across his jaw, and he seems pleased with my outfit choice. "We could maybe skip dinner."

"Or not. Let me just get these in a vase, and then we can… Wait, what are we doing?"

"You're going to put the roses in a damn vase while I wait here so I don't rip that damn dress off of you and order in dinner." He props his arm over his head against the door. I remain in a stoic expression, and he cracks his signature grin. "A dinner surprise. And excuse me, it's been a day. Envi-

sioning you under me aside, you really do look beautiful."
He's sincere.

It causes me to blush, and I need to speed us along, otherwise I will give in too. He waits for me at the door, and I quickly pop into the kitchen to fill the flowers in a vase, then return, grabbing a coat in the process. At the elevator, he steps to the side to let me go in first, and this is my sign that many doors will be opened for me tonight. A man of manners.

In the elevator, I quickly glance at my phone. "Sorry, I haven't heard from Savannah yet. Everything okay with dropping Lola off?"

He punches a button on the wall. "Yep. No need to worry."

"Are you sure?"

He observes me and lets out a laugh. "Completely."

I glance at a message from Savannah.

SAVANNAH

Your kid is the worst. I need her to misbehave, otherwise Julian will want to speed up our family-planning timeline. Enjoy tonight.

Swiping my screen closed, I ease it back into my purse, but I still feel the fluttering in my stomach. "It's silly. I've left her alone with them before. I'm just..."

Hayes steps forward and touches my elbows. "Nervous? Never left her because you're on a date? Nervous because of us?"

I look away, my smile straining, because he has me figured out. "Something like that. But my phone is away now, and I promise not to look again."

He holds out his palm. "Give it to me."

"What?"

His fingers indicate that I should hand it over. "Your phone. Give it to me." He steps forward, causing me to lean against the wall. I already feel the heat between us intensifying. Then his lips nuzzle against my forehead. "I want your undivided attention, and trust me, you won't want to be distracted either." His murmur is pure swelter.

I lift my nose, our faces inches apart as I give him my phone. "Is that so?"

"Very."

We're saved by the elevator opening because my instinct is to kiss him, and not a peck, either. We create space again, and already my body is heightened for the night ahead.

He stuffs my phone into his coat pocket. "Good girl." Those two words and his low voice cause goosebumps because it is hot as hell. We're not even ten minutes in, and I'm already fanning myself.

The driver is waiting for us when we exit the building, and even though I've been in this car a handful of times now, tonight feels different. It's not part of a routine. Hayes opens my door and waits for me to slide into the back seat, and he follows.

When the car moves, my curiosity is at its peak. "The plan is?"

"You'll see." The corner of his upper lip snags as he seems pleased with himself.

"Hmm, a man of mystery."

He gives me a wide-eyed facial expression. "Let's not tie me to a mystery considering how that panned out for us last time."

"True."

The rest of the short drive, we chit-chatted mostly about

our day at the office. Hayes didn't want to give any clues away.

With the car now at a stop, I barely notice when Hayes gets out and holds the door open for me. I'm too engrossed in studying where we are. It's basically a back door at the beginning of an alley.

"Okay, now I'm really lost." I accept his hand and get out of the car.

His smirk is comforting. "It's the back door to Two Tomatoes."

"Really? I guess I've never been here. Only heard about it."

"New owners, new location, apparently. Easton recommended it."

"We are out of the office, so I can say with honesty that, considering who gave you this recommendation, I'm a little concerned. This is probably his location for his many conquests in the women department. I'm going to assume you did some vetting before this."

"*Oh*, I did."

The man waiting at the door nods a hello before opening, and we walk on in. It's dimly lit, and I hear the sound of a busy restaurant in the distance, but we are led straight down the hall, allowing only a glimpse of the 1920s-inspired dining area. It's classy. Not a single pair of jeans in sight, either.

I vaguely hear Hayes chatting with the staff member leading us, but it's all mumbled to me, as I'm too focused on the excitement that is filling me. I already sense that this is a well-thought-out night.

We arrive at a separate dining room where booths line the walls, with very thick, maroon-colored curtains around each table to provide privacy and block noise. I only noticed because a waiter opened one to deliver somebody's order.

With the staff member indicating this is our table, Hayes and I slide in, and the heavy curtain is closed.

It already hurts how much I'm smiling. "This is knocking me off balance. Nothing in my library of options had us sitting in some secret club."

"It's not a secret club. I just didn't want to bother with the front door and running into someone who would want to try to have a conversation. Here." He slides me a pineapple with an umbrella. I didn't even notice them.

I stifle a laugh. "What is this?"

He scoots closer to me, his arm outstretched behind me on the back of the booth. "Your pineapple drink."

I touch the little paper umbrella. "This doesn't seem like a type of drink on the menu here."

His suaveness is in full swing. "It's not. A special request. Even though I'm positive you actually hate pineapple drinks. It's how I met you."

There is a pinch in my chest. Not painful yet scary. It's deep, and it's because of him. "Wow…" For once, I can't rely on my humor, so I turn my head to catch his gaze fixed on me. "A little detail and a reminder of how we first met, and now I'm positive you are a hopeless romantic," I mention softly.

"Maybe. You'll have to stick around to find out."

I chuckle. "I didn't plan on going anywhere… I'm famished and need to eat."

"Truthfully, me too. Let's have a look."

He yanks me closer as we peruse the menu reserved for VIP guests. A special selection of courses the chef is making this week, but in the end, we both order a salad to start. Hayes opts for a steak, and I go for a stuffed chicken breast.

The entire dinner conversation was about growing up and

the places he has visited. It's when he finishes talking about his trip to Sweden that he notices that I've gone a little quiet.

"Are you okay?"

I smile to ease him. "Yeah. I was just thinking that most of the time, I forget that we have an age difference. But with your long list of life experiences, I'm reminded."

He scoops up my hand and traps it between the table and his palm. "Does it bother you?"

I snicker at his mere suggestion. "No. In case you missed the memo, I don't care. If I did, then we wouldn't have Lola, trust me."

He grins. "Okay, just checking."

"Anyway, maybe it will come up when my dad meets you. More in a joking way… I hope."

"I'm looking forward to it." I stare at him skeptically. "Kind of," he admits. "I am interested in discovering more of Everhope, though. Last time was a little intense, so I missed the recommendations for the best place for coffee or the memo that sitting on a bench may lead to town speculation." His hand moves to rest on my thigh. It's not even in a sensual way. His touching me is natural, the way couples do. No thought process behind it. I barely notice because it feels right.

"It's a great place. A community. Gosh, I love all the festivals, and yes, Foxy Rox has the best coffee. Savannah's aunt owns the River Bell, the restaurant on the old steamboat. Maybe we can bring our families together there. Public spaces are safe."

His cheeks have a dimple as he is still smiling, even as he takes a sip of wine. When he sets his glass down, his fingers twist the stem of the glass. "You never want to move back?"

"Sure. It may be great for Lola. The town spends a lot of money on playgrounds and schools. But career-wise, the options are limited. Plus…" Do I say it? It could backfire. "I now need to make decisions together with you when it comes to her."

The little bell of the curtain rings to let us know they are about to open, and I'm saved. When the curtain opens, it isn't the waiter; instead, it's a woman with a cart and what seems to be various gadgets of bowls and beakers, almost like it's a science project, but then I notice a giant bar of chocolate.

"Time for dessert?" She smiles at us.

"This one, sure." Hayes squeezes my thigh under the table as I pick up my glass of water. My pussy contracts from his innuendo.

"Perfect. I'm here to create your own chocolate truffle. I'm going to infuse the chocolate based on your mood and desires," she announces.

I almost choke on my drink, and Hayes looks at the woman, impressed by the direction this conversation is going.

"Some sort of potion?" Lines form on my forehead.

"Yes," she so easily answers.

None of this was anywhere on my list of potential or future date options, and I love this. Judging by Hayes's wry smile as he watches the lady and me, I believe he does too.

She explains the process and the options, but ends on the topic of sex, which is perfectly fitting. "Chocolate is, of course, known as an aphrodisiac and a dessert of love. Partly due to the small kick of caffeine for energy, or the Love Molecule, as they say, which triggers a chemical in the brain to fall in love and increase pleasure. Plus, we have a serotonin increase as well, the happy molecule. You two seem happy together, but it is a Friday, so perhaps I can infuse your chocolate for an extra special evening."

"By all means," Hayes casually agrees as he leans back against the booth.

My jaw juts out as my eyes swing between him and the chocolatier, and then my theory is pretty much set in stone. He probably knew this was coming.

"We have a few options if we are going in the romantic direction. Strawberry champagne or raspberry liqueur are classic and safe options. A sweet gesture. However, if you really want to experience chocolate at its finest, then I recommend chili honey, which is warm and represents slow-blooming warmth mirroring sensuality."

"Sounds promising," Hayes comments.

I'm trying to maintain a straight face, but I'm struggling.

She continues. "Anything with espresso caramel also brings the slow anticipation factor and adds indulgence. I can inject any of these flavors into the chocolate truffles. What are you both thinking?"

I'm stifling my laugh. "That you must have a lot of people here who end up having sex behind the curtain." My hand flies to my mouth because I can't believe that just flew out of it.

Luckily, the woman laughs it off, and Hayes licks his lips, still smiling wryly.

"I can't believe I just said that." Should I be mortified? But then I think about it for a second, and I'm not. I'm having fun and enjoying a night that is about me and a man, nothing else. "But definitely no sweet gestures. Some guy brought me flowers already tonight."

"Slow-blooming passion it is," Hayes clarifies to the lady. "Indulgent is also very much fitting. How about we have both?"

She nods in agreement and takes her little syringes, working her magic before placing the intricate truffles on a small plate in front of us. "Bon appétit and enjoy your evening." She pushes her cart to allow space for her to close the curtain and leave us.

Instantly, I arrow my gaze straight into Hayes. "You planned this. Didn't you?"

He begins to laugh and holds his hand up to stop me. "Maybe. Honestly, I didn't think we would be going down the aphrodisiac route. I just thought having somebody make our own chocolate would be a nice touch. The other benefits kind of slipped my mind."

I grimace at him before returning my focus to the delicious chocolate. "You're in luck. I do love chocolate, and I'm far too curious."

He yanks me closer to him by wrapping his arm around my hips. He picks up one of the truffles and brings it to my mouth, but he stops short of letting me take a bite. Instead, he glides the chocolate along my lips, back and forth as he captures my eyes. It's already sensual, and I haven't even taken a bite. His eyes drop slightly to my lips as he slowly moves the chocolate that is beginning to melt against the heat of my body.

I attempt to take a bite, but he removes the chocolate to taunt me.

Instead, his lips land on mine. It's calculated. Slow, and his tongue swipes once along the seam of my mouth. I'm beginning to taste the chocolate now on his lips, and the tip of his tongue touches mine. He hums as he pulls away.

"Chili. But you are already indulgent," he rasps.

Gosh, this man gets the highest rating for date experiences.

———

We walk side by side to my door, our arms grazing. When we stop in front of my door, I turn to face Hayes.

"Well, this is me," I announce and hold up my key.

"It is." His eyes are bolted to mine.

"Thank you for a lovely night," I add. I'm trying to keep my laugh from bubbling up.

"Will there be a second date?"

I slowly nod my head. "I think so."

"Think?" His brows knit together, unimpressed with my word choice.

"There will be. Would you maybe like to come in?" I hitch my hand holding the keys over my shoulder.

He snatches my keys, and in a flash, he presses me up against my front door. "Very much so. Now, if I have to play another second of your little game, then so help me, I'll flip you around and take you right now."

My mouth turns into an O shape. "So I shouldn't go for the come in for a nightcap routine?"

He manages to open my door. "Fuck no. We have things I want to do with you."

When his lips find mine and he shuts the door behind him with his foot, I'm already falling into our little world.

And I think I'm falling for him, too.

18

HAYES

Vaguely, I hear the door slam shut behind us, but I already feel her fingers gripping my shirt through my open coat. The tension all night has been palpable. I've been desperate for the minutes on the clock to disappear so we could end up in this very moment with my mouth on hers. Every kiss is shameless because our tongues are quick and our mouths slick and warm.

"If this is great sex, then I'm going to give credit to the chocolate," Elodie murmurs against my mouth as our lips struggle to part.

I rumble a chuckle in my throat as I back her farther into her apartment. "Someone might be getting spanked for that, and I would much rather go slow with you right now."

She smiles against the corner of my mouth. I'm testing my restraint because I've wanted her naked since the moment I saw her in this black dress. Her coat disappears along our journey toward her room, and my fingers find the zipper of her dress. I really need to pace myself because I want to trace every curve of her, but she is clawing at my shirt, and it seems we're desperate.

I snake my arms around her to hoist her up. Her legs wrap tightly around me as I lead us straight to her room and deposit her onto the bed, quick to slide off her loose dress, leaving her in her matching black lace lingerie and her hair splayed on the mattress.

Taking a step back, I hiss with my grin. "Indulge, I shall." In harsh movements, I take off my shirt while I watch her lift one knee up, and her finger finds the corner of her mouth to nibble. But it's her eyes that will be my undoing. Hers narrow with challenge and an invitation.

We are both sure about all of this. Every minute of tonight. We don't need to discuss it; it's all blatantly obvious.

I continue to appraise her and the way she squeezes her thighs tightly. Joining her on the bed, I'm careful not to smother her as I pin her body to the mattress.

"Fucking beautiful," I whisper to her before I trace the curve of her neck with my teeth.

Her breath is already heavy, and her body arches up off the blanket, summoning my body to be closer.

I nip near her collarbone. "Slow," I remind her.

"Hayes," she groans in a playful way.

I wrap my hand carefully around her throat, applying just enough pressure to keep her in place but not enough to hurt her.

"I'll show you what we do when we wait," I say against her skin as my free hand parts her thighs open. "I can already feel how wet and needy you are, and I'm not even touching your pussy yet."

My thumb strokes her inner thigh, feeling her hot skin.

"You're going to make me beg tonight, aren't you?" she asks quietly.

I release her throat, and my long finger taps her mouth. "And we're going to love every second of it."

I slither down the mattress and position myself between her knees, which I spread, and I notice the way she shivers. Ensuring our eyes lock, I begin to kiss her softly up her skin with purposely slow movements. Her skin is silky and smells good. A mixture of her coconut soap and the smell of her arousal. Both my tongue and my cock crave the taste.

Every small touch of skin and our shared gaze only tightens the rope between us. This isn't physical, our emotions have already bound together some time ago. We just needed a night to take the time to soak in every realization.

Another kiss high enough on her thighs, both sides, and she moans because I am so close, yet it's not enough for her. This is restraint because I crave things in life, and she is the best of them all.

The tip of my tongue near her crevice coaxes her apart. At last, my mouth meets her flesh with a single brush of my tongue over her drenched panties, and it's all it takes for her to gasp my name. It encourages me to press my thumbs deep into her thighs while I drag up and down her pussy in a stroke. My nose repeats the action, inhaling as I do, before I slide the fabric to the side.

Finally, I taste her, directly on the source, and she's even better. I bury my face between her legs and let her vibrate against my tongue. Every flick earns a twitch of her hips, every gentle suck a near-silent plea for more. I'll be damned if I don't get to have her reacting to me this way for the rest of my life. I'm only using my mouth and still need to fill her with my cock.

Her fingers tangle in my hair to anchor herself, and the room echoes with her reaction when I insert one digit inside of her. I peer up to see her fisting the sheets, and pride booms as I circle her clit.

"Fuck."

I smile to myself while I continue my pursuit. I've learned that Elodie might appear to be a woman who follows the rules in the office and raises our child with patience and manners. But oh, this woman can have a mouth.

And I love it.

Even when she mumbles my name through curses, the sound goes straight to my cock. I'm not stopping until she comes on my mouth. Her hips buck, and I continue my mission. I had her in bed years ago, hell, I've shared a bed with her the other week to sleep. But having her in bed with me doing this to her? It's obscenely different.

My fingers curl, and my tongue speeds up, and when she begins to let out her orgasm, I stay on her clit as she shudders, clinging to me until her wave breaks. I give her a second to recover.

I expect her to say something, but after a few moments she propels her body slightly up and captures my mouth for a kiss as her hands begin to lower down my abs to my unzipped pants, together we work them off.

She wraps her hand around my cock, and my body ripples from her touch. "I have an IUD." Her voice is scratchy with lust.

"Good, because I don't want any barrier between us; we have enough obstacles in our lives right now." Her head falls back as she giggles. Inside, I picture her the way she would have looked pregnant, beautiful, and what she would have felt like carrying my child. That just sends me on a track of determination to be inside her. I lead her back down until she is flat on the mattress, and I lie on my side next to her.

Elodie rubs her body against mine, needy and impatient. She pumps my cock, exploring my length while my mouth covers hers. I sling her leg around my waist. My hand captures her, interlaces our fingers, and stretches above her head along the mattress.

I take one of her nipples into my mouth, and she moans. "Your breasts are more beautiful than I remember." I gaze at the other. It doesn't slip my mind that her breasts have changed because of our child. I release her wrist, but she stays put as my hand travels down the slopes along the side of her body before I position my cock.

Our eyes lock, and I make no mistake that this isn't exactly meaningless between us, nor wild like the bathroom. We're intentional with our chemistry now.

When I push up inside her, slow and deliberate, she gasps, the nails of one hand sinking into my shoulders. Fuck, she's snug, heat smothering every inch of me. I grit my teeth and go slowly. She moans, low and desperate, rolling her hips up to meet me as we lie on our sides, our bodies so tightly entwined. I dig my fingers into her waist, hold her steady, and give her another inch.

"Hayes," she chokes out. "You feel—oh..."

"Like you're mine?" I finish her sentence and thrust a little harder.

Her breath is heavy, and her pussy is slick for me as she nods. I curse under my breath, feeling her tighten around my shaft, binding us tighter together, and I press farther in and pick up my speed, grunting as I slam into her, but she takes every inch. I'm no longer delicate, only intent on staying buried inside her because this woman has the power to make me unhinged, and I'm lost in her.

We move together, my hand finds the back of her neck, and I fist some of her hair to ensure our eyes don't break contact. She begins to dig into the skin of my arms as our moans collide.

One jolt and I have her completely on her back, her legs

binding around me and her nails scraping along my shoulders and back. The walls of her pussy squeeze, and I'm losing control.

"Elodie." My voice sounds gravelly against her neck.

We are completely tangled yet one body, especially as I push deeper. Everything intensifies, and my middle begins to clench.

"Come for me," I demand, struggling to keep my cock waiting. Slowing our thrusts only magnifies our connection. Our foreheads touch as we sink into the feeling of one another.

We stay in sync until she insists that we pick up our pace, our mouths fused, and when she unleashes her moan, I follow her trail of an orgasm, collapsing on top of her but staying at home inside her.

Our hearts are racing, and I feel her chest rising and falling under my cheek.

"Did you feel that?" My voice is ragged.

"Mmhmm," she answers drowsily.

I have a crooked half-grin. "You have the power to undo me every time." I'm not sure I should be admitting that aloud, but I need to make it clear to her that she has a hold on me. In our dynamic, as much as I could hold power over her, she gets to have some too.

Her heavy eyes snap open as her hands cradle my face, and she doesn't say a word, only pulls me into a messy kiss, and we lie there, two completely spent bodies well aware that we are both unraveling into something more.

———

WE HAVE ridiculous smiles on our faces where we lie in bed after waking up a minute ago. The sun is out in full force on a morning that appears chilly. This bed? Quite the opposite. Body warmth does wonders, and Elodie has been in my arms most of the night as I spooned her from behind. Fucked her a few more times from that position as well. But now our sleepy somberness is disappearing, and she rests her chin against my bare chest as I lie back and she stares up.

"What happens now?" she mentions quietly with a shade of humor in her voice.

My eyes grow large. "Thinking of a post-sleeping-together exit strategy that doesn't involve disappearing?"

She licks her lips and grins. "Nah."

"Whip me up some frozen waffles?" I joke.

Quickly, she pinches me and straddles me with her on top, dragging the sheet with her to cover her breasts. "I'm making breakfast now?"

"You make it sound like we're domesticated. I call it refueling."

She shakes her head, entertained. "We have a few hours before I need to pick up Lola."

"Let's do something with her this afternoon," I suggest.

"Sounds like a good idea, just…"

I turn my facial expression into a stern warning because I have a feeling of where this is going.

"Let's be mindful of what we say or do when it comes to us."

There it is. I thought this would come up, even if it is logical.

"Don't want her to get any ideas?" I'm prying because I need to know the long-term plan. Last night isn't a one-off. I won't let it be.

"I mean, I think I already saw her refer to Berry and Bagel as Mommy and Daddy before they kissed. We have to tread carefully. Not until we are…"

"Certain," I supply, and she nods. "Well, you might want to hurry it up on the train. It's moving."

She appraises me for a second before she crawls off me to sit on the edge of her bed with her back to me, and I'm quick to judge that this is her way of hiding what's inside her head.

Sitting up, I kiss her shoulder. "Just say it," I tell her.

"You are so persistent and sure."

"I'm also always right." It's not cockiness, it's confidence.

Elodie looks down at her feet dangling near the floor. "Maybe that scares me... You weren't even in my life six weeks ago."

"Time doesn't matter, so you better catch up, sweetheart."

She rolls her eyes at me. "Is that your way of twisting inside of me and softening my resolve? Calling me sweetheart with just a tad bit of a southern drawl in it? You know, sometimes names of endearment can really fuck with a woman. Congratulations, you unlocked that."

I give her a self-assured grin. "As I say, I only succeed. Now let me show you what our mornings are like." I begin to pull her arm to reel her back into bed.

She gives in, and I soon have her underneath me while I distribute my weight with my forearms, careful not to crush her. Our eyes are in a deadlock with an apparent intensity.

"You're ahead of me, but I'm still trailing behind, not finding another path," she whispers. "Tell me you and I won't screw things up."

"We won't," I promise.

She lifts her head to kiss me fervently.

Our date was a success.

Now I just have more to conquer with her.

19

HAYES

Foster assesses the PowerPoint he's swiping through on his tablet. We have been sitting in my office seating area for the past hour, going over numbers, and every time we swipe to a new slide, he's unreadable. Sure, we've had solid conversations when a question came up, but the overall theme of my proposal requires deep thought.

"I mean, at least we wouldn't be letting anybody go," he points out as he closes the cover and sets the device on the coffee table.

"We have too much overhead, and we need to distribute it better. Too many hands on deck; it's better to combine divisions. That doesn't need to be a bad thing," I remind him.

He scratches his chin and seems to consider. "Budget allocation could be better distributed, I agree. It's my job to make the numbers work with what others consider to make sense. As long as I don't have an auditor up my ass, then I'll do that. I'll have a look so that the next C-level team meeting can be riveting to all. Get ready for Olivia from HR to sling shade Easton's way. They might have to work together on internal comms if this goes forward."

I get comfortable in my leather chair as our conversation takes a casual turn. "Yeah, I noticed they have some issues."

Foster scoffs in agreement. "Never a dull moment at Haven Crossroads. Speaking of which, let me ask off the record and as a friend. How is it going with my employee?"

An instant smile hits me. We've done our best to maneuver around our schedules and Lola. It's pretty much been stolen time for us alone, especially as we try to keep work separate, which means the office is a no-go zone.

"Good. She's coming around. Exploring beyond parenting. Speaking of which, my mom is coming to town tonight to meet Lola and Elodie. I'm also meeting Elodie's parents."

He laughs privately to himself. "Damn. I thought my family Thanksgiving dinners were hell enough with my asshole brother. But you both? Piling all of that on at once. I wish I had front-row seats." He crosses his arms and lifts his chin at me. "Scared of her dad? I bet that's gotta be shaking you up."

A tiny bit of me, yes, but I'm not going to admit that out loud, especially not to Elodie, as she is already nervous. "Whatever he may think doesn't matter. It doesn't change what has happened or what will happen. Besides, I might need to rein in my mom. I'm not 100% sure she won't say something to Elodie about the not-knowing-her-grand-daughter factor."

"Eek. The thing with Elodie is that she does have a bit of quick wit at times that might ruffle feathers. I love it when dealing with accounts, but I'm not sure that will go down well with your mommy dearest."

"That's a good quality."

He nods with his lips quirked out. "I'm not going to lie,

between you and Julian and your adamancy when it comes to the women in your lives, I should either deeply admire it or be extremely concerned. Do you even give her the option to run away if she finds you repulsive and not at all suitable for a relationship?"

Smirking to myself, that is the easiest answer there could be. "Nope. It's only going to go one way, Foster. One day, maybe you will understand."

"Or I'm just logical," he flatly replies.

"Logic can still be part of the process of giving no options. Elodie is the mother of my child; it's logical that we go through this hard time together. But there is also something else between us, and that's why I'm so sure that we're only going in one direction."

Foster grins at me as he stands. "God, your arrogance could be persuasive."

"I'll remind you if you ever actually have a successful date two with somebody," I call out as he leaves. Once the door shuts, I look at my watch, suddenly aware of the time.

———

I'VE NEVER SEEN Elodie nervous in this way. We're in my living room, and she's visibly pacing next to the fireplace, shaking out her hands, while I casually sprawl across the chaise lounge. On the ground, Lola plays, occasionally holding up a toy and telling me what it is.

"What the hell am I supposed to do with a basket of knitting supplies? Watch from the side knitting socks while your mom glares at me?"

I grin because I thought the gift was a nice idea. Shows I consider her de-stressing activities. Although appreciative, she thinks it was a ridiculous idea.

"It will be fine," I promise Elodie.

She stops mid-pace and snaps her gaze to me. "How can you sit there so calmly?"

"Because she is my mom and this has to happen."

I had my driver pick up my mom from the airport. In hindsight, maybe not the right move—I could've used that car ride to clue her in about Elodie's nerves. Instead, I came home. Elodie grabbed Lola and rushed straight here. She wanted Lola settled, but right now, it's Elodie who needs calming.

"She doesn't blame you." That's what Elodie needs to hear. It might be meh, 90% true, but I see the nerves on her.

"She thinks I kept…" Her eyes drop down to Lola, then bounce back up to meet my gaze. "From you."

I quickly leave the sofa and walk straight to her. Scooping up her wrist, I give her a little yank to clue her in on the need to follow me. The moment we have enough distance where Lola can't see us but we can see her, I sling Elodie straight against my body, and my hands cup her face before I kiss her.

"I'm calming you," I whisper, and it's accompanied by a tiny smirk.

"Not the worst of ways to do it."

My hand slides down to squeeze her ass, and she gives me a knowing look. "There is a better way, we just don't have the time for it."

"Yeah, because nothing is better than the 'Mom, this is the younger woman who had my baby, just found out, and I just fucked her' look," she says flippantly.

A chuckle rumbles in my throat, and I love the way her fingers resting against my chest always get to me somehow. A perfectly innocent touch, yet at any second, they could turn into sultry little claws.

"I'll take control of this situation."

"Surprising." Her tone is flat.

I pull her into a hug. "It will be fine. Everything is about Lola."

She inhales a sharp breath. "Right."

"And she kind of knows that we're back at it. You and I."

Elodie's beautiful blue eyes turn to saucers. "Does she now?" I shrug a shoulder and give her my best boyish grin. "What is it exactly you said?"

I'm about to answer, but my phone begins to vibrate in my pocket, and we both know it is probably reception downstairs letting me know my mom is here. A quick answer, and it's confirmed.

Stuffing my phone away, I kiss Elodie's forehead. "Don't worry. Trust me." For a split second, I wonder if she does. Are we at the point of complete trust yet?

She nods numbly and walks back to Lola.

I'm a bit nervous about this, but calmer than most would guess. I reach the door, open it, and wait as the elevator dings. When my mom steps out carrying her bags, I grin.

Her grays are freshly covered with blonde, and her understated earrings contrast with her colorful scarf. She appears healthy, which matters.

Her wide smile greets me as she approaches, her arms already outstretched and ready to hug me. "There's my son." Her hug is big.

I roll my eyes at the ridiculousness of her over-the-top greeting. The man from reception gives me a knowing smile as he places her bags down by the door and leaves us be.

"You're in good spirits." She's already about to walk herself in, but I step in front of her. "Wait a second." I close the door halfway and lower my voice as my mom stares at me peculiarly. "Just before we go in there, get whatever it is that might make this awkward out of your system."

"Don't be silly. There's nothing," she says, her smile too bright. She shifts to move past me, but I hold steady, arching a brow. Her facade crumbles. "Fine. Maybe I'll never get over you not knowing about Lola for two years. What would've happened if she never found you? What if Lola would have questions one day? I still think you should put something on paper to protect you."

"I'm also to blame for the lack of exchanging details not just Elodie. But okay, you've said it now. No need to say it to her. Anything else?"

She rolls her lips in and thinks for a second. "Not that I can think of." It's a lie, but I don't press further.

"We go in there and no over-the-top hellos. Let's not scare my kid before she can even utter the word grandma."

"Mimi, I decided I want to be Mimi," she corrects me with excitement, and it causes me to grin. "It sounds younger."

I grab the handle of her roller bag and notice it's heavy. "What the hell is in here?"

"Gifts."

"Oh, missed the memo on going over the top then. Come on." I make a point to get in front of her, and she follows me toward the living room. I ensure we take a snail's pace while I leave her bag in the hall and approach.

Part of me is nervous because I want to show her that I'm a good father, I'm everything my own was. The standard is high, and I'm fulfilling it. I want her to be proud and have the feeling that I'm honoring my dad. Now is her first impression of her son as a father.

"Easy," I mutter once more to her.

But the moment we cross the threshold and Lola enters our view, it's hopeless.

"Oh my goodness." My mom's happiness is apparent as

she zeroes in on Lola. Elodie swings her gaze to my mother, unsure of what to do. "She looks just like you." Lola looks up with her pony toy in hand and stares peculiarly at the woman.

Thankfully, my mom reins herself in, resisting the urge to dive talons-first and snatch time with her grandchild.

Clearing my throat, I gently tap her arm. "Uh, how about we get a drink in the kitchen?"

She looks over her shoulder at me and grasps my clue. It's only when I lead her straight to the counter at the open kitchen that she pauses when she sets her purse on the stool. Blinking a few times, she finally notices Elodie. I make no mistake, and notice her giving Elodie the once-over, and Elodie smiles politely through the process.

"This is my mom, Colleen."

"Hello, it's great to finally meet you."

My mom gives her a genuine smile. "Likewise." She takes a few steps in Elodie's direction. "So you are the one to give me a granddaughter."

"That's me." She smiles nervously.

Oddly enough, I know better than to interfere; I brew tea and watch—quiet, calculating.

My mom glances at Lola, then back to Elodie. "There is a resemblance. Both, I mean, you and my son."

"I think so."

"My son is a good father?"

The way Elodie breaks out in a giant goofy grin weakens me. "He is amazing at it," she gushes with pride.

"Would have been great if he were around from the beginning—"

That's my cue to intervene. "To make tea. Camomile is fine, right?"

"Lovely." Everybody gives their attention to Lola, our princess, who will break the conversation if needed.

"I'm hungry. Bunnies hungry." Lola speaks up as she stands.

"Her stuffed bunnies," Elodie clarifies as she crouches down to wait for a tottering Lola.

"Dinner sounds good," I say.

"Doesn't it? We can really talk and get to know one another. I'm assuming you and my son missed that memo a while back when you first met," my mother quips.

Elodie's jaw goes slack, and I wince from that sudden turn. "Wow."

She looks between us all. "I'm joking!" But she still mutters something under her breath.

Elodie and I ease but still might need an extra second to recover.

"We start from today, okay? We'll have all evening to get to know one another and breakfast, too," my mother adds.

"Oh, I won't be here at breakfast. Lola will stay here tonight so you can have one-on-one time with her. I'm going home later," Elodie explains. It's a disappointment I already knew, but I also get it. We are in unknown romantic territory, and my mother's presence adds an extra element. Elodie doesn't live here and has the option to escape this overwhelming situation before tomorrow's big dinner.

My mother begins her exaggerated cackle. "Really? You two are… Don't feel the need to leave on my account. We are past the waiting-for-marriage part. I just assumed that you two are shari—"

"Subtle," I comment as I see Elodie's face bloom red. A smile begins to etch on my face because, truthfully, as much as my mom is questionably witty today, it's good to see. I haven't seen her this way since before my dad passed.

Elodie begins to bounce Lola on her hip. "Okay, dinner for the princess." She turns her attention to my mom. "I hope you don't mind that we're keeping it simple. She eats early, and we figured it's better to stick to routine as everything is a lot. Maybe more for the adults than her. Don't worry, the mac n' cheese is for her, the orzo bake is in the oven is for us."

"Perfect."

My mother keeps her gaze locked on Lola, and Elodie notices and gives me a sidelong glance for a clue as to what comes next.

I turn the stove off and give up on my mom's tea before I circle around the kitchen counter to join them standing by the island, and I tap Lola's arm. "Hey, kiddo, there is someone you get to meet."

She looks at me with her wide eyes.

I point to my mom. "Your mimi. My mom. Another grandparent. Do you understand that?"

She wiggles in Elodie's arms to swing her gaze between my mom and me. She doesn't seem to understand, but she waves at my mom anyway.

Elodie smiles and kisses her little forehead. "You're very good at welcoming people to the family," she partly jokes.

Even with my mom now cooing her way to Lola and holding out her arms, my ears were already sealed in on the word family and the way Elodie said it so easily.

Because that's what we essentially are, right?

One another's family.

"I'm here," I whisper delicately to Hayes as we lie on our sides facing one another in his bed. Something feels stronger between us just from the way we lie in bed together. A smile plays on my lips because of last night.

His hand is already traveling along the curve of my hip, his palm warm. "I'm happy you are."

Sputtering a laugh, I'm going to highlight the obvious. "Because your mom strong-armed me."

"She likes you."

"Really?" I'm doubtful.

He scoots closer so the crook of my neck is within reach of his lips. "Yes. You both talked for hours."

We did. Initially, I was petrified of being judged. But once Colleen got her few snarky, half-serious comments out of the way, the walls between us broke down, and we got to know one another. She had so many questions about Lola, and I was happy to share. Lola took to her instantly and even let her read the night's bedtime story. It's not that I didn't want to spend the night, I always do if Hayes is involved.

But I figured that he and his mother would want some

bonding time alone. I'm trying to avoid everyone's eyes on Hayes and me in the romance department. I don't need the added pressure from our families, but as the night went on, I realized that it doesn't matter. No matter what we do, there will be opinions, and we shouldn't factor them in. And that's how I ended up spending the night. It doesn't faze me, though, that Colleen is in the room down the hall.

"Lola is lucky to have her now in her life."

He agrees with a mumble. "But I don't want to talk about it anymore." His stubble scrapes against my skin. My body is turning to liquid again as he touches me the way he wants.

I begin to open my legs, and he's already shifting down the bed until he's on his belly with his hands braced on either side of my hips. The gentle kiss from his mouth on my inner thigh causes my clit to throb due to anticipation of what is coming next. He moves purposely slow, and I'm not sure he wants me to beg or if taunting me revs him up just as much as me. Hayes looks up at me with dark eyes as his tongue taps my clit, causing me to grind up against his mouth.

Then he licks me, open-mouthed and painfully slow, up and down. It's so good my back arches off the mattress. He laps at me, steady and confident, circling just right. The prickle of his stubble against my warm skin intensifies the feeling.

Remembering that we have a child and a guest in the house, I bite my finger to keep my moans in check as I drift away, both drowsy and so alive at the same time.

Hayes growls against my pussy as he spreads me wider, the whole time his tongue working me into a frenzy.

His mouth gets slicker, his own moan vibrates against my flesh, and his eyes, occasionally catching my own, don't need approval; he's already satisfied with his efforts.

"Ahh," I rasp, and it only eggs him on to work me

methodically, tongue and lips teasing. "Is this your way of calming me?" I breathe heavily.

"It's my way of waking up with you." His voice is low and thick with lust before he continues to explore me.

He dips his tongue inside me once before circling my clit with speed.

It sends me straight into a world of stars, and I'm completely spent from my orgasm.

He slithers up my body, satisfied with his efforts, and kisses my lips to ensure I taste myself. "I need to taste you more often on my lips. One of these days, I will lock the door in my office and do it when I'm craving you."

I swat him with my drowsy smile intact. "Don't do that. I've lost focus on life right now. I don't need that at the office."

My hand searches for his cock, and I feel him hard. I want him in my mouth now, and I squeeze him.

"Breakfast is needed." And he gets that I 100% mean him in my mouth.

Hayes eases my body to my side to enter me from behind. "No time. Now be a good girl and stay quiet while I quickly fuck you."

"Yes, sir." And I shimmy against his body.

AFTER A SHOWER AND A CHANGE, I enter the kitchen and see Colleen cutting up toast for Lola.

"Morning," I greet her, and she gives me a smile.

"Good morning. I woke a little while ago as east coast time kicked in. I figured I would get her ready."

Yawning, I stretch as I tread over to the coffee machine. "Yeah, a good idea, thanks."

"You made her dress that was laid out?"

I nod my head with a hint of pride. "I did."

"It's beautiful. Working on anything right now?"

"A sweater that I'm knitting, but I've kind of forgotten about it lately due to… life." I'm so occupied with this life change that I haven't taken a moment to unwind.

We both listen to the grinding of the coffee machine, and it's quiet until I join them. I'm quick to notice that she is lost in thought as she watches me take a sip from my mug.

"My son is a family man. His father's influence. Hayes takes pride in that. He's a provider, too. The first thing he did when the money started rolling in for him was rebuild the kitchen at my house because I've wanted that forever. Don't ever be resistant to his commitment to provide."

"When it comes to Lola, I would never."

"Lola is lucky, you are lucky. Hold on because you won't ever want to let it go."

Huh, we're starting deep for the day.

"He truly is wonderful with Lola. I'm not blind to that."

"And with you." Her stoic expression reflects her seriousness. I sense it enough, her undertone warning that I'm not going to hurt her son.

"My eyes are wide open, Colleen."

"Hmm, good. Some might say he is a little traditional, but he has ten years on you, has no reason to wait if he feels he has the missing puzzle piece."

I bite the inside of my cheek because I want to smile, and I'm not sure it's because she's coming on strong.

Our eyes hold as we accept the magnitude of the situation. I'm relieved when Hayes enters the room to break the mood.

Now freshly showered and dressed, he claps his hands once. "Okay, ladies, ready for the day? The caterer will be delivering things at any moment."

She gives Hayes a stern look. "I'm not sure this is right. I could have had a turkey in the oven by now and Irish soda bread freshly baked."

He shrugs it off. "It's easier this way. You don't need to worry about anything."

"I'll remind you of this error of judgment for eternity." She only half jokes and returns to checking on Lola's plate. "I thought I would take Lola to the playground. You can have some alone time with Elodie's parents."

"Maybe that's a good idea," I say, my voice uneven. "Lola always loves the playground. She probably wants to wear the new coat you got her as well."

"Then it's settled," she replies.

She has a point. This is the first time Hayes has met my parents.

A while later, they're gone, and Hayes and I are in the reversal of roles from yesterday, except he doesn't have an ounce of nerves, or at least it isn't showing as we sit together on the sofa.

Still, I feel the need to remind him. "They know the score and don't blame you for not being in Lola's life. They're even excited to meet you."

"Great," he says so coolly. The sex appeal to him today is extra. Granted, he always wears dark jeans and a neat shirt, whether a t-shirt or a buttoned shirt; he most definitely chose his button-up with intention today.

I give up on cracking his exterior to discover if he is holding up a charade; instead, I decide that I'll do something that might calm me. Finding my way to straddle him, I give him a sultry, mischievous smirk as I begin to play with his belt.

"Sure I can't help ease any concerns you might have?"

The corners of his mouth twist. "Tempting." His hands

clasp my wrists. "But not now. My thoughts are too dirty for this time of day. Having you on your knees with your mouth stuffed with my cock is only the beginning of how I will ruin you."

I'm aching for him again, and I pout because he won't give in, which turns out to be a blessing. The front desk phoned that they sent my parents up in the elevator, I'm the one rushing to the door to wait for them, and when the elevator door opens, I spot my mom carrying white boxes with pies inside them right away.

"Hey, guys."

They're already carrying their coats, and I see my dad in his usual polo with his favorite hockey team's logo on the chest. My mom is wearing a long skirt and a cream-colored sweater, and both look in good spirits. My mom gives me a side hug. "I know Hayes handled food, but pie from Everhope is a must."

"I agree." I quickly hug my dad. "Okay, Lola is with Colleen, and they will be back soon. Just Hayes and us for now. You've only ever told me that you will let us do things our way. Please show me that it's true." I feel vulnerable right now. This *is* a big deal. They're meeting their granddaughter's father for the first time.

"Of course," they both agree in unison.

My body eases, and my head tips in one direction. "Come on."

I take the boxes from my mother's hands and feel slightly weighed down by my parents following me. We take a moment to deposit their coats in the hall. Soon, comfort finds me when we arrive in the open living room to Hayes standing by the window with that swagger that infuses an air of confidence and dominance. He walks to us with his hand already outstretched to shake theirs.

"These are my parents, Janet and Michael."

"I think he gathered," my mom teases me.

Right away, my eyes fall to Hayes shaking my dad's hand. I'm not sure whose grip is tighter, but it's sending a message between them. I have a strange feeling it's my father with a warning to treat me right, and Hayes isn't fazed.

"So great to finally meet." Hayes turns to my mom, who has a wide smile; she's already mentioned a few times how handsome he is.

"Great for Lola," she compliments.

"Thanks. Please, come in. A drink, perhaps? Coffee, tea." He checks his watch. "Something stronger."

Covering my mouth, I'm teetering on a laugh, and all eyes fall on me. "What? I think strong drinks might be a necessity right now," I defend.

My mom rubs my shoulder as we enter the living area.

"Drinks can wait," my father insists, and it surprises Hayes.

Hayes extends his arm to show the seating area, suggesting we all sit down, and we do. They're on one sofa, and Hayes and I are on the other.

"Finally," I announce awkwardly with a bit of dramatic pep in my tone.

Hayes sets his hand on my knee, and my parents, for some reason, zone in on that gesture, and Hayes most definitely notices and clears his throat. "Let's break the ice, shall we? The situation is unusual, but it seems we've all fallen into place."

My father nods. "Indeed. Lola has her father, and my daughter has the support."

Hayes is quick to answer, his stoic expression adamant. "No question about it."

"Good." My father seems satisfied. "I've been wondering

for the last two years where Lola got her stare-down technique for bedtime negotiation from, and it seems to be you."

It causes the corner of Hayes's mouth to stretch. "Probably did get that from me." He's proud of that. "We've discussed implementing quarterly reviews for her stuffed bunnies, too." Wow, he is breaking out the jokes. "Now, hopefully, we will have a nice afternoon. My mother, obviously, has only just met Lola and is already crazy in love. We can all get to know one another, and Lola will have a great day."

"She's the best," my mom gushes.

"Perfect. Pleasantries over, and we can check that off our list," I'm thrilled to announce and hop up with intent to make drinks.

Hayes gently touches my hand, a feathery touch but just enough to stop me from moving. "Why don't you go on ahead with your mother. I'll show your father the place and chat."

I sway my gaze between the men, or rather, I squint my eyes at Hayes, attempting to digest his thoughts. It's pointless. The man is insistent on whatever he's up to.

"Sure."

My mom and I leave them be and head into the kitchen. We can't hear them as they begin to walk around the penthouse. I feel the tug on my sweater and turn to my mom.

"You two doing well?"

"Yeah. We have everything figured it out with Lola, so it's going fine."

She raises her brows at me. "Not what I mean."

I can't hide a blush from my mom. It's not that we're best friends like some mother-daughter pairs are, but we're close enough. I stay diplomatic.

"Mmhmm." She grins. "Anyways, his mom?"

I begin checking the stack of plates on the counter I pulled out earlier and take inventory of the count. "Actually, really okay. She completely lights up with Lola, and I see the way Hayes is with her. I have a better understanding of her relationship with Hayes. Obviously, she's protective of him, maybe more than most, now that his father has passed. But in the end, I'm Lola's mother, and she respects that."

"It will be nice to have someone join the grandparent club. A shame she lives so far away."

"I think she'll visit more."

My mom leans against the counter, taking in her surroundings. "How's the office?"

"Also fine. Or are you trying to pry and ask how it is at the office *with* Hayes there?" She has a Cheshire smile in response. "We're on the down-low. I mean, people know we have a child together, but we don't make a point to display it. Well, most of the time."

"Not what I meant. I'm just pointing out that there are some power dynamics that maybe a mom should worry about. Age, money, and a high role in the company where you work. You're an adult, it just crosses my mind."

When she states it like that, then it triggers me slightly. For the next few minutes, while we check the table settings, I ponder more. Perhaps I haven't held the lens from that angle. Maybe I should do more. After all, in the first few days, he was adamant that lawyers get involved. He has a lot to hold over my head.

Yet I feel completely safe.

Especially when I see him reenter the living area with a reassuring grin, my father next to him, in good spirits.

Hayes walks straight to me while my father joins my mom, who has just headed back to the kitchen. I cross my arms and just stick my chin out as Hayes arrives in front of me.

"What was all that about?"

His hand touches my arm in a soothing gesture. "Nothing for you to worry about. Just a little man-to-man conversation."

I roll my eyes. "When you say that, then maybe I should worry," I joke.

He encourages me to join him on his side to walk together with his arm wrapped around me. "Trust me, you never need to worry when you're around me."

And I don't think he's wrong.

Because I've already begun to feel that way for a while now.

21

ELODIE

Behind my desk, I listen as Blair complains. "Please, Elodie." She brings her hands together in prayer as she sits across from me. "I'm going to lose my mind."

I smile, and while I understand her frustration, there is no way around it. "Sorry, every intern needs someone to shadow. You have Katie shadowing you, and I'm not going to switch around. She's only here for a few weeks as part of her college course."

Blair stares at me blankly. "She told everyone in the breakroom that Hayes is really hot until someone pointed out your connection, then she mentioned 'hashtag cute couple' as part of an actual sentence. Even I don't do that."

Having to hide a chuckle wouldn't have been me six weeks ago. I would've been mortified by this situation, but I'm not concerned by a 20-year-old intern or what people think.

"You must be desperate if you just brought that up." Because, as much as I'm sure people gossip, nobody actually says anything to my face.

She slumps in her chair, then leans forward as she pleads. "I'm sorry. I'm just dying here." She looks genuinely desperate.

I pick up a pen with no intent to use it. "Besides, 'hashtag cute couple' is all speculative in her head. But please do get her back on focus."

Her eyes widen slightly. "Sure," she replies dryly, then pushes herself up from the chair, her shoulders drooping as she turns to go.

I watch her walk away, only for Sutton to appear at my door, and my smile turns big. "Hey! What are you doing here? I thought you weren't coming until tomorrow?"

Sutton is neatly dressed in a fitted knee-length dress with a matching charcoal-gray blazer. "HR asked if I could change days to go over their job offer and sign, but it works out better because of the long weekend we just had and visiting Everhope."

She enters the room and takes the vacant seat. Savannah and I have spent the past week trying to persuade Sutton to accept the job offer. HR even contacted me to ask for suggestions on how to convince Sutton to join the legal department, since they are eager to have her do so.

I drop my pen onto the desk. "So, did you sign?" I wonder about her final decision.

She has a warm, honest smile. "I did."

I beam. "Yay!"

"I came borderline and calm, partly because I have two offers from other companies. I don't need the job, you know. But I had the tour, and everyone said the right things."

I wiggle my brows at her. "It was also, of course, 'I'll join my bestie, Elodie, at her place of work.' Although we will rarely cross paths unless it's for coffee. I don't work with legal much. Foster deals with that stuff."

"Having you here is still a bonus. Anyhow, give me the gossip on Thanksgiving and your family?"

"Fine. Everyone has met, and we can just focus on moving forward. Hayes's mom went back last night. Hayes has to leave later tonight for a business trip. But that's not unusual, we puzzle the schedule to ensure Lola stays with him some evenings."

"But not you?" She smirks as she glances at her heeled shoe hanging half off her foot as she sits with one leg crossed over her knee.

I swivel on my chair. "Sometimes, maybe. It's hard, to be honest. At first, I thought we should be very cautious around Lola, and her parents spending the night together might put ideas in her head. Now, I just think that she's two and has no idea what any of it means, especially as I believe we would be doing things all three of us together even if Hayes and I were not involved."

"That's true. Not to put pressure on you, but as a friend," Sutton brings her hand to her chest, indicating herself, "I need to ask the trigger question of at what point do you believe you both will work out and begin to take the step to something else? I mean, living together, marriage, I don't know. You guys still kind of sneak around, no?"

"Not enough if I have an intern deciding I'm gossip material. But anyhow, we're private people, which means it isn't sneaking around."

My phone goes off, and I see that it's my apartment building management. They had called earlier to ask if they could check inside my apartment because the apartment upstairs had a water pipe issue.

I hold my finger up to ask Sutton to hold on a second. "Hi, it's Elodie." I listen to him explain the situation, and dread fills me to the brim. Nothing about the story is reassuring. "Thanks. Yeah, I will probably think of… I will stop by in an hour or so to check." Cringing as I hang up, I guess this isn't going to be a great day.

"What's up? You look like you just sank to the bottom of the sea."

Growling, I rub my forehead and temples as I mentally adjust. "Well, my apartment just might. The apartment upstairs had a burst pipe while they were away for the weekend. Guess who apparently has water seeping through her ceiling?" I raise my hand. "Yep, yours truly."

"Oh no, what does that mean?"

"Well, they have to get drywallers in to fix my ceiling, but it has to dry first before they can come. I can't have Lola in the apartment while they do this. It's going to take at least a week or two, maybe more. The building takes care of this stuff."

Sutton pretends to check her nails. "Oh my, look what fate just threw at you. Hmm, I wonder where you could stay?"

Sighing, it's a mix of my apartment issue and knowing where my day is going. "Sure. I'm going to ask Hayes, but it's because of Lola, and she has a room there. As for Hayes and me living together, that's a different situation, I'm positive he will point out. This is temporary."

"Sure. Whatever you say." She doesn't sound convinced. "Anyhow, I would say let's grab lunch, but I think you have bigger fish to fry right now. Hopefully, they are not swimming in the ocean in your apartment." She stands.

"Wait." I grab my phone as I rise. "I'll join you, as I need to…"

She looks at me wide-eyed, aware of what I'm doing. "See Hayes?" she finishes the sentence.

"Yep."

"I'm happy there are company perks here, and that is that I'll get to have a front-row seat to the Elodie and Hayes show."

"At least I'll have another friend around."

We leave together, and once in the elevator, the door is about to close but slides back when a hand stops it. Foster appears and joins us.

"Morning, Elodie," he greets me, and his finger stabs the number for the floor where the logistics department is. His eyes drift, and I follow his line of sight which lands on Sutton, who gives him a courteous, feeble smile.

They both linger a second more than they should.

For fuck's sake.

"Sutton. Her name is Sutton," I announce blandly. *"Friend,"* I stress to Foster, and he returns his attention to me.

"How convenient." He doesn't sound thrilled.

Sutton struggles to grasp the message between Foster and me. It's our own communication style, developed over the years of working together.

"So he gets to know my name, but I have no clue who he is?" She teasingly complains to me.

"Foster. Friend of Julian. Executive team member at the company you are going to work at, and my manager." I'm lacking pep in my tone.

Something clicks in Sutton's head. "Ah, yeah. I've heard about you before. You'll also be at the big wedding."

"Big wedding?" He's a little confused.

"Savannah and Julian," she clarifies.

It registers for him. "Of course, that extravaganza."

"I mean, we could probably add Hayes and Elodie to the season, complete with a wedding gift registry for a new toaster." She glances sideways at me with a smirk.

Foster chuffs a laugh and looks at the arrow above the door, indicating his floor is next. "You are going to fit in around here." As the door opens, he adds, "Have a good day, ladies." He definitely gave Sutton one last once-over.

When the doors close, I turn to Sutton with my best unimpressed look, even if there is a tiny laugh wanting to escape me.

She shrugs at me. "What? He is part of the inner circle out of the office."

I can't argue. My mind's already somewhere else.

———

CAUTIOUSLY, I glance around to make sure no one is watching as I quickly exit the elevator and head to Hayes's office. Once inside, I close the door securely behind me with a definitive click and lean against it, as if bracing myself.

Hayes's eyes drift up from his laptop screen, and he notices me. Lines form on his forehead in confusion before a smirk slowly draws on his face.

"Well, well, well." He stands and buttons his blazer as he rounds his desk. "What a surprise. You never come in here. Avoid this place like the plague." He perches on the front of his desk. "What brings you here, Elodie?"

I'll never get tired of the way my name rolls off his lips.

I step away from the door, and I slowly approach him to close the distance. "I kind of need to talk to you about something."

His brows knit together. "Oh? Sounds kind of serious. Here I was thinking I could finally have my way with you on my desk." I roll my eyes, as I should have known that cliché was coming. He holds out his hands because he also understands that humor might not be needed. "What is it? We survived the weekend, right? Is it Lola?"

I accept his hands with my palms landing on his. "She's fine, but this is kind of about her. My building attendant phoned, and the apartment upstairs has a burst pipe."

He winces. "Yikes. I have a feeling I know where this is going. Your apartment has some damage?"

"Yeah. They're going to need to fix it with drywall and everything. It falls under their liability insurance, thankfully. I hate to ask, but I need a favor."

"Huh," he scoffs. "You hate to ask." His wry smile tells him he is a tiny bit amused.

Ignoring his comment, I move on. "Since Lola has a room at your place and you are away this week anyway, would it be possible for us to—"

"Sweetheart, this doesn't require a question, as this is just perfection. You and Lola will be living exactly where you are supposed to." His eyes bolt me in.

I chew on my lip and wonder if I should already lay down the ground rules. "You and I are going slow, so it's only temporary."

"Sure." I've never heard an answer so disbelieving.

"It's not like we're living together."

"Yet." A smirk ghosts his mouth.

Nervously, I keep a knowing chuckle in my throat and hold onto a pasted soft smile. "This is a dangerous move, isn't it?"

He breaks our contact to walk back behind his desk. "That depends," he responds simply and casually searches for something on his desk.

"Well. I guess I'm taking my chances on that."

"Good. You should skip the suitcase and just pack a few

boxes. I'll meet you at home before I go, just to check you have everything you need." Now he is diplomatic in his tone.

All the more concerning that he's plotting.

Inside me, something switches because I don't want him to believe he has the upper hand. With purpose, I take calculated steps to the door that I lock, ensuring our eye contact doesn't break. Stalking forward to get closer to him again, I throw on my best sultry look until I stop by his side, touching his arm to get his attention.

"You may own the home that I'll be sleeping in, but let's be very clear that I own every reaction you are about to have," I rasp as I lift my gaze because he's taller than me and believes he is on his throne, anyhow.

His cheekbones rise as he is intrigued. "Is that so?"

I nod gingerly, while inside my chest my heart speeds. My fingers begin to crawl down his arm until they reach his belt, the sound of the metal jingling. His face shows no sign of hesitation. There's none. His jaw is set, mouth a stern line, but his eyes—his eyes are hungry. For me. The woman who would never dream of doing this, but many things around this man don't make sense to me, yet I only run closer.

Moving, I give myself ample opportunity to use two hands to unbuckle him, springing him free from the restriction. I don't waste time and curl my fingers around the band and lower his boxer briefs slightly, taking a second to admire his thick cock that I've noticed is always ready for me. Bending, my knees dent into the expensive carpet. His breath catches, and this would be his moment to protest, but he won't. Instead, his facial expressions dare me. I inspect his cock now at my eye level while I feel his eyes drilling into me.

He is in no way self-conscious; instead, he stands ready and waiting. I stroke my thumb along the base of him, feeling the weight of his balls, and the corner of my mouth snags at the fact.

"You are so heavy."

"Because I didn't get to empty my cum inside that pussy of yours this morning."

This plan may backfire because he is turning me on in an impossible way to solve right now if I want to be the one in control.

I squeeze him tighter. "If you're lucky, then you might get to in my mouth." My tongue darts out to touch his tip, tasting the salt of his pre-cum. He jerks, and it causes me to feel powerful.

Closing my lips around him, my eyes flutter up as I watch him and hear his silent groan. It's so easy to take him deeper, and I'm not sure if it's greed or if I just want to impress him, but I take it up a notch. I circle him again, slow, deliberate, before I pull back and let my teeth just barely graze his skin. He jerks, and then I take him deeper into my mouth, and his hands find my hair to hold.

My jaw is wide, but my lips are tight, keeping my teeth hidden. I want this to be perfect. My hand grips his base, steadying him in my mouth, and my other hand cups his balls.

"Elodie." He hisses my name, and the pleasure in his voice is praise to me.

I bob lower, careful not to gag. But if I'm honest, this is intoxicating. The man who always wants to call the shots is at my mercy. The change in his breath makes me braver to bring him deeper into the back of my throat.

"Fuck." He breathes out in a rough, throaty voice, low enough for only me to hear. His hips tip forward, taking him deeper. On the challenge, I begin to pump him in my mouth until his hands hold my head in place, refusing to let me move as I hear him grit through his teeth as he twitches in my mouth and his cum slides down my throat.

I've succeeded. I may be on my knees, but only I can make him orgasm like that.

I suck him clean before I ease off, let him slip nearly free. I don't even notice how or who tucks his cock back into his pants. He drags me up, steadying me. I feel that my lips are swollen and my clit is throbbing too, but I stay focused on my original mission.

"You like this? Me losing it for you?" His breath gives away that his heart rate is a little high.

I let my eyes slide up to his face, and I'm met with his jaw locked and eyes darkened with heat.

"Yes," I faintly say.

Hayes drags his thumb across my bottom lip. "You may be a very naughty girl, but don't mistake my desire for you as weakness, Elodie. I'm very much the one holding all the cards."

Before I can figure out what he means, his mouth dips down to kiss me.

And I'm lost all over again.

WHEN I GET to Hayes's place, Lola heads straight to her corner of the living room, which was never intended as a play area, yet somehow her toys have found their new home there. I head to the fridge to figure out dinner, and Hayes must have had his housekeeper stock up earlier today, as I see new groceries already unpacked. Of course he did.

I'm not used to being taken care of in so many ways. It's always been Lola and me. Sure, friends and family have been around, but it's the little things that have thrown me off. I don't even need to check, I'm positive the cleaner refreshed all the sheets, too.

Scavenging the fridge, I opt to just make a grilled cheese sandwich for Lola and me. I'm exhausted from the day, so I quickly ran home to check the damage and collect a few things. It's not great, but it could be worse. Either way, I anticipate my stay here to be longer than I might have planned.

And that's the way Hayes probably wants it.

Surprisingly, I'm not hitting a panic button either.

"Daddy!" I hear Lola call out, and I duck around the fridge door to see Hayes arrive home. I've been so lost in my thoughts that I missed hearing him arrive.

One look across the living area, and I notice the way he neatly tosses his blazer onto the back of the couch and rolls up his sleeves as he beelines it to Lola, and it smolders in a different way. He picks her up, and I soften from the image.

"How are Berry and Bagel today? I heard you get to stay here." He tickles her belly, and she laughs.

Swinging her around on his hip, he faces me with the sweetest smile, all because of our daughter.

I stride a few steps to the island. "Are you in a rush to get to the airport?"

"Nah, I have an hour to spare. Plus, I forgot my personal tablet in case I need it for certain things." He flashes his eyes at me.

Video sex was not on my agenda, but neither was giving him a blowjob in his office, and look how that panned out.

I only chirp a hum in response.

He sets Lola back down, and she runs back to her area. "Also wanted to check that everything is alright here?"

"Just fine. I can make you a gourmet dinner of grilled cheese before you go."

"Tempting, but I'll eat on the plane with Julian. Do you have a minute?" He tilts his head in the direction of the hallway entrance.

Strange but also not. I follow his lead, and when we get to the hallway, he quickly grabs and presses me against the wall, instantly thrilling me.

He drags his mouth with warm breath up to my temple. "I'm assuming you're sleeping in my bed while I'm away."

"Oh? But there is a guest room," I feign my choice.

He rumbles a chuckle in the back of his throat, and it vibrates along my spine. His hand braces against the wall right by my ear, the other cradling my jaw

"I'm sure my shirts can be of service when you need something to wear to bed." His hand tilts my head, baring my throat. "But next time I come home, you'd better be in nothing at all in my bed," he growls, a request or is it a warning?

His mouth cascades down my face, and his lips brush along mine, taunting me. Just when I think he is about to kiss me, he steps back and abandons me. The swelter I just experienced from him eases.

"It's good that you and Lola are here. I'll be back on Friday. You have already made this place your home, even if you don't realize it." He's serious. "You should begin to think about that a little more." He tucks a tendril of my hair behind my ear, his thumb brushing my skin. "Use this week to do that." He begins to head back in Lola's direction.

I open my mouth to speak, but words have run dry.

Probably because deep down, I think he might be right.

22

ELODIE

The week has been moving fast, and I'm not sure if my feeling rested is due to the world's most comfortable bed or simply feeling at peace with where I'm currently living. Either way, I'll take this mood and feeling.

Lola gives me a cute little wave when I begin to leave the daycare, and I'm confident as always that she'll have a great day. Life is easy when clay, crustless sandwiches, and playing with other kids are involved. It's me who is tasked with taking on serious matters.

I opt to grab a quick coffee from Beans, and I'm busy buried in my phone scrolling the latest news when I feel the presence of a man in a sharp suit.

"Morning, Elodie," Julian greets me.

I offer him a polite smile. "Most people here would be concerned that the CEO is talking to them in the line at Beans when all he has to do is snap his fingers and people will part ways so you can skip the line."

He cracks a grin. "Most people don't have their fiancée's

best friend working at their company. And speaking of which, their best friend's girlfriend, too."

Raising my brows, the lines on my mouth are in a thin line due to a smile. "Is that my title now?" Hayes and I skipped the discussion on titles. We are by far more than just two people who date casually. Our connection will forever be stronger. But I like to hear someone else calling me Hayes's girlfriend. "Didn't realize I've been promoted." We begin to move with the current of the line toward the register.

"I'm not sure what your label is, but I love adding confusion to people's relationships if it means it gets them to think."

I pretend to peruse the menu that I learned by heart years ago. "What is it that I might be thinking about?"

"Look, Hayes is a good guy. His intentions are always pure in everything he does on this earth, even if he can be stubborn and impossible. Just keep that in mind."

Jutting my chin out, I'm both listening but taken aback that he is bringing this up in line for coffee.

"Has Savannah been talking to you?" I wonder.

"Nope."

"Hayes?"

"Nope."

"So, you just thought you would casually highlight Hayes's characteristics before my caffeine hit."

His suave grin appears. "Yep. It's a friend duty he doesn't realize I've taken on, and Foster works too closely with you to cheer you two on in your weekly meeting."

Taking a deep break, I look around and note that nobody is taking notice of us. "Since we're on this topic, anything else you wish to add?" It's not to humor me, I'm genuinely curious.

"He's loyal and devoted. Keep that in mind when it comes

to responsibility. You never have to worry that will go haywire, no matter what path you two take." Damn, he just slipped in that subtle hint about my situation should Hayes and I fail. The translation is simple either way: the family part of our equation will be okay.

I do my best to show no emotion. Julian doesn't need to know that he just sent my thoughts into a tailspin. "Thanks for the insight."

We're almost at the register and he checks his watch. "Listen, sometimes someone else needs to remind you of what is right in front of you."

"I'm sure that pre-Savannah this 100% isn't the conversation we would be having."

"Fuck no," he agrees. "Instead, the roles were reversed, so I'm repaying the favor as an outside observer."

True. Somehow, I ended up helping him see reason in his pursuit of Savannah.

"I'll take your views into consideration," I comment simply.

"Good. Now, if you'll excuse me, I have an actual coffee machine in my office."

When he walks away, the pondering begins, and it sticks with me all day.

———

AFTER MY SHOWER, I walk down the hall, tightening the tie on my satin robe as I peek inside Lola's room to see her sleeping peacefully. Hayes will be back tonight, and as much as I want to wait for him, I already feel my tiredness kick in. But then I hear noise from the living room. As much as this would be the moment in the movie that I grab a baseball bat in fear, it's the complete opposite. I'm staying in a fortress, and the faint sound of hockey on the television informs me that it could be only one person.

Most of all, I feel him around because my heart is already palpating.

I don't deny that there is an angelic smile forming on my mouth because I'm delighted by this early surprise, and even more when I see him standing by the floor-to-ceiling window looking across the city. His suit jacket gone, his sleeves rolled revealing his silver watch, and it's an image that is always sexy. He's eating from a plate with the game on in the background.

I don't announce my entry, nor am I sure that he sees my reflection in the window.

Except… "I thought you were in the shower," he says without looking my way. Maybe he heard me or saw me, or simply the sixth sense that we've grown for one another makes it pointless to announce my arrival.

"You're back early." I walk to him, then lean against the window next to him, causing his heated gaze to draw a line straight to me.

"I had the opportunity to take an earlier flight. Grabbed the chance, as I wanted to see my girls."

Swoon.

My girls.

That brings a different type of pattern to my heart. It's saccharine yet clenches my chest.

"I was in the shower. Lola is asleep already, has been for a while."

He pops a piece of food into his mouth. "I know. I did a quick check and thought I would let you enjoy your shower," he mumbles through chewing.

My eyes narrow in on his plate, and I began to laugh. "Are you eating dino nuggets?"

Hayes has a boyish grin as he swallows. "These things are the best. I threw some in the air fryer while I was waiting."

I cover my mouth to control my giggle. "Is this why the freezer was packed with an absurd amount of nuggets?"

"Completely." He takes a step and reaches to set the plate on the table then spins back to snake his arms around me and pull me close.

"There is something kind of hot about seeing a grown man after a day's work in a suit and eating his daughter's dino nuggets."

He smirks right before he kisses me. "Missed me?"

"A little. Your bed smells of you, but it isn't the same. Although, I think I might have actually slept more than with you in it."

I interlace our hands, and I notice he gives a little space between us while his eyes run up and down me before he gives a tug on my belt for my robe to fall open, revealing my matching nightie with thin straps, stopping mid-thigh.

"Arriving back early has its payoffs," he says huskily. "MILF appeal, and you're still getting carded at bars."

Instantly my mouth gapes open from his humor, and I prod his chest with my finger. "I'm 27, don't ever use MILF in a sentence again!"

He chuckles. "Sorry. The joke popped into my mind, and I had to let it out."

"Ha-ha," I mock.

"Reminding me that you're younger doesn't help tame me. You are also the mother to my kid, and I have every intention of fucking you tonight."

My thighs tighten together because I'm not sure how long we will last before we begin to rip off fabric from one another.

But he surprises me when he takes my hand and tows me

along toward the couch, and in the process he picks up the remote and turns the TV off. "Before I have my way with you, tell me how it has been here this week?"

"Don't want your dino nuggets for this catch-up?" I wisecrack.

He bobbles his head side to side. "I am hungry."

"Me too, I guess."

With that, we took a few minutes to grab some snacks and a bottle of wine, and Hayes changed into some sweats and a white tee. For some reason, we opted to sit on the floor between the couch and coffee table while we enjoyed more food fit for a two-year-old paired with an expensive white wine from France. I caught him up on the week, and I'm relieved it's the weekend.

"So tomorrow she has ballet and then maybe we can—" I begin to list. I'm interrupted when he touches my arm to indicate for me to stop.

"Lola is all good. Why don't you tell me something that has nothing to do with logistics of our daughter and laundry."

My smile is perhaps appreciative because I acknowledge he's right. "Sorry. I'm just…" I press my lips together because maybe I'm doing my best to avoid the obvious which I probably shouldn't keep in anymore.

Hayes looks into his wine glass. "Avoiding us. Ouch." He takes a decent sip.

"Nah. I missed you a lot while you were gone. You have a lot of business trips and long days. We're used to it. But this time it hit different." I swirl my fingers in the air. "Probably because I'm living here right now. Reminders of you everywhere."

He listens with deep interest in his eyes. "And?"

"The last few weeks even when we weren't here, when you would be away, I put it down to missing you because of

Lola and I understand how she might feel." I quirk my lips. "Well, I mean she has no concept of time, but you get my drift. But it's no longer that. I miss you because of us. It's taken my head a bit to de-compartmentalize, maybe."

"Come here." He loops his arm around my shoulders to reel me in closer to his body, until I'm straddling him. "I'm going to try and do this without needing to tie you to the bed, but I'll do it if I need to. Let's go through this, Elodie. This isn't just about Lola."

Faintly, I shake my head in agreement.

Hid hands come up to frame my face. "It's obvious. Let's go back to the very day we met. What would have happened if we'd actually exchanged our names. Do you think about that?"

"All the time," I admit softly.

His eyes sear into me with an intensity that feels earth-shattering. "I'll tell you what would've been next. I'd call you and say it's crazy and I'm in another state, but would you like to meet up? I could come to you, or I'd fly you down all because you stayed in my mind."

"I'd say okay."

"Because?"

"The same, I couldn't forget you. What I did with you on the island wasn't like me. I don't just connect with someone and go to their hotel room on the same day. Nor would I think a weekend when we live quite a distance apart would be a good idea. But you don't make me think rationally."

The softness of his fingers tucking hair behind my ear is soothing. "Ditto, sweetheart. Then we would enjoy a long weekend, then another. And when you thought you were pregnant, I would have been there. Every step of the way. When you discovered you were, then I would have been on a plane so fast, and we would've figured it out. It wasn't planned, but I don't believe it was an accident when it comes to us. Everything we do is unexpected. Then when I got to you, I'd have held you and repeated that it was your choice, while I would secretly wish that you made the one I wanted, and lucky for me you did."

"What next?" I'm in a trance of relaying our what-if.

"Moving here, living together, getting a ring on your finger and you with my last name."

I snicker a tiny smile. "That's a lot."

"Ask me about the secret," he urges in a whisper.

"What secret?"

"Even if there weren't Lola, that all would have still happened."

He leaves me speechless. How can it be that the last few minutes have given me a different mirror? The one with a realization that we very well probably would have happened had fate been different.

"Hayes—"

He shushes me with his finger on my mouth. "I'm crazy about you. You're with me on this, right? You're mine."

"I'm yours." It's honest, and I loop my arms around his neck.

"Good. Because this…" he motions between us as he grips my hips to lift me a few inches tighter to his waist, "is where you belong."

"Going to trap me in your castle?"

"Tempting, but we need you at the office for your work ethic," he jokes.

I touch his forehead with my own, and my fingers play with the hairs on the back of his neck. "What am I going to do?" I purr.

He nuzzles his nose against mine then kisses the corner of my mouth. "You have me," he murmurs.

As I'm lost in the trance that he always puts me in, somehow my thoughts and feelings connect as pieces fall into place. I'm not overthinking.

It's the reason why I confess so easily in a whisper, "I've fallen in love with you."

23

HAYES

Elodie and I sit down at a new little coffee spot a few blocks from the office. The place is bustling with people on a late weekday morning, but we managed to find a small Parisian-style table after ordering. Holiday lights and garland fill the place.

It's been a week since she confessed that she's falling for me. I can't say much has changed, since we were already developing a rhythm as a family. The only thing I notice is that both our feelings have been laid on the table, which has made things easier. She seems more comfortable, too. Maybe she was walking on eggshells before because she was keeping it all in. That's not the case anymore. Me? I feel rejuvenated. I have her where I wanted her to be. Running away wasn't an option for her, whether she realized it or not.

"Finally got you to sneak off." I grin.

She adjusts her coat on the back of the chair. "Yeah, figured I can grab an early lunch. Shake things up."

Elodie has definitely become more relaxed, or rather, testing boundaries of what she is comfortable with. We arrive at work together sometimes, but I still won't see her showing up to my office, though interrupting our workday for some alone time is good.

"I'm not complaining." We both settle into our seats to wait for the barista to finish making our drinks.

She smiles brightly. "I'm sure you're not."

I pull out my phone to swipe the screen for a picture of Lola finger painting. "Did you see what daycare sent?"

"Most parents use this opportunity in a café to have normal, non-child-related moments."

"I get the hint." I stuff my phone back into my pocket.

"Subtle, wasn't I?"

"A little."

The barista arrives with our coffees and a muffin, and we thank her before she scurries back behind the counter.

"Santa has been busy," I warn her.

"Yeah, well, please tell Santa that he needs to discuss his decisions with me." She grins.

We've talked about it, and we will attempt to make this a low-key holiday season going forward. Sure, we'll have a tree. She said we have to leave the city and go to a farm called Olive Owl. It's run by the Blisswood family that has ties to Everhope, and it's tradition to go. My mom will fly in, and we'll do a repeat of Thanksgiving on the invite scale, except I've been scolded for the whole catering at Thanksgiving and am under strict orders that our moms will be cooking. Okay, I guess this isn't going to be low-key after all.

"We also have the company holiday party," she says, broaching the topic.

I struggle to fight a grin. "And? You have an issue with that?"

She rolls her eyes at me. "It just crossed my mind that people normally bring their significant others, and mine just happens to be you who already works there."

"I'm being thrown into significant-other category. That's promising."

"It will stay that way if you ensure we keep it professional at the party. I'm sure you'll be busy schmoozing with everyone."

It's a long sip of coffee for me this time. "Trying to hide me?"

"No. I just don't want to remind people that they probably think I'm sleeping my way to the top."

I reach across the tiny table and take hold of her hand, interlacing our fingers. "I respect that. But one day when you have my last name, you'll have to let it go."

Her lashes flutter. I wasn't joking. I've fallen hard for this woman.

She clears her throat, removes her hand, and it's the sign that she'll move on from my words. "Uhm, I've heard from my apartment management."

I pause mid-whiff of the strong vanilla undertone of my brewed coffee as I hold the mug near my nose. "Oh?"

"Everything will be dry and good as new in the new year," she mentions casually.

Getting a read on Elodie right now is difficult. Is she telling me this as a matter of fact, or is she nudging me with a reminder that, officially, she and Lola don't live with me?

"There's no rush." I pretend to be unaffected and take a sip of the half-decent coffee.

"Right. I know. Just thought I would update you." She spoons the milk foam and looks away.

Is she trying to give me a prod into what she needs to hear? My mouth tugs from her cute nervousness.

"If I haven't made my intentions clear, then let me repeat them."

I scoot my chair forward, causing a screeching sound

against the tile. We're close enough that under the table, I'm able to hook my hand around her chair leg and yank her chair closer to me.

My hand stays in place, and I lean in, locking our eyes and ensuring our orbit is only ours. The room around us is somewhere in the distance.

"I'm crazy about you, Elodie. I love you. If you don't fucking cancel that lease, then I sure as hell will do it for you," I tell her in a low voice with grit and firmness present.

Her beautiful glossed lips part open, and I've come to learn it often happens when I'm direct with her in very close proximity.

"Understand?" I run my hand along her thigh before I return to sitting normally. Picking up my mug, I take a sip as casually as possible while she remains quiet, probably contemplating. "Mmm, decent coffee," I comment.

She snickers as she leans back. "Your way or no way, right?" She sounds amused, which is a small relief, because defensive is the last thing I was going for.

"I'm older and wiser, Elodie," I humorously remind her.

She tears a piece of muffin away for a small bite. "I'd be careful labeling yourself older because that gives me full ammo to completely push your buttons one day in a few years from now when you might actually begin to look like a Greek god who no longer has the effects of age-defying water."

That's when I point out the obvious. "A few years? We should talk about that long-term timeline you just mentioned."

Is she blushing? Because her cheeks tighten and she's biting back her smile. "We're stuck with one another. We have Lola." She's being coy with me.

"No other reason?" I play along.

She shrugs a shoulder. "I mean, there is this old guy that I kind of like a lot. We're new."

Now, I grin and tickle her leg under the table, which causes her to break into laughter.

The people at the table next to us glance over, and I guess to everyone we're two people in love, enjoying life.

That's partly true.

I'm just searching for something even more certain.

———

EVERY CHANCE I get in the morning, I find myself in this euphoria. Today, Elodie's hips are curved into my hands again as she braces herself on all fours, hair wild, and her body jiggles on every thrust. It's a nice view when I take her from behind. She isn't shy, audible enough. I love the way she lets out little gasps when I fuck her harder.

She throws me a look over her shoulder, and it's mischievous.

Sometimes, we can be more physical than sentimental. Today, we're on a compressed schedule. I've been slammed at work and need to be on time, earlier if I can manage.

I'm not going slow, using brute force, which is the reason she's clinging to the sheets.

I press my thumbs into her lower back as my fingers dig deeper into her hips.

"Hayes." She tries to muffle herself with a pillow, but it's a fail.

I slow the next pump, more to taunt her than to change my rhythm, but the delay gives us both agony.

"We don't have time for that today," she warns me in a groggy voice.

"Fair point." And I pick up the pace again.

Leaning down, I cup her breasts as I continue to move, with her back slick against my chest.

"You feel fucking good, sweetheart."

She releases a blissful sound. I've noticed that whenever I call her sweetheart, she always twitches a smile.

I don't stop pounding into her until she begins to clasp harder around my cock and presses herself against me. She begins to make inaudible sounds, and I feel her orgasm coming until she shudders.

Inside, I burn from my own impending orgasm.

I let the sound of her, the shudder and choke and gasp, burn into the deepest parts of me as I chase her orgasms, with my own roaring through my body.

We both explode until she slumps forward, boneless, and I pull my cock out at the same time. I collapse on the bed next to her.

I've recently realized that my heart is full when it comes to Elodie. It's for her, I'm not entirely sure she gets that.

We enjoy a peaceful moment with my arm slung over her as she lies on her belly. This is our routine. We get a minute or two before the daily grind begins.

"Breakfast duty," she whispers, her voice gritty and lazy.

I kiss the top of her head before I roll out of bed. "My guess is we have five minutes before she wakes."

Elodie shuffles to a sitting position, energy blooming as we begin our day. She laughs when she checks her thighs to see my mark. "I get the shower first."

Still naked, I walk into the closet. "Dirty girl," I say.

"Ha-ha. I'm showering quickly, then I'll make banana oatmeal. Or toast. Whatever is fastest, depending on Lola's morning mood."

I search for my suit option of the day. "Yeah, yesterday was a bit brutal. We're going together today, though, right?"

That's been happening more. Elodie seems more at ease when people see us together in the office. It's not a daily occurrence, as my meeting schedule is a bit more demanding, but it still happens a few times a week.

"We'll try, but I don't want to rush. For my own sanity."

I chuckle at that. Looking to the side, I check out the view as she's about to head into the bathroom. "Elodie," I call out.

"Yeah, yeah, I like you a lot, too," she teases me.

We both know that "like" is an understatement, and what's between us is strong, but we avoid deep conversations.

Smirking to myself, I'm satisfied enough.

But it still dances in my mind that we need to have a real discussion about what comes next between us.

————

"I'M GOING A LITTLE CRAZY," I say.

Foster is in my office, and we're sitting at my table about to eat lunch. My assistant had subs delivered, and I'm famished, but I also need a listening ear.

"You don't like uncertainty, but who does? Just talk to Elodie." He bites into his sandwich.

I inspect my own, happy that it's turkey. "I feel like we've been half doing that lately. But I think it's time to get a little more serious. She mentioned that her apartment will be ready again. As much as I've given every indication that she and Lola have moved in now and won't be moving out, I'm not 100% until I have the logistics done and dusted. I think like that sometimes."

"It makes sense to stay if she's already there." He speaks with his mouth full, holding the sandwich over a plate as he decapitates it. "But it has to be because she wants to be with you long-term. Not just because of Lola."

Opening a packet of mustard, I've been listening. "That's maybe the issue. If she moves back to her apartment, then what happens logistically? Sure, we'll end up spending nights together, but…" I fear what thought crosses my mind.

Foster drops his sandwich onto the plate and sinks back into the chair. "Ah. Got it. The fine print."

"Something like that." I'm not sure I have much of an appetite right now. "My lawyer emailed me because I want to finalize Lola's trust. But he reminded me that even though it isn't needed, I did originally ask him about custody arrangements."

Foster winces when I say that. "That's a little extreme, no? Do you think it's really needed?"

I shake my head. "Not at all. Right now, we are both committed to putting our daughter first, and we are something more than just co-parents. There isn't a need for paperwork. It's something on the backburner just in case something were to ever change. But even with no paperwork,, there can't be any gray areas between Elodie and me."

"If she's in a shitty mood tomorrow in my department meeting, then I can blame you."

Rubbing my thumb along my chin, I debate what's next. "I'll just talk to her. It sounds so simple."

"Humans hate confrontation," Foster states the obvious. "But you can put on your big boy shoes."

"Thanks." I smile contritely at him, then take a bite of my own sandwich.

He picks up a chip. "You're welcome. That's the good thing about being single. I get to watch from the sidelines and analyze."

"Yeah." I laugh. "How is that going for you? Any future prospects for the wife title?"

"Nope." His P is sharp. "Much to my family's

dismay." He comes from old money, and I'm positive his family has expectations for him to carry on the name.

"A friend of Elodie is joining the company. Apparently, she finds you remotely attractive."

He develops a cocky grin. "Oh yeah? I saw her in the elevator with Elodie. Sutton, right? I threw her my best look, the one I know women like. Suave, yet it says I make my own rules. Which would be what I've learned from you and Julian. No way am I getting involved with workplace entanglements."

"To be fair, Elodie and I make a point not to cross paths here. The only time is the occasional lunch or when we pick up or drop off Lola."

Foster grabs his sandwich again and huffs with skepticism. "I guess it's true that you both don't exactly flaunt your relationship, but people are aware. Eventually, she will be your plus-one to whatever business dinner someone thinks requires a date. You'll both, at some point, make it more public outside the office. If she feels you two are serious and endgame, of course."

Inside of me boils at the thought that there could even be another option. I also need people to know that she is *mine*.

"Trust me. There is only one way this could go. I just need to check off the confirmation, and that has to come from her."

"Good luck."

I don't need it. I'm still a little nervous, though. That's what she is capable of. Making a man who is completely unnerved by life lose his balance.

And my tolerance for that has reached its limit.

———

ELODIE HUMS while she cleans up Lola's mess on her highchair. She waited until Lola was asleep to spruce up the area.

I watch her while I sit quietly at the kitchen island, pretending to read my emails. When she carries the sponge to the sink, now mollified with her efforts, she turns and leans against the sink to face me.

"Want to watch a movie or something? I'm actually not exhausted for once."

This is my in, and I slide my phone to the side. "Actually, can we talk about something?"

Her mood quickly shifts to concern. "Sure. Everything okay?"

I leave my seat and circle around the counter, closing our distance when I lean against the opposite counter. I'm careful to give a little room to ensure we have a serious conversation that can't be turned into intimacy until it needs to.

"The lawyer is sending you more documents for Lola's trust. You've been pushing it off. It's really important that you read it over and sign it. It's for her college fund, ensuring she'll be taken care of from now until infinity, even if something happens to me. I don't want to stall," I explain.

"Right. Sure. I keep forgetting to look over that stuff. If you really feel it needs to be done, then of course. I'm okay with it," she replies sincerely.

My lips twitch, not quite ready to commit to a smile. "Good. And you gave up your lease, right?"

"Oh." She seems taken aback and briefly drops her eyes to the ground. "No. Not yet."

I lift my chin, and a sound of confusion rumbles in the back of my throat. "Why the hesitation? You see us as long-term, right?"

She stuffs her hands in her back pockets. "Of course, I mean—"

"This isn't me moving fast, it's me being logical. Others might co-parent well apart, and that's great for them. But us? It doesn't make sense for you to move back, hesitate, or make us live a life apart every day. You're living here now, and it's going pretty damn well, no?"

She shrugs a shoulder. "It is."

"Take Lola out of the equation. I need to hear you say that you are 100% invested in you and me. We're not together because you're the mother of my child, and you're not with me because I'm Lola's dad. We can have it all. You just need to be committed. I feel the answer, but I need to hear the words."

Her lips press and slide to the side. "Hayes, you're a lot." She half smiles. "It's been a whirlwind since you walked into that BBQ."

"I don't think any BBQ will ever be the same," I joke.

"The first few days were a little rough. You really threw a lot at me. Well-intentioned threats, and then you turned them all into clear goals. Me." Luckily, her angelic look remains. "It's a lot for a woman. But I'm here. I haven't been in a situation where someone so close to me is all-in. It's been only me the last few years. Now it's not. I wanted to wait until I'm certain I'm not caught in a moment. You're charming, in case you didn't notice." She lunges forward to close our distance and scoops up my hands into hers. "This is where I should be. My brain is catching up. If it didn't, then what would you do?"

I hiss a breath and flex my jaw. "I'm not sure you would like that answer."

She flutters her lashes, not pleased with my answer. "What does that mean?"

Squeezing her hands, I've got to keep our touch from breaking. "It doesn't matter. Just persistence, I guess."

"So, right now, if I said that it's better if we were only friends, then what would happen?" By her tone, I'm guessing I might have triggered a slight fear.

"Let it go," I insist.

She grumbles and makes a point to let go of my hands, shaking me away. "Now I'm frustrated with your vague answers. I don't want to get hurt, and this is what happens."

I'm quick to grab her wrist to prevent her from walking away. "I would never hurt you, and you know that."

Again, she breaks free from my hold. "I'm going to bed."

"Avoidance?"

"Yes," she answers bluntly.

"We love one another, you know."

She is already halfway out of the kitchen area. "We do," she confirms. It's her voice when she's annoyed, but at least she isn't angry.

I give her 20 minutes to cool off, and when I arrive in the bedroom, she's sitting up, sewing, and wearing one of my shirts. She doesn't look up but knows I'm there.

"Still in avoidance mode?" I can't help but find her cute.

"No," she intones. "I just needed a minute."

I off my shirt to get ready to join her. "My fault." There is a little guilt there.

"It is."

We have a minute of quiet until I slide under the covers, and she sets her supplies on the side and looks at me as I sit up. "Is this us fighting? Because I don't want to."

A smirk dances on my lips. "Then we don't. Only trying to have a realistic conversation. We didn't fight. It was a small argument."

"You're right. It makes no sense for me to hold off if we already know that we can be something."

"Good. I'll end the lease for you."

She breaks out into a wide smile. "I'm sure you already wrote the email."

I dive to wrap my body around hers. "You know it."

We kiss, and this has all been what I needed to hear.

"Make-up sex?" she initiates.

Another way to my heart. "You don't even need to ask."

It's a long night.

———

BUT THEN MORNING COMES, and our usual routine comes to a halt when I walk into the kitchen and find her leaning over the counter, staring at her phone, and fury on her face.

"Your lawyer emailed me."

I search for the coffee beans, surprised that Elodie hasn't used the machine yet. "Oh yeah?"

"I didn't check my email last night." Her voice chokes off, and I can hear something is horribly wrong.

Giving up on the coffee, I turn to face Elodie, who looks up with tears pooling in her eyes. "The trust papers. We discussed that, so fine. But then he added something, and it got me thinking about what you said last night about how I wouldn't like your answer if I said we had no future."

I'm cautious to approach her; something in my chest pings, and it hurts.

She swallows. "He sent me custody papers. Was that your plan all along?"

It takes me a few seconds to dissect what she just said, then it hits me what exactly she means and that a serious error happened. My entire stomach sinks, because this wasn't supposed to happen at all. The lawyer was told not to send those because they are no longer relevant. Now he has completely pissed me off, and Elodie is an emotional wreck. Holding my hands up, I'm quick to try to stop her from misunderstanding. "Elodie, listen to me. He sent those by mistake." And is now officially fired.

"Who the fuck cares. They were obviously on your mind."

Shaking my head fervently, I'm trying to disagree. "No."

"If I denied what was happening between us, then you would play hardball and resort to legal means? I mean…" She laughs sadly. "You think we couldn't even find an understanding as two normal adults?"

"We would."

"Have you just been… gosh, is this all to ensure that you have the fine print signed? I mean, you have rights, so you could. But I thought…"

I rush to her and grip her arms to ensure she looks at me. "I'm telling you. He sent them by mistake," I seethe out as our eyes meet in an intense stare. "I'm madly in love with you."

Her breathing is heavy as her anger is apparent. "Congratulations. Now we are really fighting. I need space."

And she storms off, leaving me to slam my hand on the counter. Angry she won't listen, furious with a stupid piece of legal paperwork, and worried that this is going to push Elodie and me back a step.

But I'll respect her wish for space—until I can't.

ELODIE

"It wasn't the best morning," I relay to Savannah and Sutton as I peruse my old apartment to survey the work that has been done. A distraction from me reeling for the past two hours. I've noticed that I subconsciously keep saying "old" apartment as if it were part of the past.

"At least you have a new ceiling," Sutton highlights, and we all stare up at the pristine white paint that makes it appear like nothing ever happened. The extra support from my friend has been a bonus since she started working at the office the other week.

I'm heading into the office in an hour, and Savannah was waiting here for me on the sidewalk when I arrived, complete with coffee in hand. Sutton followed a minute later. Updating them on what happened with Hayes, they didn't say anything, only nodded and hummed.

I appraise the work that the contractor has done, and the place now looks new, or just foreign. Sure, there are still the personal touches I made, and Lola's toys have been pushed to one corner. Not that it matters, she has an entire toy store at Hayes's.

"Time to chat," Savannah encourages by touching my arm and guiding our steps to the couch in the living room.

Plopping down next to her, I sigh. Sutton sits on the floor, resting against the coffee table with her coffee, keen and ready to listen.

"It's a misunderstanding," she says bluntly, and it causes Savannah to gawk at Sutton.

Savannah smiles at me, supportive yet nervous. "What she is trying to say is that it is a serious matter. If Hayes truly means it is a misunderstanding, then perhaps you really need to consider it."

"Even lawyers screw up. The guy probably just lost one of his major clients, and potentially his track to partner, which will make his wife unhappy, but humans screw up," Sutton, the lawyer herself, points out.

"Boyfriends screw up, too," I deadpan.

"Are you sure you really want me to send a list of lawyers that might help you? I mean, I have a friend from college who handles custody cases here in the city, but it's a route that you need to be ready for," Suttons asks.

I asked her because my headspace has been pulled in too many directions. "I need to be prepared for worst-case scenarios. He once mentioned 50/50 custody. I can't even imagine having Lola only half of the time."

Sutton shifts to get more comfortable in her position. "Look, I don't want to play the legal card right now, or sound like the worst friend ever, but you can't be mad at him, as he actually has every legal right to ask for a custody agreement if he really wanted to. You're not married to each other, and even perfectly content parents still have one. I understand how scary it can be and how it can cause an array of emotions. That's why it is really important for me to tell you that you don't need to worry. It can be a normal step. But I also know BS, how else would I deal with my profession? With full confidence, I can say that all indications from what I've seen or heard about Hayes is that he honestly has no intention of doing anything other than to make you his wife one day."

"Totally agree," Savannah says, adamant.

My eyes travel between them and bring my hand to my heart, my pulse to my palm. "In a split second, it's like I had a heart attack. The very idea that Lola would get taken away from me just unleashed me."

"Um, not sure it's really that." Sutton winces.

Savannah glares at her again. "Really, don't want to soft land her into this?"

Sutton rolls her eyes. "We don't have time for that." She turns to me. "Either you feel you don't know him enough to trust he won't hurt you—"

"Or you do," Savannah adds, "but confrontation about a permanent future scares the hell out of you because you believe it's going to happen with him."

"Can't a girl just be angry?" I complain.

"For sure, but this isn't an angry he left a dish in the sink kind of issue," Sutton reminds me.

I huff out a big breath. "The only thing he has continued to do is show me how much he wants Lola and me. It's just, gosh, why did I have to get that email?" I shrug my shoulders in exasperation. "What am I supposed to do?"

"Give it a day. Decompress. Talk to him when you're calm," Savannah advises, shaking her cup to gauge how much coffee is left.

Sutton brightens. "Ooh, go back to Everhope this weekend. There's a donut festival—a perfect escape from the city."

"Great. Carbs and misery," I say, sarcastic.

"And your alternative would be?" Her challenge drags on. She has a point.

The knock on the door, with the sound of my building's super, prompts me to call out that he can come in.

"Sorry to interrupt." He's already talking before he rounds the corner to my living room, and once in view, his smiling face and large frame greet us. "I won't be long. Just wanted to check if the work is up to standard or if I need to call the contractor back."

"It's all fine. Wouldn't realize at all that there was water damage."

"They were very careful to ensure everything dried out so that mold couldn't form."

Savannah and Sutton contort their faces from the image of it.

"Appreciated."

"The leasing office also wanted to know if you've reviewed the lease renewal? There's new language about building liability after the incident."

A long exhale leaves me. "Not yet. I've been a bit... occupied."

"Alright, well, have a nice day, and let me know if you need any help moving anything back in." He happily bids us a good day and leaves.

I feel my friends' eyes heavy on me.

"Uh-oh, that was just added to your mountain of current life choices," Sutton taunts in a loving way.

I rub my forehead, already exhausted, and I haven't even made it to the office yet.

Savannah affectionately touches my shoulder. "You've already made the choices, you just need to safely wallow in them before admitting it."

The problem is that my brain and heart are so fogged up right now that I'm not sure I'm even wallowing.

———

I'M curious as to how long Hayes has been staring out his office window to the sky with flurries of snow, hands in pockets, deep in thought.

"I think your work avoidance is my fault," I announce from the door.

He glances briefly over his shoulder at me. "I'm not sure it's a good sign when you drop by my office. You are a fan of office boundaries."

Slowly, I close the door and step into his office. "Boundaries, rules, laws—does it matter? You make your own."

He turns around, and his gaze is sharp, going straight through me. "It was an error from the lawyer," he repeats with insistence. "When I first found out about Lola, it's what any smart man would consider."

I sigh heavily. "Fair enough. But those documents are a little reminder that you can dangle taking custody over my head like a fucking carrot."

"And one could argue that you're with me only so that I don't use the fucking carrot," he seethes, clearly hurt from my words.

I cross my arms to keep my body in check; he might see how much I hurt right now. I'm doing my best to stay firmly in place because I'm not weak.

He pinches the bridge of his nose out of frustration for his turn of mood, and with one sigh, he returns to somberness. "I wouldn't. Deep down, you believe it, too. We're past that stuff. Now it's you and me, on the same road together."

I run my tongue along my teeth to give me a second. A

little more cooling down is still needed. "Anyhow, I just wanted to say or ask, considering that's how joint custody would work," I mock, "I want to take Lola to Everhope. My parents have seen her less than normal since they've been giving us time to let us three bond, fall in love, all that jazz," I say dryly. "Do I have your permission?" Now, I'm plain flippant.

He rolls his eyes. "You never need permission when it's about her family. Your parents will love seeing her."

"Good. We'll be back sometime later in the weekend."

"Sure." He lifts his shoulders.

My eyes squint because I'm skeptical as to why he is so calm. "That's it?"

"Should I be doing something else? I've explained what happened. I've said sorry. I've made it clear already for a long time what I want. You don't need to worry about the document. And I love you," he says. "That means the ball is in your court, and if you need a little space, then fine. I'm not a fan of that approach, but it's what I'll do for you… only you." He taps his fingers on his perfectly clean desk.

It makes me angrier that he is remaining calm throughout the last five minutes, and he hasn't even once touched me. I miss his touch. It feels cold between us without it. Maybe I was expecting him to rush and try to persuade me to forgive him this very instant. I'm not used to Hayes being the one with patience.

I swallow the lump in my throat. "I just need time. Do you know what it feels like to run through every scenario for two years, and then you get the one you want only for a flicker of the bad? Because that's what this is."

He doesn't respond.

For a moment, our eyes catch and linger. It's not even tense; it's somber, yet hope is laced somewhere in it.

Sighing, I straighten my shoulders and turn to leave.

"Drive safe," he calls out softly.

"Will do."

That was that.

Why do I feel disappointed? Is it the situation, or Hayes respecting space and not lunging forward to hold me in his arms and tell me it will all be alright?

Deep down, I know the answer.

25

HAYES

I absently peel the label off my beer bottle as I lounge on the new couch in Julian and Savannah's weekend home in Everhope. Tonight is supposed to be a guys' night with Foster, Easton, and Julian, but it's clear this has turned into our impromptu support group. Savannah has gone to dinner with Sutton, and I assume they've both already visited Elodie today.

"She has no idea you're in Everhope right now?" Easton comments more than he asks.

Faintly, I shake my head side to side. "I want to give her space."

Foster, sitting next to me, bumps my arm. "And wanted to be close, so you pushed for Everhope as our hangout spot tonight," he says, calling me out.

Easton raises his bottle. "Hey, great move. There is a wholesomeness to the women out here that just grabs ya."

"Is that why you're volunteering to go to the store and pick up more beer?" Julian suggests.

Easton is fun, sometimes goofy, and we know underneath it all that there has got to be some piece of him that will surprise us all. But until that's unveiled, then serious conversations not business-related with him are not his forte.

He's already standing and pulling his car fob out of his pocket. "Yep, I'm going. I can take a hint. Enjoy whatever the hell you are going to say to this guy." He hikes his thumb at me.

When he's out of the room, the guys turn quiet. We're all waiting for another one of us to talk, and when it doesn't happen, I growl, frustrated, and begin. "It was a fucking mistake."

"*Oh*, that is clear. I heard you yelling at the lawyer on the phone before our 9 o'clock meeting this morning," Julian states.

"I'm confident we'll be okay, but this is hard. I'm giving her space and hoping she solves whatever is bothering her."

"Solid approach," Foster supports.

Briefly, I look around my surroundings and notice how Julian and Savannah, who have only been together for not even a year, have made this place their weekend oasis. The living room feels as though they've made this their home, even if they're not here too often.

"You're happy with your weekend investment?" I wonder.

Julian instantly breaks out in a grin. "Yeah, Everhope grows on you. Nice to be away from the grind of the city, and the charm of the town grew on me fast. Why? Thinking of buying something?"

"Nah, I mean, unless Elodie wants to, then I would for her. But I think her parents would lose it if we came to Everhope for the weekend and their grandchild was staying somewhere else."

The room fills with the sound of a cap popping off a

bottle as Foster opens the whiskey. "I'll have to explore this town tomorrow. Thanks for letting us crash here."

Julian chuckles as he throws his feet up on the coffee table. "We have like four extra bedrooms."

Foster slides three tumblers on the table and begins to pour, glancing at me as a form of question.

"Go on. Beer seems too subdued for my mood, anyhow."

Foster pours a decent amount and hands me the glass. "Remember when we were in college, and you both said that you would never be the type of guy who fights for a woman? Well, look at you two now." Foster lifts his glass to toast.

I chuff a sad laugh. "Well, now I'm the guy who accidentally has to argue over custody papers that I don't need."

"*But…* should things really not work out between you both on a romantic level, would you need them? Playing devil's advocate here," Julian challenges.

A pit in my stomach sinks because it's natural for the thought to cross my mind. "Elodie thinks I'm holding it over her head to strong-arm her. That's the scary part. I'm not sure she believes that or was just caught in the moment. I don't have a reason to need them, we could be solid co-parents." The thought causes me to take a long sip of my drink. "But it's not going to fucking happen. We're only going one way." My words come out sharp. "Me and her together. This isn't about Lola, it's about us. If we had actually exchanged our real names on that island, then we would still be together. I think Lola is the easiest part of this all. We both want the best for her."

Foster winces. "Even if being better means not staying together or slowing things down?" He's pressing me hard tonight.

One look at Julian, and he shrugs at me that our friend might have a point.

"Like I said, Elodie and I are endgame," I reiterate to the room.

"Geez, you are as stubborn as a fucking mule. We're just trying to get you to see all angles because we're not too convinced that you do," Foster defends.

"I briefly did, and I'm sure only one direction is needed." My voice rises an octave from the frustration of this conversation. I calm down for a second, but the annoyance still runs strong. "One day you will be in my fucking shoes, Foster. Minus the secret-kid part, but even so, you'll consider yourself lucky."

He grows silent, and Julian awkwardly moves his mouth as he stares down into his glass. It's a stiff silence until he plasters on a bright smile. "I believe we are supposed to watch a hockey game. They're on the road, otherwise we would have had box seats."

I rub my eyes, wanting with everything inside of me to push the last day to the side.

For now, all I can do is pretend to watch a game.

———

LOCKING my car with one click of the button, I wait as Foster gets out of his own car, which he parked next to me on this chilly morning. We'll be going our separate ways after this. It's cloudy out, cold but tolerable, and the parking lot next to Main Street only has a few spots left.

"I'll show you around, but as soon as I see her, I'm abandoning you," I remind him.

He grins as he closes his car door. "I'm very aware." Then he clicks his key fob as we both walk away from our cars.

"You're very confident that Elodie is around here. Couldn't you just text her?"

"I'm supposed to be giving her space, but that doesn't mean an accidental run-in can't happen. Plus, I'm ready to ask to talk, and if Lola is at her grandparents' and Elodie isn't in a great mood, then there is a strong chance that she's at the coffee shop, Foxy Rox."

The moment we walk onto Main Street, we see an older couple slowly walking into the post office that has a giant wreath on the door. He has a cane, and she's holding his arm steady, and they both smile as they greet a woman holding the door open for them.

Foster nudges my arm. "That could be you with Elodie one day."

"I should be so lucky."

He continues to survey the town curiously. "Point me in the direction of a boutique shop or something. It's my neighbor's birthday, the big seven zero. She lives a few floors down but always leaves me a tin of baked cookies at reception. Not quite sure why, but I like cookies."

"There are a few places, I guess."

I'm not moving slowly as I focus on the sidewalk, as I still have two blocks until Foxy Rox, but I stop when I feel Foster touch my arm to stop me. "We know her, no?"

I look up and see Sutton, who recently started at the office, slow her approach, and we do the same. I joined her and Elodie for a coffee the other week, and my impression was she has a laidback calm approach to life.

"Hey, Hayes," she preambles with sympathy.

"Hi, Sutton," I greet her, scratching my cheek. "You know Foster by now, I guess."

They catch one another's gaze, and I notice the way he displays his best suave grin, and her wry smile seems to challenge his cocky approach.

"I believe we've seen one another in the elevator, wasn't it?" She tilts her head slightly to the side.

"The newbie in legal, right?"

I roll my eyes and cross my arms, not patient enough to watch whatever is unfolding. I don't try to be a good friend or keep this meeting pleasant.

"I'm going to assume I'm going to find Elodie where I think I will?" I check with Sutton.

Her attention drifts back to me, and she sinks into the real situation. "I may be pleading the fifth on this."

My facial expression might show how unimpressed I am with her approach.

"Don't do that." She sulks and drops her shoulders. "Turn broody and ridiculously over the top, maybe borderline deranged on the tenacious scale."

"And?" I simply reply.

She takes a beat to study me before she grumbles with herself. "Gah, okay, fine. Elodie has *perhaps* calmed since yesterday. I'm not sure how it was last night when she was with her parents, so perhaps stay clear of her dad for a while," she attempts to joke. "But this morning, I saw her while Lola was with her grandparents at the donut festival. Elodie wanted to skip that. A shame, as they are criminally good."

I raise my brows, giving her the sign that she needs to shorten her answers.

Sutton presses her lips together, takes a deep breath, and then gives me a comforting look. "Yeah, you know where to find her. No need to ask."

I pinch the bridge of my nose and exhale a large breath. Partly from nerves, a little from not needing to search too long, and a major part relief that I know Elodie so well now. I also feel her, as though I'm telepathically experiencing her hollow stomach and mixed emotions swirling in her chest.

"I'm sure you can show Foster where to go."

"Yeah, sure."

They both look at me, and I nod goodbye.

You would think that I would run down the street to Elodie.

Instead, I slowly pace, each step feeling heavier than the last.

Because Elodie is honest, she's love, she's everything I want.

And for once, I learned not to rush to get what I want; it requires delicate maneuvering because it's so perfect it could break.

26

ELODIE

It's crazy how a simple bench can be the center of the universe, where people come to contemplate life. My hometown of Everhope has the best one, perfectly placed for people-watching on Main Street. Normally, I'd rejoice that good coffee is just across the street. Today, though, I'm only using my to-go cup to keep my hands warm. I'm not rejoicing, but I'm not drowning in sorrow, either.

The feeling of someone approaching is strong. It's an all-too-familiar presence of someone who is persistent, arrogant, and I wouldn't change a thing about him.

"Thought I might find you here." I hear Hayes's voice and, in my peripheral view, notice the way he takes a few steps cautiously before he slides onto the bench. There is a little distance between us, but not so much that all I would have to do is take my pinky to touch his.

"Not many places to go here unless I'm at my parents'." I keep watching people entering and leaving Foxy Rox.

"Is it a coincidence that this is also where we talked the first day we walked back into one another's lives?"

When he puts it like that, my stoic face softens because I

find it both funny in a way and poetic. For a moment, amusement wins out over restraint. "We've come full circle," I say, looking at him, feeling a bittersweet warmth.

Even though it's been two days, the reverence in Hayes's eyes remains the same. Sure, he doesn't appear to have slept, and the stubble on his face is the perfect length to scrape against my thighs. But as I watch him, I shift from worry to noticing something peculiar: his patience. There is more of it than before, and that quiet change soothes me.

"A lot has changed since then, I get that." He outstretches his arm across the back of the bench. "But to me, it's only good."

I laugh dryly. "Then you were some high-powered guy holding legalities over my head."

He clears his throat, and his face contorts. "I'm aware. To be fair, I was in major shock."

I nudge his shoulder with mine and begin to smile. "Why? It was a completely normal BBQ. Potato salad included."

"The fact you just joked is maybe promising."

"I needed time to think or cool off. But now that I've had that, then I'm certain of a few things." I roll my lips in and debate the best way to explain myself, feeling hesitant at first. "Sometimes I think who we were on the island are two completely different people than who we are now. Then I remind myself that it has to be. Those were carefree moments, and now we have responsibilities, whether at work or, more importantly, with Lola. We're not the same people now." As I say it, I feel the weight of change settle over me, blending nostalgia and acceptance.

He collects the cup of coffee from my hand and sets it down on the ground under the bench. Scooting closer, I feel his arm wrap behind me to bring me a tad in his direction. "Can I tell you a little secret?"

"That you like the real world a lot better?"

His brows rise. "Reading my thoughts again?"

"Easy to do when I feel the same. Also, disagreeing with you really sucks."

He tips his head to the side. "No argument there."

"I love the way you won't let anything happen to not only Lola but me. I love the way you can be stubborn and romantic at the same time, and it's annoyingly hot even if it can twist my mind. Actually, some may say you are a walking red flag because of your insistent personality. Except, I've come to learn it's your protectiveness and possessiveness for your family. Apparently, that's the kind of man I want to be with. But I think I finally know how to navigate you. The direct and tender sides of you. Plus, waking up with you is perfect. I mean, I should probably give credit to your mattress for that one," I tease him.

"Cute."

I smile wider. "I love our breakfasts and dinners that make me happy. Or how lucky I feel to catch your eye at work for an extra second because you're mine."

"Only yours," he whispers and squeezes me closer.

"Good, otherwise lingering stares in the office would be awkward," I retort.

He quirks his lips out in agreement. "Anything else that I should know?"

"Communication is key. That's why when I took a step back and had a chance to breathe, I do believe that your idiot lawyer—"

"Ex-lawyer," he corrects.

"He made a mistake, but at least it forced us to confront everything. I'm a broken record. Whether I meant to or not, Lola was hidden from you, and you have every right to process and navigate how to handle that in your own way.

But these last months, I've hidden my own heart. I didn't want to confuse a fantasy in my head that I've only imagined before I saw you again. Everything must be for the right reasons. The truth is the connection between me and you is ours, always has been. That also means you have the power to break it. That scared me."

Hayes swoops up my hands into his. "Trust me. I'm going to cling to the trust you've given me, which means I will hold on carefully and confidently."

"I want us, and all our future brings."

"Marriage, more babies, in case you need clarity."

I glare at him playfully. "I'm sure it would be tomorrow if I said yes."

He shrugs. "You're not wrong. I'm not getting any younger, and I already got your dad's approval." He winks.

Was that what he and Dad talked about at Thanksgiving? "That was fast."

Shrugging a shoulder, I see vulnerability appear. "Maybe honorable, as my dad would say. But I already knew then that it is far more than infatuation with you. It's too strong."

Sighing, I partly turn to rest my head against his shoulder while lacing our fingers together. "The future comes up a lot on this bench." I joke.

"Last time on this bench, you told me you didn't expect things from me out of obligation."

Bubbling a laugh, the memory comes to me. "I'm independent. But then you entered the picture, and I learned that I don't need to be. I have someone supportive who wants to give me the world. And I want to make him happy."

"Sweetheart, I've never agreed with you more."

I peer up to meet his eyes. Everything in my chest feels strong, I'm teetering on the edge of complete happiness, and the best part is I know it's there when I fall. "Thanks for not trying to end my lease without me."

A smirk crawls on the corner of his mouth. "How do you know I didn't?"

"Because I contacted them to end my own lease." I smile at the cocky look he gets on his face at the win. "And while I'm at it, you're right. We piece together like a puzzle to make sure Lola has the best, and I need to remember that I'm not parenting alone anymore. I shouldn't second-guess or refuse opportunities. So I've told Foster that I'll go to the conference in Houston. I have you now, and she'll love extra alone time with you. Just don't spoil her too much. I've been demoted a few times on the who-she-cuddles-first scale."

"I'll say no to cookies a few times or buy a balloon to even the playing field again."

He lowers his mouth to meet mine for a soft kiss, a brush across my lips, really. "I love you, Elodie."

"Me too. I mean, I love myself, but what I meant was me too, as in I love you," I begin to ramble.

He grins before his long finger plants on my mouth. "I know what you meant. Don't be adorable right now. Not when I'm trying to figure out the fastest way to get you somewhere to show you how much I love you."

"Here I was thinking that I could finally enjoy my coffee since the serious conversation was over."

He shakes his head and fakes exhaustion from my antics. "Since I'm in a small town in the middle of nowhere, and I'm positive the farmer walking out of the shop with a box of donuts is watching us, then I will abide by your let's have a coffee reunion."

I bring my hand to his cheek, feeling his skin against my own, with certainty swirling inside me. "Trust me, that could be an idea. However, I was thinking one more sip of coffee, your car, and this spot outside of town, perfectly secluded." I flash my eyes at him.

"And that is why you're my future. Such a smart woman," he jokes.

I stand up and offer him my hand. "Come on."

―――――

MY BODY MOLDS TO HAYES. After yesterday—a quickie in his car and our choice to return to the city—I should be exhausted. Instead, I soak him in as he drags his mouth along my shoulder while I straddle him. I breathe in his warmth in what is now our bed. His hand roams from my hips to my ribcage under his shirt that I'm wearing, mapping me. I lock eyes with him, my fingers splayed across his chest.

We woke to find ourselves in this position, just lying here for a while, limbs entwined on a lazy Sunday morning. But that's about to change because I lower my mouth to his.

"I want you inside me," I whisper.

He smiles against my lips. "Me too," he murmurs and deepens our kiss. It's smooth, soft, but pure reverence.

Sneaking my hand between us, I feel his hard cock under his boxer briefs that presses against my wet center. We're both ready for one another.

I begin to move to align him but freeze when I notice Hayes's facial expression change to panic.

"I can't sleep." Lola stands in the doorway, still in her pajamas, holding her two stuffed bunnies that hang from her hands.

I almost bolt off him at the same time as he tries to toss me off his body, shifting the blanket even though I'm in a shirt that falls to my knees.

Hayes awkwardly chuckles as he adjusts the sheets.

"That's because it's morning." Lola begins to patter our way. "I thought that safety thing on the side of the bed was to keep her in bed," he mumbles under his breath and holds a tight smile.

"Falling out is not the same as climbing out," I mutter.

We both begin to scoot and make space for her in the middle of the bed.

"What brings you here?" I ask our daughter. "Hungry, I bet."

She nods her head and looks between us. "Toast jam, please."

"Of course, your highness," I promise as we cuddle in together.

"Want to go swimming today?" Hayes asks her, and Lola instantly lights up and bounces, which gives us her answer. "Maybe we can convince Mommy to join us in her bikini." He winks at me.

"Or I can supervise?" I tease.

Lola begins to pull my arm. "Come swim."

Rolling my eyes, I won't be able to decline the suggestion. "Fine. Breakfast first, though."

"Okay." Lola begins to wiggle away from us and crawls to the foot of the bed to carefully slide off, and she runs.

"Whoa. Where ya heading?" Hayes checks.

She pauses in the doorway. "Swimsuit."

We both laugh. "Or breakfast first," I repeat.

Already at two, she has defiance and runs away anyhow.

Hayes leans in to kiss my cheek. "Raincheck on having you on top of me, and I'll go handle this." Then he scampers out of bed too quickly and heads straight to his dresser for a shirt.

I scratch the back of my head with wild hair. "We'll need to tell her that this is her permanent home now," I remind us.

His signature grin appears. "I'm not sure that's going to be difficult."

He's right. I'm not sure Lola ever grasped the dynamics of living space. I wave him off. "Meh, you have a pool. She'll be in heaven."

He yanks down his shirt as he approaches the bed and crawls onto it quickly to kiss me. "I think her mom is too."

The back of my knuckles run along his rough cheek as I smile. "How observant of you."

One more quick kiss, and he disappears.

Sighing, I fall back and rest my head on the pillow. Somewhere in my head, a list develops of laundry, breakfast, and where we left the pool floaties. But it's quite noisy because I'm still relaxed after the last five minutes.

All because I'm no longer hiding anything, my heart is no longer hidden, and I've laid my heart bare. Lola is where she should be, and I'm where I want to be.

EPILOGUE : HAYES

4 MONTHS LATER

"Can't we try just one? Maybe the pink one—or the bunny-shaped balloon? I mean, she's okay with Easter eggs. That's the same shape, just doesn't float in the air," I ask Elodie quietly, snaking my arms around her waist from behind as she leans forward to peek into Lola's room. Together, we watch Lola sleep, Bagel clutched tight, sprawled on her bed beneath the big nap blanket. Her pink dress is laid out on the chair in the corner. A dress that Elodie made herself.

"I mean, be my guest. She does need to learn. Any meltdowns are your responsibility, though."

I smile because I have a feeling that Elodie is my mirror, looking on with pure affection. "Our little girl is three," I remind us.

"Yeah… she is," Elodie laments.

It's also my first birthday celebration with Lola. She had her birthday already, but with it being so close to Easter, we decided to combine the occasions. Bunnies are her favorite animal, after all. Last week, a wave of sadness hit me. I've missed all of this stuff the last few years. Elodie noticed my quietness every single time—she always gently placed her arm around me and whispered, "You're here now." Only now will Lola actually begin to remember celebrations.

Hence, why I'm going a little overboard.

Elodie took a stand when I nearly hired a magician—more for me than our daughter, honestly. Who doesn't love reliving their childhood? Instead, she convinced me a face painter with unicorns was the better bet.

We're keeping it low-key at our house: some kids from daycare and her dance class, plus close family and friends. My mom was here a few weeks back for St. Patrick's Day in Chicago, and now she has returned and blessed us with another stay. I'm going to get her own place once an apartment a few floors down becomes vacant. We are very thankful that my driver drove her to the grocery store because she wanted to inspect avocados herself for a salad she wants to make. Gives us a little breathing space.

Elodie let me hire a caterer for the adults but insisted on spending three hours cutting toddler food into shapes. Apparently, bunny-shaped, crustless peanut butter and jelly sandwiches are essential.

The smell of Elodie's coconut shampoo invades my senses as she closes the door. I kiss her hair above her ear, then guide her aside and press her gently against the hallway wall.

"Careful there. Lola will wake soon, and we still have things to do," she purrs. True.

My response is to pull her tighter, the heat between us immediate. "And," I whisper, my lips brushing her ear, "we don't need a lot of time... for now." My heart pounds with anticipation at her closeness.

The sneaky little vixen brings her hand between us to cup my bulge that is hardening. "Ooh, someone wants me."

"I do. So will you be a good girl and let me take off your panties underneath this dress?" I'm already beginning to drag up the fabric, and she gives me a firm squeeze.

"I mean, it would be a nice de-stressor. There have been so many things to do." Her voice is sultry.

My nose nestles into her neck. "That sounds promising," I rasp.

"Uh-huh, just a shame that we have..." Her hips buck into me, causing our middles to touch. "*Too* many things to do." She pouts before her finger boops my nose. Her smile straightens, and her rejection stings.

I grin at her as she wiggles out of our bubble. "I'll get you for that later."

"Please do," she says over her shoulder as she heads in the direction of the kitchen. "Plus, don't you have a ring to find somewhere?" she casually adds as she turns the corner.

My grin falls. "Wait, what?"

I move fast, straight to the kitchen, where Elodie seems to have been waiting for me. She has a wry smile as she leans against the long counter, where, at one end, appetizers are covered, prepared earlier by the caterer.

"What did you say?"

"You know, you and Lola are really cute together. She's also learning new words every day, so imagine my surprise when she mentioned, what was it..." She brings a finger to her chin. "Ring. Daddy. Box. I believe the sentence was 'Daddy, ring, Mommy.'"

A reluctant smile tugs at my lips as I pinch the bridge of my nose, stifling a laugh. "Clearly, our daughter has not developed secret-keeping skills."

Elodie shakes her head. "Nope. Also, when she

mentioned the ring, then I kind of bribed her with an extra cookie."

"That's not playing fair." I approach her slowly, grinning despite myself. I stop in front of her, hoist Elodie up onto the counter so she's seated between my legs, and gently place my hands on her hips to steady her. "And what did her mommy have to say after that?" I ask. Looking up, I catch her soft smile as her eyes meet mine.

"That she shouldn't tell you that I know." She laughs once.

I'm not going to lead us around this playful circle. "Fine. Let me be more direct. I wanted to respect your pace and have been waiting for a sign. We've talked about it before. What it would mean. How if Lola gets a sister or brother then we don't want to have too much of an age difference between them. Those are all indicators. So yes. There is a ring, a box, you, me, a wedding, a marriage."

"Oh, am I agreeing to this?" she pretends and teases me.

I shake my head because this woman isn't going to make it easy. I would have had a romantic dinner planned for this, but instead, we are about to enter party chaos. But I think this suits us. Elodie and I have always been about having conversations when planning. Since we reentered our lives, we have been extra careful not to miss details. We learned our lesson already. So, asking her to marry me this way might be fitting.

"Elodie," I firmly state her name. "You are agreeing. I'm asking you to marry me, but I'll only accept one answer." Her face softens, and I see her eyes turn misty. I bring the palms of my hands to her cheeks, our gaze fully locked. "Marry me," I rasp.

She leaves me waiting for a few seconds, but I'm not worried. "Yes," she whispers.

"Good. We agree." I smile at her before I slam my mouth

onto hers. A hard, confirming kiss as she hooks her knees around my waist, keeping me locked in as though she'll never let go. And she won't. She smiles and makes that sound that I love when our tongues dust. I break away briefly. "There is a ring."

She shushes my mouth with hers. "And I'll love it. But today is about Lola. You can show me later tonight. Let's enjoy this change just us for a day or two before everybody finds out."

"Fair enough." I steal one more peck of a kiss from her. "I love you."

"I love you, future husband."

"Want to head to the courthouse next week? During lunch break, instead of grabbing a sandwich?"

She rolls her eyes at me. "Ha. Not happening."

We stay in the embrace and bask in our news for a few minutes. Soft kisses and whispers of nothing.

An hour later, guests fill our living room, while the kids sit at a special table in the corner where two women are painting faces on the little girls and the others decorate eggs. This is going to go wrong somewhere, I feel it. Messy, for sure. Then Elodie is going to taunt me with the reminder of having the wrong-colored sofa for kids, which will result in me having a new one delivered ASAP.

"Loving the party vibes," Savannah compliments in passing, holding up a bottle of something as she heads to where Elodie is busy in the kitchen with Sutton.

"Thanks," I call out as I finally sink onto the sofa after wrangling the kids to their table and ensuring our family had drinks because apparently watching the kids is their idea of fun. Elodie's parents cornered me about grandkids and us living together, but no ring, even though I already asked her dad's permission. Now he's watching the clock. I really need a breather.

"The lack of balloons at a kids' party is a little weird, but I'll let you go because the 500-dollar bottle of champagne for the adults is a nice touch," Julian mentions as he finds a spot on the opposite sofa. "We'll need it when the kids start reaching their sugar high."

Easton and Foster arrive, chatting with drinks in hand, and find places to sit and join us.

"Is this the place where we watch the insanity unfold? Only for you am I at a kids' party on a Sunday afternoon." Easton grins cheekily, then huddles in toward the coffee table. "And what are the chances you know if the face painter with a talent for bears is single?" he asks in a low voice.

Chuckling to myself, I'm not surprised. "I don't know. You can ask her *after* the party."

Foster rolls his eyes at Easton's antics, then brings his gaze to me. "How does it feel to have a three-year-old?"

"Amazing. I kind of wish there were a way for her to stop growing." In September, she'll start preschool. Affection fills me to the brim. I'm truly lucky—Lola is the sweetest little girl.

"She sleeps through the night, right?" Foster is curious.

I nod. "Yeah, always has, I think. Only wakes if she's sick or there's a storm."

Julian squints his eyes as he examines across the room. "Prepare yourselves, gentlemen, the ladies are stirring up some drinks."

We all shoot our gaze in their direction where Elodie appears to doubt what Savannah is mixing, only to shrug her shoulders and grab another glass. My guess is they are heading down the pink mimosa route.

To my side, I notice that Foster is staring at them all in a different way. He's not in tune, and when I follow his line of sight, it leads me to Sutton, who smiles weakly at Elodie's side while she holds a plate of food.

Easton draws our attention back. "We know it's the princess's big day, but what are the chances that we can turn on the hockey?" He grimaces.

I check on Lola well across the room, and my future wife is far too busy to notice. "Fine. But the game goes off during cake time, present time, and any meltdowns that require calm in the room," I warn him.

"Deal."

"The remote is…" I look around me as I stand, my phone vibrating in my pocket. "Somewhere."

He can figure it out. I quickly pull out my phone and see that it's the front desk downstairs. Answering, they let me know more dessert has been delivered, and I tell them I will come and get it. Normally, they would bring it up, but I could use a moment to process this day.

"I need to head downstairs real quick. The dessert's here," I inform my friends.

Easton and Julian swing their gaze to the dining table, where a giant three-tier tower of carrot cake cupcakes and lemon meringue pies from Everhope are on display.

"You already have dessert," Julian points out.

"Yeah, then Elodie woke this morning and my mom questioned about the lack of hot cross buns. Elodie freaked out that my mom disapproved and insisted we fix it. I don't question the process, just made some calls to calm her down," I explain.

"I'll join you." Foster follows. For some reason, I sense he could use a breather, too.

A minute later when the doors to the elevator close, we

both sigh from the lack of squealing kids. We lean against the wall and stare forward at the light above the door.

"Never thought I would say hot cross buns better be good. It's from some up-and-coming bakery. If I'm going to have a lifetime supply of leftover sweet bread in my freezer, then it might as well be worth it."

"Right." Foster remains distant, in his own world.

"What's up with you?"

"It's Sutton."

Now I'm curious. I know there was something from a while ago, or it's something office-related. "What about her?"

"She's pregnant."

My eyes nearly pop out. I look at him, and he meets my gaze, eyes piercing.

"She just doesn't know it yet."

"What the fuck does that mean?"

Guilt floods his face as I wait for his reply.

www.ingramcontent.com/pod-product-compliance
Lightning Source LLC
Chambersburg PA
CBHW051504030726
47592CB00006B/2082